HIGHEST PRAISE FOR OCTAVIA E. BUTLER

♦♦♦

"Butler's books are exceptional. . . . Butler is a realist, writing the most detailed social criticism and creating some of the most fascinating female characters in the genre . . . the hard edge of cruelty, violence, and domination is described in stark detail . . . real women caught in impossible situations."

—*Village Voice*

♦♦♦

"A new Octavia Butler novel is an exciting event. . . . She is one of those rare authors who pay serious attention to the way human beings actually work together and against each other, and she does so with extraordinary plausibility."

—*Locus*

♦♦♦

"Butler sets the imagination free, blending the real and the possible."

—**United Press International**

more . . .

"Butler's exploration of people is clear-headed and brutally unsentimental. . . . If you haven't read Butler, you don't yet understand how rich the possibilities of science fiction can be."

—*The Magazine of Fantasy & Science Fiction*

"Butler is among the best of contemporary SF writers, blessed with a mind capable of conceiving complicated futuristic situations that shed considerable light on our current affairs. Her prose is lean and literate, her ideas expansive and elegant."

—*Houston Post*

"Her books are disturbing, unsettling . . . her visions are strange, hypnotic distortions of our own uncomfortable world. . . . Butler's African-American feminist perspective is unique, and uniquely suited to reshape the boundaries of the genre."

—LA Style

"Butler's strength is her ability to create complete and believable characters."

—San Francisco Chronicle

"Butler's spare, vivid prose style invites comparison with the likes of Kate Wilhelm and Ursula Le Guin."

—Kirkus Reviews

Also by Octavia E. Butler

*Available from Warner Aspect
†Also available in the omnibus edition *Lilith's Brood*

OCTAVIA E. BUTLER

MIND OF MY MIND

WARNER BOOKS

A Time Warner Company

For Octavia, M.,
Harlan
and Sid.

WARNER BOOKS EDITION

Copyright © 1977 by Octavia Butler
All rights reserved.

Aspect® is a registered trademark of Warner Books, Inc.

This Warner Books Edition is published by arrangement with the author.

Cover design by Don Puckey
Cover illustration by John Jude Palencar

Warner Books, Inc.
1271 Avenue of the Americas
New York, NY 10020

Visit our Web site at
www.warnerbooks.com

 A Time Warner Company

Printed in the United States of America

First Warner Books Printing: August, 1994

10 9 8

· Prologue ·

DORO

Doro's widow in the southern California city of Forsyth had become a prostitute. Doro had left her alone for eighteen months. Too long. For the sake of the daughter she had borne him, he should have visited her more often. Now it was almost too late.

Doro watched her without letting her know that he was in town. He saw the men come and go from her new, wrong-side-of-the-tracks apartment. He saw that most of her time away from home was spent in the local bars.

Sometime during his eighteen-month absence, she had moved from the house he had bought her—an expensive house in a good neighborhood. And though he had made arrangements with a Forsyth bank for her to receive a liberal monthly allowance, she still needed the men. And the liquor. He was not surprised.

By the time he knocked at her door, the main thing he wanted to do was see whether his daughter was all right. When the woman opened the door, he pushed past her into the apartment without speaking.

She was half drunk and slurred her words a little as she called after him. "Hey, wait a minute. Who the hell do you think you—"

"Shut up, Rina."

She hadn't recognized him, of course. He was wearing a body that she had never seen before. But like all his people, she knew him the instant he spoke. She stared at him, round-eyed, silent.

There was a man sitting on her couch drinking directly from a bottle of Santa Fe Port. Doro glanced at him, then spoke to Rina. "Get rid of him."

The man started to protest immediately. Doro ignored him and went on to the bedroom, following his tracking sense to Mary, his daughter. The child was asleep, her breathing softly even. Doro turned on a light and looked at her more closely. She was three years old now, small and thin, not especially healthy-looking. Her nose was running.

Doro touched her forehead lightly but felt no trace of fever. The bedroom contained only a bed and a three-legged chest of drawers. There was a pile of dirty clothes in one corner on the floor. The rest of the floor was bare wood—no carpeting.

Doro took in all this without surprise, without changing his neutral expression. He uncovered the child, saw that she was sleeping nude, saw the bruises and welts on her back and legs. He shook his head and sighed, covered the little girl up carefully, and went back out to the living room. There the man and Rina were cursing at each other. Doro waited in silence until he was sure that Rina was honestly, in fact desperately, trying to get rid of her "guest" but that the man was refusing to budge. Then Doro walked over to the man.

The man was short and slight, not much more than a boy, really. Rina might have been able to throw him out physically, but she had not. Now it was too late. She stumbled back away from him, silent, abruptly terrified as Doro approached.

The man rose unsteadily to face Doro. Doro saw that he had put his bottle down and taken out a large pocket knife. Unlike Rina, he did not slur his words at all when he spoke. "Now, listen, you— Hold it! I said hold it!"

He broke off abruptly, slashing at Doro as Doro advanced on

him. Doro made no effort to avoid the knife. It sliced easily through the flesh of his abdomen but he never felt the pain. He abandoned his body the instant the knife touched him.

Surprise and anger were the first emotions Doro tasted in the man's mind. Surprise, anger, then fear. There was always fear. Then yielding. Not all Doro's victims gave in so quickly, but this one was half anesthetized with wine. This one saw Doro as only Doro's victims ever saw him. Then, stunned, he gave up his life almost without a struggle. Doro consumed him, an easy if not especially satisfying meal.

Rina had gasped and begun to raise her hand to her mouth as the man slashed at Doro. When Doro finished his kill, Rina's hand was just touching her lips.

Doro stood uncomfortably disoriented, mildly sick to his stomach, the hand of his newly acquired body still clutching its bloody knife. On the floor lay the body that Doro had been wearing when he came in. It had been strong, healthy, in excellent physical condition. The one he had now was nothing beside it. He glanced at Rina in annoyance. Rina shrank back against the wall.

"What's the matter with you?" he asked. "Do you think you're safer over there?"

"Don't hurt me," she said. "Please."

"Why would you beat a three-year-old like that, Rina?"

"I didn't do it! I swear. It was a guy who brought me home a couple of nights ago. Mary woke up screaming from a nightmare or something, and he—"

"Hell," said Doro in disgust. "Is that supposed to be an excuse?"

Rina began to cry silently, tears streaming down her face. "You don't know," she said in a low voice. "You don't understand what it's like for me having that kid here." She was no longer slurring her words, in spite of her tears. Her fear had sobered her. She wiped her eyes. "I really didn't hit her. You know I wouldn't dare lie to you." She stared at Doro for a moment, then shook her head. "I've wanted to hit her though—so many times. I can hardly even stand to go near her sober any more. . . ." She looked at the body cooling on the floor and began to tremble.

Doro went to her. She stiffened with terror as he touched her. Then, after a moment, when she realized that he was doing nothing more than putting his arm around her, she let him lead her back to the couch.

She sat with him, beginning to relax, the tension going out of her body. When he spoke to her, his tone was gentle, without threat.

"I'll take Mary if you want me to, Rina. I'll find a home for her."

She said nothing for a long while. He did not hurry her. She looked at him, then closed her eyes, shook her head. Finally she put her head on his shoulder and spoke softly. "I'm sick," she said. "Tell me I'll be well if you take her."

"You'll be as well as you were before Mary was born."

"Then?" She shuddered against him. "No. I was sick then too. Sick and alone. If you take Mary away, you won't come back to me, will you?"

"No. I won't."

"You said, 'I want you to have a baby,' and I said, 'I hate kids, especially babies,' and you said, 'That doesn't matter.' And it didn't."

"Shall I take her, Rina?"

"No. Are you going to get rid of that corpse for me?" She nudged his former body with one foot.

"I'll have someone take care of it."

"I can't do anything," she said. "My hands shake and sometimes I hear voices. I sweat and my head hurts and I want to cry or I want to scream. Nothing helps but taking a drink—or maybe finding a guy."

"You won't drink so much from now on."

There was another long silence. "You always want so damn much. Shall I give up men, too?"

"If I come back and find Mary black and blue again, I'll take her. If anything worse happens to her, I'll kill you."

She looked at him without fear. "You mean I can keep my men if I keep them away from Mary. All right."

Doro sighed, started to speak, then shrugged.

"I can't help it," she said. "Something is wrong with me. I can't help it."

"I know."

"You made me what I am. I ought to hate your guts for what you made me."

"You don't hate me. And you don't have to defend yourself to me. I don't condemn you." He caressed her, wondering idly how she could want life badly enough to fight as hard as she had to fight to keep it. In producing her daughter, she had performed the function she had been born to perform. Doro had demanded that much of her as he had demanded it of others, her ancestors long before her. There had been a time when he disposed of people like her as soon as they had produced the number of offspring he desired. They were inevitably poor parents and their children grew up more comfortably with adoptive parents. Now, though, if such people wanted to live after having served him, he let them. He treated them kindly, as servants who had been faithful. Their gratitude often made them his best servants in spite of their seeming weakness. And the weakness didn't bother him. Rina was right. It was his fault—a result of his breeding program. Rina, in fact, was a minor favorite with him when she was sober.

"I'll be careful," she said. "No one will hurt Mary again. Will you stay with me for a while?"

"Only for a few days. Long enough to help you move out of here."

She looked alarmed. "I don't want to move. I can't stand it out there where I was, by myself."

"I'm not going to send you back to our old house. I'm just going to take you a few blocks over to Dell Street where one of your relatives lives. She has a duplex and you're going to live in one side of it."

"I don't have any relatives left alive around here."

He smiled. "Rina, this part of Forsyth is full of your relatives. Actually, that's why you came back to it. You don't know them, and you wouldn't like most of them if you met them, but you need to be close to them."

"Why?"

"Let's just say, so you won't be by yourself."

She shrugged, neither understanding nor really caring. "If people around here are my relatives, are they your people too?"

"Of course."

"And . . . this woman I'm going to live next door to—what is she to me?"

"Your grandmother several times removed."

Rina's terror returned full force. "You mean she's like you? Immortal?"

"No. Not like me. She doesn't kill—at least not the way I do. She's still wearing the same body she was born into. And she won't hurt you. But she might be able to help with Mary."

"All for Mary. She must be important, poor kid."

"She's very important."

Rina was suddenly the concerned mother, frowning at him worriedly. "She won't just be like me? Sick? Crazy?"

"She'll be like you at first, but she'll grow out of it. It isn't really a disease, you know."

"It is to me. But I'll keep her, and move, like you said, to this grandmother's house. What's the woman's name?"

"Emma. She started to call herself Emma about one hundred fifty years ago as a joke. It means grandmother or ancestress."

"It means she's somebody you can trust to watch me and see that I don't hurt Mary."

"Yes."

"I won't. I'll learn to be her mother at least . . . a little more. I can do that much—raise a child who'll be important to you."

He kissed her, believing her. If the child had not been such an important part of his breeding program, he would not have put a watch on her at all. After a while he got up and went to call one of his people to come and get his former body out of the apartment.

EMMA

Emma was in the kitchen fixing her breakfast when she heard someone at her front door. She hobbled through the dining room toward the door, but before she could reach it, it opened and a slight young man stepped in.

Emma stopped where she was, straightened her usually bent body, and stared a question at the young man. She was not afraid. A couple of boys had broken in to rob her recently and she had given them quite a surprise.

"It's me, Em," said the young man, smiling.

Emma relaxed, smiled herself, but she did not let her body sink back into its stoop. "What are you doing here? You're supposed to be in New York."

"I suddenly realized that it had been too long since I checked on one of my people."

"You don't mean me."

"A relative of yours—a little girl."

Emma raised an eyebrow at him, then drew a deep breath. "Let's sit down, Doro. Ask me the favor you're going to ask me from a comfortable chair."

He actually looked a little sheepish. They sat down in the living room.

"Well?" said Emma.

"I see you have someone living in your other apartment," he said.

"Family," said Emma. "A great-grandson whose wife just died. He works and I keep an eye on the kids when they get home from school."

"How soon can you move him out?"

Emma stared at him expressionlessly. "The question is, will I move him out at all? Why should I?"

"I have a youngster who's going to be too much for her mother in a few years. Right now, though, her mother is too much for her."

"Doro, the kids next door really need my help. Even with guidance, you know they're going to have a hard time."

"But almost anyone could help those children, Em. On the other hand, you're just about the only one I'd trust to help the child I'm talking about."

Emma frowned. "Her mother abuses her?"

"So far, she only lets other people abuse her."

"Sounds as though the child would be better off adopted into another family."

"I don't want to do that if I can avoid it. She's probably going to have a strong need to be among her relatives. And you're the only relative she has that I'd care to trust her with. She's part of an experiment that's important to me, Em."

"Important to you. To you! And what shall I do with my great-grandson and his children?"

"Surely one of your apartment complexes has a vacancy. And you can pay a baby sitter for the kids. You're already providing for God knows how many indigent relatives. This should be fairly easy."

"That's not the point."

He leaned back and sat looking at her. "Are you going to turn me down?"

"How old is the child?"

"Three."

"And just what is she going to grow up into?"

"A telepath. One with more control of her ability than any I've produced so far, I hope. And from the body I used to father her, I hope she'll have inherited a few other abilities."

"What other abilities?"

"Em, I can't tell you all of it. If I do, in a few years she'll read it in your mind."

"What difference would that make? Why shouldn't she know what she is?"

"Because she's an experiment. It will be better for her to learn the nature of her abilities slowly, from experience. If she's anything like her predecessors, the more slowly she learns the better it will be for the people around her."

"Who were her predecessors?"

"Failures. Dangerous failures."

Emma sighed. "Dead failures." She wondered what he would say if she refused to help. She didn't like having anything to do with his projects when she could help it. They always involved children, always had to do with his breeding programs. For all but the first few centuries of his four-thousand-year life, he had been struggling to build a race around himself. He existed ap-

8

parently as a result of a mutation millennia past. His people existed as a result of less wildly divergent mutations and as a result of nearly four thousand years of controlled breeding. He now had several strong mutant strains, which he combined or kept separate, as he wished. And behind him he had an untold number of failures, dangerous or only pathetic, which he had destroyed as casually as other people slaughtered cattle.

"You must tell me *something* about your hopes for the girl," Emma said. "Just what kind of danger are you trying to expose me to?"

He laid a hand on her bony shoulder. "Very little, Em. If you have a hand in raising the girl, she should come out reasonably controllable. In fact, I was thinking of giving you the whole job of raising her."

"No! Absolutely not. I've raised enough children. More than enough."

"That's what I thought you'd say. All right. Just let me move her and her mother in next door, where you can keep an eye on them."

"What are you going to do with her after she's matured?—if she's a success, I mean."

He sighed. "Well, I guess I can tell you that. She's part of my latest attempt to bring my active telepaths together. I'm going to try to mate her with another telepath without killing either of them myself. And I'm hoping that she and the boy I have in mind are stable enough to stay together without killing each other. That will be a beginning."

Emma shook her head as he spoke. How many lives had he thrown away over the years in pursuit of that dream? "Doro, they've never been together. Why don't you leave them alone? Let them stay separate. They avoid each other naturally when you're not pushing them together."

"I want them together. Did you think I had given up?"

"I keep hoping you'll give up for the sake of your people."

"And settle for the string of warring tribes that I've got now? Not that most of them are even that united. Just families of people who don't like their own members much even though they usually need to be near them. Families who can't tolerate members of my other families at all. They all tolerate ordinary people well enough, though. They would have merged back into the general population long ago if I didn't police them."

"Perhaps they should. They would be happier."

"Would you be happier without your gifts, Emma? Would you like to be an ordinary human?"

"Of course not. But how many others are in full control of their abilities, as I am? And how many spend their lives in abject misery because they have 'gifts' that they can't control or even understand?" She sighed. "You can't take credit for me, anyway. I'm almost as much of an accident as you are. My people had been separated from one of your families for hundreds of years before I was born. They had merged with the people they took refuge among, and they still managed to produce me."

And Doro had been trying to duplicate the happy accident of her birth ever since. She had known him for three hundred years now, had borne him thirty-seven children through his various incarnations. None of her children had proved to be especially long-lived. Those who might have been were tortured, unstable people. They committed suicide. The rest lived normal spans and died natural deaths. Emma had seen to that last. She had not been able to keep track of her many grandchildren, but her children she had protected. From the beginning of her relationship with Doro, she had warned him that if he murdered even one of her children, she would bear him no more.

At first Doro had valued her and her new strain too much to punish her for her "arrogance." Later, as he became accustomed to her, to the idea of her immortality, he began to value her as more than just a breeder. She became a companion to him, a wife to whom he always returned. Both he and she married other people from time to time, but such matings were temporary.

For a while, Emma even believed in his race-building dream. But as he allowed her to know more of his methods of fulfilling that dream, her enthusiasm waned. No dream was worth the things he did to people.

It was his casually murderous attitude that finally caused her to tire of him, about two centuries into their relationship. She had turned away from him in disgust when he murdered a young woman who had borne him the three children he had demanded of her. For Emma, it had finally been too much.

But, by then, Doro had been a part of her life for too long, had become too important to her. She could not simply walk away from him, even if he had been willing to let her. She needed him, but she no longer wanted him. And she no longer wanted to be one of his people, supporting his butchery. There was only one escape, and she began preparing herself to take it. She began preparing herself to die.

And Doro, startled, alarmed, began to mend his ways somewhat. He gave her his word that he would no longer kill breeders who became useless to him. Then he asked her to live. He came to her, finally, as one human being to another, and asked her not to leave him. She hadn't left him. He had never commanded her again.

"Will you take the mother and child, Em?"

"Yes. You know I will. Poor things."

"Not so poor if I'm successful."

She made a sound of disgust.

He smiled. "I'll be seeing you more often, too, with the girl living next door."

"Well, that's something." She reached out and took one of Doro's hands between her own, observing the contrast. His was smooth and soft. The hand of a young man who had clearly never done any manual labor. Her hands were claws, hard, skinny, with veins and tendons prominent. She began to fill her hands out, smooth them, straighten the long fingers until the hands were those of a young woman, attractive in themselves but incongruous on the ends of withered, ancient arms.

"I wish the child were a boy instead of a girl," she said. "I'm afraid she isn't going to like me much for a while. At least not until she's old enough to see you clearly."

"I didn't want a boy," he said. "I've had trouble with boys in . . . in the special role I want her to fill."

"Oh." She wondered how many boy children he had slaughtered as a result of his trouble.

"I wanted a girl, and I wanted her to be one of the youngest

11

of her generation of actives. Both those factors will help keep her in line. She'll be less likely to rebel against my plans for her."

"I think you underestimate young girls," said Emma. She had filled out her arms, rounding them, making them slender rather than skinny. Now she raised a hand to her face. She passed her fingers over her forehead and down her cheek. The flesh became smooth and flawless as she went on speaking. "Although, for this girl's own sake, I hope you're not underestimating her."

Doro watched her with the interest he had always shown when she reshaped herself. "I can't understand why you spend so much of your time as an old woman," he said.

She cleared her throat. "I am an old woman." She spoke now in a quiet, youthful contralto. "And most people are only too glad to leave an ugly old woman alone."

He touched the newly smooth skin of her face, his expression concerned. "You need this project, Em. Even though you don't want it. I've left you alone too long."

"Not really." She smiled. "I've finally written the trilogy of novels that I was planning when we lived together last. History. My story. The critics marveled at my realism. My work is powerful, compelling. I'm a born storyteller."

He laughed. "Hurry and finish reshaping yourself and I'll give you some more material."

PART
ONE

· One ·

MARY

I was in my bedroom reading a novel when somebody came banging on the door really loud, like the police. I thought it was the police until I got up, looked out the window, and saw one of Rina's johns standing there. I wouldn't have bothered to answer, but the fool was kicking at the door like he wanted to break it in. I went to the kitchen and got one of our small cast-iron skillets—the size just big enough to hold two eggs. Then I went to the door. The stupid bastard was drunk.

"Hey," he mumbled. "Where's Rina? Tell Rina I wanna see her."

"Rina's not here, man. Come back around five this evening."

He swayed a little, stared down at me. "I said tell Rina I wanna see her."

"And I said she's not here!" I would have shut the door in his face, but I knew he'd just start kicking it again unless he managed to understand what I was saying.

"Not here?"

"You got it."

"Well." He narrowed his eyes a little and sort of peered at me. "How about you?"

"Not me, man." I started to shut the door. I hate these scenes, really. The idiot shoved me and the door out of his way and came on in. That's what I get for being short and skinny. Ninety-eight pounds. At nineteen, I looked thirteen. Guys got the wrong idea.

"Man, you better get out of here," I warned him. "Come back at five. Rina's the whore, not me."

"Maybe it's time for you to learn." He stared at me. "What's that you got in your hand?"

I didn't say anything else. I had done my bit for nonviolence.

"I said what the hell you got in your—"

He lunged toward me. I side-stepped him and bashed his stupid head in. I left him lying where he fell, got my purse, and went out. Let Rina or Emma see to him.

I didn't know where I was going. I just wanted to get away from the house. I had a headache, and every now and then I would hear voices—a word, a scream, somebody crying. Hear them inside my head. Doro said that meant I was close to my change, my transition. Doro said that was good. I wished I could give him some of the pain and the craziness of it and let him see how good it was. I felt like hell all the time, and he came around grinning.

I walked over to Maple Avenue and there was a bus coming. A Los Angeles bus. On impulse, I got on. Not that there was anything for me in L.A. There wasn't anything for me anywhere except maybe wherever Doro was. If I was lucky, when Rina and Emma found that idiot lying in our living room, they would call Doro. They called him whenever they thought I was about to blow. The way things were now, I was always about to blow.

I got off the bus in downtown L.A. and went to a drugstore. I didn't remember until I was inside that the only money I had was bus fare. So I slipped a bottle of aspirin into my purse and walked out with it. Doro told me a few years ago that he'd beat the hell out of me if I ever got picked up for stealing. I had been stealing since I was seven years old, and I had never been caught. I used to steal presents for Rina back when I was still trying to pretend it meant something that she was my mother. Anyway, now I knew what I was going to do in L.A. I was going "shopping."

I didn't try very hard, but I got a few things. Got a nice little Sony portable radio—one of the tiny ones. I just walked out of a discount store with it while the salesman who had been showing it to me went to stop some kid from pulling down a display of plastic dishes. Got some perfume. I didn't like the way it smelled though, so I threw it away. I took four aspirins and my headache kind of dulled down a little. I got a blouse and a halter and some junky costume jewelry. I threw the jewelry away, too, after I got a better look at it. Trash. And I got a couple of paperbacks. Always some books. If I didn't have anything to read, I'd really go crazy.

On my way back to Forsyth, somebody screamed bloody murder inside my head. Along with that, I felt I was being hit in the face. Sometimes I got things mixed up, I couldn't tell what was really happening to me and what I was picking up accidentally from other people's minds. This time, I was getting onto a bus when it happened, and I just froze. I had enough control to hold myself there, to not scream or fall on the ground from the beating I felt like I was taking. But you don't stop half on and half off a bus at Seventh and Broadway at five in the evening. You could get killed.

I wasn't exactly trampled. I just kept getting shoved out of the way. Somebody shoved me away from the door of the bus. Other people pushed me out of their way. I couldn't react. All I could do was hang on, wait it out.

And then it was over. I was barely able to get on the bus before it pulled away. I had to stand up all the way to Forsyth. I did my best to knock a couple of people down when I got off.

I didn't want to go home. Even if Rina and Emma had called Doro, he couldn't have gotten there yet. I didn't want to hear Rina's mouth. But then I started to wonder about the john—how bad I had hurt him, if maybe he was dead. I decided to go home to see.

There was nothing else to do, anyway. Forsyth is a dead town. Rich people, old people, mostly white people. Even the southwest side, where we lived, wasn't a ghetto—or at least not a racial ghetto. It was full of poor bastards from any race you want to name—all working like hell to get out of there. Except us. Rina had been out, Doro told me, but she had come back. I never have thought my mother was very bright.

We lived in a corner house—Dell Street and Forsyth Avenue—so I walked home on the side of Dell Street opposite our house. I wanted to see if there were any police cars around the corner before I went in. If there had been any, I would have kept going. Doro would have gotten me out of any trouble I got into, I knew. But then he would have half killed me. It wasn't worth it.

Rina and Emma were waiting for me. I wasn't surprised. There was this little drama we had to go through.

Rina: Do you realize you could have killed that man! Do you want us to go to prison!
Emma: Can't you think for once in your life? Why'd you leave him here? Why didn't you at least—at least—come and get me? For God's sake, girl. . . .
Rina: What did you hit him for? Will you tell us that?

They hadn't given me a chance to tell them anything.

Rina: He was just a harmless old guy. Hell, he wouldn't have hurt—
Emma: Doro is on his way here now, Mary, and you'd better have a good reason for what you did.

And, finally, I got a word in. "It was either hit him or screw him."

"Oh, Lord," muttered Rina. "Can't you talk decent even when Emma is here?"

"I talk as decent as you taught me, Momma! Besides, what do you want me to say? 'Make love to him?' I wouldn't have loved it. And if he had managed to do it, I would have made sure I killed him."

"You did enough," said Emma. She was calming down.

"What did you do with him, anyway?" I asked.

"Put him in the hospital." She shrugged. "Fractured skull."

"They didn't say anything at the hospital?"

"The way he smelled? I just shriveled myself up a little more and told them my grandson drank too much and fell on his head."

I laughed. She used that little-old-lady act to get sympathy from strangers, or at least to throw them off guard. Most of the time when Doro wasn't around, she was old and frail-looking. It was nothing but an act, though. I saw a guy try to snatch her purse once while she was hobbling down the street. She broke his arm.

"Was that guy really your grandson?" I asked.

"I'm afraid so."

I glanced at Rina with disgust. "You can't find anybody but relatives to screw? God!"

"It's none of your business."

"I wouldn't pretend to be so disgusted with the idea of incest if I were you, Mary." Emma sort of bared her teeth at me. It wasn't a smile. She and I didn't get along most of the time. She thought she knew everything. And she thought Doro was her private property. I got up and went to my room.

Doro arrived the next day.

I remember once when I was about six years old I was sitting on his lap frowning up into his latest face. "Shouldn't I call you 'Daddy'?" I asked. Until then, I had called him Doro, like everybody else did.

"I wouldn't if I were you," he said. And he smiled. "Later, you won't like it."

I didn't understand, and I was a stubborn kid anyway. I called him "Daddy." He didn't seem to mind. But, of course, later, I didn't like it. It still bothered me a little, and Doro and Emma both knew it. I had the feeling they laughed about it together.

Doro was a black man this time. That was a relief, because, the last couple of visits, he'd been white. He just walked into my bedroom early in the morning and sat down on my bed. That woke me up. All I saw was this big stranger sitting on the side of my bed.

"Say something," I said quickly.

"It's me," he said.

I let go of the steak knife I slept with and sat up. "Can I kiss you, or are you going to jump me, too?"

He pulled back my blankets and ran his hand down the side of the bed next to the wall. Of course he found the steak knife. I kept it sheathed in the tight little handle you're supposed to use to pick up the mattress. He threw it out the door. "Leave the knives and frying pans in the kitchen, where they belong," he said.

"That guy was going to rape me, Doro."

"You're going to kill somebody."

"Not unless I have to. If people leave me alone, I'll leave them alone."

He picked up a pair of jeans from the floor, where I had left them, and threw them in my face. "Get dressed," he said. "I want to show you something. I want to make a point in a way that even you might understand."

He got up and went out of the room.

I threw the jeans back on the floor and went to the closet for some clean ones. My head was aching already.

He drove me to the city jail. He parked outside the wall and just sat there.

"What now?" I asked.

"You tell me."

"Doro, why did you bring me here?"

"As I said, to make a point."

"What point? That if I'm not a good little girl, this is where I'll wind up? God! Let's get away from here." Something was wrong with me. Or something was about to be wrong. Really wrong. I was picking up shadows of crazy emotions.

"Why should we go?" he asked.

"My head . . . !" I could feel myself losing control. "Doro, please. . . . " I screamed. I tried to hang on. Tried to just shut down, the way I had the day before. Freeze. But I was caught in a nightmare. The kind of nightmare where the walls are coming together on you and you can't get out. The kind where you're locked in some dark, narrow place and you can't get out. The kind where you're at a zoo locked up like the animals, *and you can't get out!*

I had never been afraid of the dark. Not even when I was little. And I'd never been afraid of small, closed places. And the only place I had ever seen a room where the walls formed a vise was in a bad movie. But I screamed my head off outside that jail. I started flailing around, and Doro grabbed me to keep me from jumping out of the car. I almost made him have an accident, as he was trying to drive away.

Finally, when we were a good, long way from the jail, I calmed down. I sat bent over in the seat, holding my head.

"How long do you suppose you could stay even as sane as you are in the midst of a concentration of emotions like that?" he asked.

I didn't say anything.

"Most of the prisoners there aren't half as bothered by their thoughts and fears as you were," he said. "They don't like where they are, but they can live with it. You can't. Wouldn't you rather even be raped than wind up in a place like this even for a short time?"

"You got any aspirin?" I asked. My head was throbbing so that I could hardly hear him. And for some stupid reason, I had left my new bottle of aspirin at home on my night table.

"In the glove compartment," he said. "No water, though."

I fumbled open the glove compartment, found the aspirin, and swallowed four. He was stopped for a red light, watching me.

"You're going to get sick, doing that."

"Thanks to you, I'm already sick."

"You don't listen, girl. I talk to you and you don't listen. For your own good, I have to show you."

"From now on, I'll listen. Just tell me." I sat back and waited for the aspirin to work. Then I realized that he wasn't taking me home.

"Where are we going? You don't have another treat for me, do you?"

"Yes. But not the way you mean."

"What is it? Where are we going?"

"Here."

We were on South Ocean Avenue, in the good part of Forsyth's downtown shopping district. He was driving into the parking lot of Orman's, one of the best stores in town.

He parked, turned off the motor, and sat back. "I want you to step out of character for a while," he said. "Stop working so hard at your role as Rina's bitchy daughter."

I looked at him sidelong. "I usually do when you're around."

"Not enough, maybe. You think we can go into that store and buy—not steal—something other than blue jeans?"

"Like what?"

"Come on." He got out of the car. "Let's go see what you look good in."

I knew what I looked good in. Or at least acceptable in. But why bother when the only guy I was interested in was Doro and nothing I did seemed to reach him? He either had time for me or he didn't. And if he didn't, I could have walked around naked and he wouldn't have noticed.

But because he wanted it, I chose some dresses, some really nice pants, a few other things. I didn't steal anything. My headache sort of faded back to normal and my witchy reflection in the dressing-room mirror relaxed back to just strange-looking. Doro had said once that, except for my eyes and coloring, I look a lot like Emma—like the young version of Emma, I mean. My eyes—traffic-light green, Rina called them—and my skin, a kind of light coffee, were gifts from the white man's body that Doro was wearing when he got Rina pregnant. Some poor guy from a religious colony Doro controlled in Pennsylvania. Doro had people all over.

When he decided that I had bought enough, he paid for it with a check for more money than I had ever seen in my life. He had some kind of by-mail arrangement with the banks. A lot of banks. He ordered everything delivered to the hotel where he was staying. I waited until we were out of the store to ask him why he'd done that.

"I want you to stay with me for a few days," he told me.

I was surprised, but I just looked at him. "Okay."

"You have something to get used to. And for your own sake, I want you to take your time. Do all your yelling and screaming now, while it can't hurt you."

"Oh, Lord. What are you going to give me to yell and scream about?"

"You're getting married."

I looked at him. He'd said those words or others like them to Rina once. To Emma heaven knew how many times. Evidently, my time had come. "You mean to you, don't you?"

"No."

I wasn't afraid until he said that. "Who, then!"

"One of my sons. Not related to you at all, by the way."

"A stranger? Some total stranger and you want me to marry him?"

"You will marry him." He didn't use that tone much with me—or with anyone, I think. It was reserved for when he was telling you to do something he would kill you for not doing. A quiet, chilly tone of voice.

"Doro, why couldn't you be him? Take him and let me marry you."

"Kill him, you mean."

"You kill people all the time."

He shook his head. "I wonder if you're going to grow out of that."

"Out of what?"

"Your total disregard for human life—except for your own, of course."

"Oh, come on! Shit, the devil himself is going to preach me a sermon!"

"Maybe transition will change your thinking."

"If it does, I don't see how I'll be able to stand you."

He smiled. "You don't realize it, but that might really be a problem. You're an experimental model. Your predecessors have had trouble with me."

"Don't talk about me like I was a new car or something." I frowned and looked at him. "What kind of trouble?"

"Never mind. I won't talk about you like you were a new car."

"Wait a minute," I said more seriously. "I mean it, Doro. What kind of trouble?"

He didn't answer.

"Are any of them still alive?"

He still didn't answer.

I took a deep breath, stared out the window. "Okay, so how do I keep from having trouble with you?"

He put an arm around me, and for some reason, instead of flinching away, I moved over close to him. "I'm not threatening you," he said.

"Yes you are. Tell me about this son of yours."

He drove me over to Palo Verde Avenue, where the rich people lived. When he stopped, it was in front of a three-story white stucco mansion. Spanish tile roof, great arched doorway, clusters of palm trees and carefully trimmed shrubs, acres of front lawn, one square block of house and grounds.

"This is his house," said Doro.

"Damn," I muttered. "He owns it? The whole thing?"

"Free and clear."

"Oh, Lord." Something occurred to me suddenly. "Is he white?"

"Yes."

"Oh, Doro. Man, what are you trying to do to me?"

"Get you some help. You're going to need it."

"What the hell can he do for me that you can't? God, he'll take one look at me and. . . . Doro, just the fact that he lives in this part of town tells me that he's the wrong guy. The first time he says something stupid to me, we'll kill each other."

"I wouldn't pick any fights with him if I were you. He's one of my actives."

An active: One of Doro's people who's already gone through transition and turned into whatever kind of monster Doro has bred him to be. Emma was one kind of active. Rina, in spite of her "good" family, was only a latent. She never quite made it to transition, so her ability was undeveloped. She couldn't control it or use it deliberately. All she could do was pass it on to me

24

and put up with the mental garbage it exposed her to now and then. Doro said that was why she was crazy.

"What kind of active is he?" I asked.

"The most ordinary kind. A telepath. My best telepath—at least until you go through."

"You want him to read my mind?"

"He won't have much choice about that. If you and he are in the same house, sooner or later he will, as you'll read his eventually."

"You mean he doesn't have any more control over his ability than I do over mine?"

"He has a great deal more control than you. That's why he'll be able to help you during and after your transition. But none of my telepaths can shield out the rest of the world entirely. Sometimes things that they don't want to sense filter through to them. More often, though, they just get nosy and snoop through other people's thoughts."

"Is it because he's an active that you won't take him? No moralizing this time."

"Yes. He's too rare and too valuable to kill so carelessly. So are you. You and he aren't quite the same kind of creature, but I think you're alike enough to be complementary."

"Does he know about me?"

"Yes."

"And?"

"He feels just about the way you do."

"Great." I slumped back in the seat. "Doro . . . will you tell me, why marriage? I don't have to marry him for him to give me whatever help I'm supposed to need. Hell, I don't even have to marry him to have a baby by him, if that's what you want."

"That might be what I want once I've seen how you come through transition. All I want now is to get the two of you to realize that you might as well accept each other. I want you tied together in a way you'll both respect in spite of yourselves."

"You mean we'll be less likely to kill each other if we're married."

"Well . . . he'll be less likely to kill you. The match is going to be pretty uneven for a while. I'd keep low if I were you."

"Isn't there any way at all that I can get out of this?"

"No."

I felt like crying. I couldn't remember when I'd done that last. And the worst of it was, I knew that, as bad as I felt now, it was nothing to what I'd be feeling when I actually met this son. Somehow, I'd never thought of myself as just another of Doro's breeders—just another Goddamn brood mare. Rina was. Emma was for sure. But me, I was special. Sure. Doro had said it himself. An experiment. Apparently an experiment that had failed several times before. And Doro was trying to shore it up now by pairing me with this stranger.

"What's his name?"

"Karl. Karl Larkin."

"Yeah. When do I have to marry him?"

"In a week or two."

I would have put up more of a fight if I had known how to fight Doro. I never much wanted to fight him before. I remember, once when he was staying with Rina, an electronics company out in Carson—one of the businesses that he controlled—was losing money. Doro had the guy who ran the company for him come to our house to talk. Even then I knew that was a hell of a put-down to the guy. Our house was a shack compared to what he was used to. Anyway, Doro wanted to find out whether the guy was stealing, having real trouble, or was just plain incompetent. It turned out the guy was stealing. Big salary, pretty young wife, big house in Beverly Hills, and he was stealing from Doro. Stupid.

The guy was Doro's—born Doro's, just like me. And every dime of his original investment had been Doro's. Still, he cursed and complained and found reasons why, with all the work he'd done, he deserved more money. Then he ran.

Doro had shrugged. He had eaten dinner with us, got up, stretched, and finally gone out after the guy. The next day, he came back wearing the guy's body.

You didn't cheat him. You didn't steal from him or lie to him. You didn't disobey him. He'd find you out, then he'd kill you. How could you fight that? He wasn't telepathic, but I had never seen anyone get a lie past him. And I had never known anyone to escape him. He did have some kind of tracking sense. He locked in on people. Anybody he'd met once, he could find again. He thought about them, and he knew which way to go to get to them. Once he was close to them, they didn't have a chance.

I put my head against his shoulder and closed my eyes. "Let's get out of here."

He took me back to his hotel and bought me lunch. I hadn't had breakfast, so I was hungry. Then we went up to his room and made love. Really. I would call it screwing when I had to do it with his damn fool son. I had been in love with Doro since I was twelve. He had made me wait until I was eighteen. Now he was going to marry me off to somebody else. I probably loved him in self-defense. Hating him was too dangerous.

We had a week together. He decided to take me to Karl when I started passing out with the mental stuff I was picking up. It surprised him the first time it happened. Evidently I was closer to transition than he had thought.

· TWO ·

DORO

Actives were nearly always troublesome, Doro thought as he drove his car down Karl Larkin's long driveway. He already knew that Karl was not in his house, that he was somewhere in the back yard, probably in the pool. Doro let his tracking sense guide him. He had thought it would be safest to visit Karl once more before he placed Mary with him. Both Karl and Mary were too valuable to take chances with. Mary, if she survived transition, could prove invaluable. She would never have to know the whole reason for her existence—the thing Doro hoped to discover through her. It would be enough if she simply matured and paired successfully with Karl. Eventually the two of them could be told part of the truth—that they were a first, that Doro had never before been able to keep a pair of active telepaths together without killing one of them and taking that one's place. This would be explanation enough for them. Because by the time they had been together for a while they would know how hard it was for two actives to be together without losing themselves, merging into each other uncontrollably. They would understand why, always before, actives had been rigidly

28

unwilling to permit such merging—why actives had defended their individuality, why they had killed each other.

Karl was in the pool. Doro could see him across a parklike expanse of grass and trees. Before Doro could reach him, though, the gardener, who had been mowing the lawn, drove up to Doro on his riding mower.

"Sir?" he said tentatively.

"It's me," said Doro.

The gardener smiled. "I thought it must be. Welcome back."

Doro nodded, went over to the pool. Karl owned his servants more thoroughly than even Doro usually owned people. Karl owned their minds. They were just ordinary people who had answered an ad in the Los Angeles *Times*. Karl did no entertaining—was almost a hermit except for the succession of women whom he lured in and kept until they bored him. The servants existed more to look after the house and grounds than to look after Karl himself. Still, he had chosen them less for their professional competence than for the fact that they had few if any living relatives. Few people to be pacified if he accidentally got too rough with them. He would not have hurt them deliberately. He had conditioned them, programmed them carefully to do their work and to obey him in every way. He had programmed them to be content with their jobs. He even paid them well. But his power made him dangerous to ordinary people—especially to those who worked near him every day. In an instant of uncontrolled anger, he could have killed them all.

Karl hauled himself out of the water when he saw Doro approaching. Then he leaned down and offered his hand to a second person, whom Doro had not noticed. Vivian, of course. A small, pretty, brown-haired woman whom Doro had prevented Karl from marrying.

Karl gave him a questioning look. "I was afraid you were bringing my prospective bride."

"Tomorrow," said Doro. He sat down on the dry end of the long, low diving board.

Karl shook his head, sat down on the concrete opposite him. "I never thought you'd do something like this to me."

"You seem to have accepted it."

"You didn't give me much of a choice." He glanced at Vivian, who had come to sit beside him. As he owned the servants, he owned her. Doro had been surprised to find him wanting to marry her. Karl usually had little but contempt for the women he owned.

"Do you intend to keep Vivian here?" Doro asked.

"You bet I do. Or are you going to stop me from doing that, too?"

"No. It will make things more difficult for you, but that's your problem."

"You seem to do all right handling harems."

Doro shrugged. "The girl will react badly to her." He looked at Vivian. "When's the last time you were in a fight?"

Vivian frowned. "A fight? A fist fight?"

"Knock-down, drag-out."

"God! Not since I was in third grade. Does she fight?"

"Fractured a man's skull last week with a frying pan. Of course, the man deserved it. He was trying to rape her. But she's been known to use violence on far less provocation."

Vivian looked at Karl wide-eyed. Karl shook his head. "You know I'm not going to let her get away with anything like that here."

"For a while, you might have to," said Doro.

"Oh, come on. Be reasonable. We have to protect ourselves."

"Sure you do. But not by tampering with her mind. She's too close to transition. I've seen potential actives pushed into transition prematurely that way. They usually die."

"What am I supposed to do with her, then?"

"I hope talking to her will be enough. I've done what I could to make her wary of you. And she's not stupid. But she's every bit as unstable as you were when you were near transition. Also, she comes from the kind of home where violence is pretty ordinary."

Karl stared down at the concrete for a moment. "You should have had her adopted. After all, I'd be in pretty bad shape myself if you had left me with my mother."

"You would never have lived to grow up if I had left you with your mother. Her mother wasn't quite as bad. And her family tends to cluster together more than yours. They need to be near each other more, and some of them get along together a little more peacefully than your family—not that they really like each other any better. They don't."

"What's the girl going to do about needing her family when you bring her here?"

"I'm hoping she'll transfer her need to you."

Karl groaned.

"I'm also hoping that you won't find that such a bad thing after a while. You should try to accept her, for the sake of your own comfort."

"What if talking to her doesn't quiet her down? You never answered that."

Doro shrugged. "Then use her methods. Beat the hell out of her. Don't let her near anything she can hit or cut you with for a while afterward, though."

MARY

I turned twenty just two days before Doro took me to Karl. Later, I decided Vivian must have been my birthday present. Somehow, Doro forgot to tell me about her until the last minute. Slipped his mind.

So I was not only going to marry a total stranger, a white man, a telepath who wouldn't even let me think in private, but I was going to marry a man who intended to keep his girl friend right there in the same house with me. Son of a bitch!

I threw a fit. I finally did the yelling and screaming Doro had warned me I would do. I couldn't help it, I just went out of control. The whole thing was so Goddamn humiliating! Doro hit me and I bit a piece out of his hand. We sort of stood each other off. He knew that if I hurt him much worse, I would force him out of the body he was wearing—into my body. He'd take me, and all his efforts to get me this far would be wasted. I knew it myself, but I was past caring. I felt like a dog somebody was taking to be bred.

"Now, listen," he began. "This is stupid. You know you're going to—"

We both moved at the same time. He meant to hit me. I meant to dodge and kick him. But he moved a lot faster than I expected. He hit me with his fist—not hard enough to knock me unconscious, but hard enough to stop me from doing anything to him for a while.

He picked me up from where I had fallen, threw me onto the bed, and pinned me there. For a minute, he just glared down at me, his face for once looking like the mask it was. There's usually nothing frightening about the way he looks—nothing to give him away. Now, though, he looked like a corpse some undertaker had done a bad job on. Like whatever he really was had withdrawn way down inside the body and wasn't bothering to animate anything but the eyes. I had to force myself to stare back at him.

"The one thing I can't do," he said softly, "is prevent my people from committing suicide." Whatever there was about his voice that made it recognizable no matter what body it came from was much stronger. I felt the way I had once when I was ten years old and at a public swimming pool. I couldn't swim and some fool pushed me into twelve feet of water. I remember I just held my breath and waited. Somebody had told me to do that once, and, scared as I was, I did it. Sure enough, I floated to the surface, where I could breathe and where I could reach the edge of the pool. Now I lay still beneath Doro's body, waiting.

He reached out to the night table and picked up a switchblade knife. "This came with the body I'm wearing," he said. He rolled off me and lay on his back. He pressed a stud on the knife and about six inches of blade jumped out.

"As I recall, you like knives," he said. He took my hand and closed my fingers around the handle of the knife. "It doesn't really matter where you cut me. Just drive the knife in to the hilt anywhere in this body and the shock will force me to jump."

I threw the knife across the room. Broke the dresser mirror. "You could at least make him get rid of that damn woman!" I said bitterly.

He just lay there.

"Someday there's going to be a way for me to hurt you, Doro. Don't think I won't do it."

He shrugged. He didn't believe it. Neither did I, really. Who the hell could hurt him?

"I loved you. Why are you humiliating me like this?"

"Look," he said, "if he has the woman there to turn to, he's a lot less likely to let you goad him into hurting you."

"I'd be a lot less likely to goad him into anything if you'd get rid of Vivian."

"You underestimate yourself," he said grimly. "Besides, he's in love with Vivian. If I made him get rid of her, I guarantee you he'd take it out on you."

"I just wish I could find a way to take this out on you."

He got up and looked down at me. "Change your clothes," he said. "Then we'll go."

I looked at myself and saw that my pants and blouse were smeared with blood from his hand. I changed my clothes, then packed the rest of my things. Finally, we drove over to Palo Verde Avenue.

While Doro introduced us, Karl and Vivian stood together looking like sister and brother and staring at my eyes. Which gave them at least one thing in common with everybody else who meets me for the first time. There were times when I wished for a nice, bland pair of brown eyes. Like Karl's or Vivian's. Oh, well.

I watched Vivian, saw how pretty she was, how nervous she was. She was no bigger than me, thank God, and she looked scared, which was promising. Doro had told me Karl wouldn't let her really resent me or feel angry or humiliated. *Wouldn't let her!* She was a Goddamn robot and she didn't even know it. Or, rather, she did know it but she wasn't allowed to care.

Karl looked like one of the bright, ambitious, bookish white guys I remembered from high school. Intense, hair already thinning. Doro had said he was twenty-eight, but he looked older. And he sounded . . . well, he sounded just the way I would have expected a well-brought-up guy to sound when he's trying to be polite to somebody he can't stand. Strained.

After the short, stiff introductions, Doro took Vivian's hand as though this wasn't the first time he had taken it, and said, "Let's let them get acquainted. How about a swim?"

Vivian looked at Karl and Karl nodded. She and Doro went out together. I watched them go, wondering about things that weren't exactly any of my business. I looked at Karl but his face was closed and cold. Then I forgot about Vivian and Doro and wondered what the hell Karl and I were supposed to do now. We were in his tennis-court-sized living room, with its wood paneling and its big white fireplace. We were sitting near the fireplace and we both stared into it instead of at each other.

Then, finally, I decided to get things started. "Do you suppose there's any way we can do this and still have a little pride left?"

Karl looked surprised. I wondered what Doro had been telling him about me. "I was wondering if there was any way for us to manage it at all," he said.

I shrugged. "You know as well as I do that we don't have any choice about that. Do you know what kind of help you're supposed to give me?"

"I'm to shield you from the thoughts and emotions you receive when they get to be too much for you. Doro seems to think they will."

"Did they for you?"

"In a way. I passed out a few times."

"Shit, I'm already doing that. It hasn't killed me yet. Did anybody help you?"

"Not that way. All I had was someone to keep me from banging myself up too badly physically."

"Then, why the hell . . . ? No offense, but why am I supposed to need you?"

"I don't know."

"Oh, well. I guess it doesn't matter. It's his decision and we're stuck with it. All we can do is try to find the least uncomfortable way of living with it."

"We'll work something out." He stood up. "Let me show you around the house."

He showed me his fantastic library first, and that helped me warm to him a little. A guy with a room like that in his house couldn't be all bad. Like the living room, it was huge, with that beautiful wood paneling. The fireplace and the windows were the only spots of wall not covered with books. Most of the floor was covered by the biggest oriental rug I had ever seen. There was a long, solid, heavy wooden reading table, a big desk, a lot of upholstered chairs. The high ceiling was wood carved in a regular octagonal pattern and hung with four small, simple chandeliers. While I was growing up, Forsyth Public Library was my second home. It was someplace I could go and be by myself. I could get away from Rina and her whining and her johns and away from Emma period. I actually liked the little old ladies who worked there, and they sort of adopted me. That was where I got into the habit of reading everything I could get my hands on. And now . . . well, old-fashioned libraries of wood and stone and books were still like home to me. The city tore down Forsyth Public a few years ago and built a new one of steel and glass and concrete and air conditioning that was always turned too high. A cold box. I went to it two or three times, then gave up. But Karl's library was perfect. I had walked away from him to look at some of the book titles.

"You like books?"

I jumped. I hadn't heard him come up beside me. "I love them. I hope you don't care if I spend a lot of time in here."

Karl made a straight line of his mouth and glanced over at his desk. His desk, right. His work area.

"Okay, so I won't spend a lot of time in here. Show me my room, will you?"

"You can use the library whenever I'm not working in here," he said.

"Thanks." I could see there was going to be a certain coldness about this library, too.

He showed me the rest of the first floor before he took me up to what was going to be my bedroom. Large, businesslike kitchen. Large, businesslike cook. She was friendly, though, and she was a black woman. That helped. Formal dining room. Small, handsome study—why the hell couldn't Karl work there? Game room with billiard table. Large service porch. As big as the house was, though, it was smaller than it looked from the outside. I thought it might turn out to be a more comfortable home than I had expected.

Karl and I stood on the porch and looked out at his park of a back yard. Tennis court. Swimming pool and bath house. We could see Doro and Vivian splashing around in the pool. Grass. Trees. There was a multicar garage off to one side, and I got a glimpse of a cottage almost hidden by trees.

"The gardener and his wife live out there," Karl told me. "His wife is the maid. The cook helps with the housework, too, when she isn't busy in the kitchen. She lives upstairs, in the servants' quarters."

"Did you inherit all this or something?" I asked. I wouldn't have been surprised if he'd said, "None of your business."

"I had one of my people sign it over to me," he said. "He was going to put it up for sale anyway and he didn't need the money."

I looked at him. The expression on his thin, angular face hadn't changed at all. I hooted with laughter. I couldn't help it. "You stole it! Oh, God. Beautiful; you're human, after all. And here I have to make do with shoplifting."

He gave me a forced smile. "I'll show you where your room is now."

"Okay. Can I ask you another question?"

He shrugged.

"How do you feel about black people?"

He looked at me, one eyebrow raised. "You've seen my cook."

"Right. So how do you feel about black people?"

"I've known exactly two of them well before now. They were all right." Emphasis on the "they."

I frowned, looked at him. "What's that supposed to mean?"

"That you shouldn't get the idea that I dislike you because you're black."

"Oh."

"I wouldn't want you here no matter what color you were."

I sighed. "You're going to make this even harder than it has to be, aren't you?"

"You asked."

"Well . . . I'm no happier to be here than you are to have me, but we're either going to have to get used to each other or we're going to have to keep out of each other's way a lot. Which won't be easy even in a house as big as this."

"Why did you and Doro fight?"

"What?" My first thought was that he was reading my mind. Then I realized that even if he hadn't seen Doro's hand, I had a big bruise on my jaw.

"You know damn well why we fought."

"Tell me. I answered your questions."

"Why does a telepath bother to ask questions?"

"Out of courtesy. Shall I stop?"

"No! We fought . . . because Doro didn't tell me about Vivian until about two hours ago."

There was a long pause. Then, "I see. How did you feel about marrying me before you found out about Vivian?"

"My grandmother married Doro," I said. "And, of course, my mother married him. I've expected to marry him myself ever since I was old enough to know what was going on. I wanted to. I loved him."

"Past tense?"

I almost didn't answer. I realized that I was ashamed. "No."

"Not even after he decides to marry you off to a stranger?"

"I've loved him for years. I guess it takes me a while to turn my emotions around."

"You probably never will. I've met several of his people since my transition. He uses me to keep them in line without killing them. And he's done terrible things to some of them. But I've never met one who hates him. Those who don't kill themselves by attacking him as soon as he acts against them always seem to forgive him."

Somehow that didn't surprise me. "Do you hate him?"

"No."

"In spite of . . . everything?" I remembered Vivian going out hand in hand with Doro.

"In spite of everything," he said quietly.

"Can you read his mind?"

"No."

"But why not? He says he's not a telepath. How could he stop you?"

"You'll find out after your transition. This will be your room." We were on the second floor. He opened the door he had stopped in front of.

The bedroom was white, and I guess you could call it elegant. There was a small crystal chandelier. There was a huge bed and a large dresser with a beautiful mirror. I'd have to be careful how I threw things. There was a closet that was going to look empty even after I hung up the new clothes Doro had bought me. There were chairs, little tables. . . .

It was just a really nice room. I peered into the mirror at my bruise. Then I sat down in a chair by the window and looked out at the front lawn as I spoke to Karl. "What do I do after my transition?"

"Do?"

"Well, I'll be able to read minds. I'll be able to steal better without getting caught—if I still want to. I'll be able to snoop through other people's secrets, even make robots of people. But. . . . "

" But?"

" What am I supposed to do—except maybe have babies?" I turned to face him and saw by his expression that he wished I hadn't said that last. I didn't care.

"I'm sure Doro will find some work for you," he said. "He probably already has something in mind."

Just at that moment, someone was hit by a car. I sensed enough to know that it was nearby, within a few blocks of Karl's house. I felt the impact. I might have said something. Then I felt the pain. A slow-motion avalanche of pain. I know I screamed then. That hit me harder than anything I'd ever received. Finally the pain got to be too much for the accident victim. He passed out. I almost passed out with him. I found myself curled into a tight knot on the chair, my feet up and my head down and throbbing.

I looked up to see whether Karl was still there, and found him watching me. He looked interested but not concerned, not inclined to give me any of the help he was supposed to give. I had a feeling that, if I survived transition, I would do it on my own.

"There's aspirin in the bathroom," he said, nodding toward a closed door. Then he turned and left.

Five days later, we were married at city hall. For those five days, I might as well have been alone in that big house. Doro left the day he brought me, and didn't come back. I saw Karl and Vivian at meals or ran into them accidentally around the house. They were always polite. I wasn't.

I tried talking to the servants, but they were silent, contented slaves. They worked, or they sat in their quarters watching television and waiting for the master's voice.

I joined Karl and Vivian out by the pool one day and what looked like a really interesting conversation came to a dead halt.

The only times I ever felt comfortable was when I was in my room with the door shut, or in the library when Karl wasn't home. He spent a lot of time in Los Angeles keeping an eye on the businesses he controlled for Doro and the ones he had taken over for his own, personal profit. Evidently he did more for them than just steal part of their profits. For me, he did nothing at all.

Doro showed up to see us married. Not that there was any kind of ceremony beyond the bare essentials. He went home with us—or with Vivian and me. Karl dropped the three of us off, then headed for L.A. Doro challenged Vivian to a game of tennis. I walked three blocks to a bus stop, caught a bus, and rode.

I knew where I was going. I had to transfer to get there, so there was no way for me to pretend to myself that I wound up there by accident. I got off at Maple and Dell and walked straight to Rina's house.

Rina was home, but she had company. I could hear her and her company yelling at each other way out on the sidewalk. I walked around the corner and knocked on Emma's door. She opened it, looked at me, stood back from the door. I went in and sat down in the big overstuffed chair near the door. I closed my eyes for a while and the ugly old house seemed to go around me like a blanket, shutting out the cold. I took a deep breath, felt relief, release.

Emma laid a hand on my forehead and I looked up at her. She was young. That meant she had had Doro with her recently. I didn't look anything like her when she was young. Doro was crazy. I wished I did look that good.

"You were supposed to get married," she said.

"I did. Today."

She frowned. "Where's your husband?"

"I don't know. Or care."

She sort of half smiled in her know-it-all way that I had always resented before. Now I didn't care. She could throw all the sarcasm she wanted to at me if she just let me sit there for a while.

"Stay here for a while," she said.

I looked at her, surprised.

"Stay until someone comes to get you."

"They might not even know I've gone anywhere. I didn't say anything. I just left."

"Honey, you're talking about Doro and an active telepath. They know, believe me."

"I guess so. I came here on the bus, though. I don't mind going back that way." I never liked depending on other people and their cars, anyway. When I rode the bus, I went when I wanted, where I wanted.

"Stay put. Doro might not have heard you yet."

"What?"

"You've said something by coming here. Now the way to make sure that Doro's heard you is to inconvenience him a little. Just stay where you are. Are you hungry?"

"Yeah."

She brought me cold chicken, potato salad, and a Coke. Brought it to me like I was a guest. She'd never brought me anything she could send me after before in her life.

"Emma."

She had gone back to whatever she was doing at her desk in the dining room. The desk was half covered with official-looking papers. She looked around.

"Thanks," I said quietly.

She just nodded.

Karl came after me that night. I answered the door, saw him, and turned to say good-by to Emma, but she was right there looking at Karl.

"You're too high, Karl," she said quietly. "You've forgotten where you came from."

He looked at her, then looked away. His expression didn't change, but his voice, when he spoke, was softer than normal. "That isn't it."

"It doesn't really matter. If you've got a problem, you know who to complain to about it—or who to take it out on."

He drew a deep breath, met her eyes again, smiled his thin smile. "I hear, Em."

I didn't say anything to him until we were in the car together. Then, "Is she one of the two?"

He gave me a kind of puzzled glance, then seemed to remember. He nodded.

"Where do you know her from?"

"She took care of me once when I was between foster homes. That was before Doro found a permanent home for me. She took care of me again when I was approaching transition. My adoptive parents couldn't handle me." He smiled again.

"What happened to your real parents—real mother, I mean?"

"She . . . died."

I turned to look at him. His expression had gone grim. "By herself," I asked, "or with help?"

"It's an ugly story."

I shrugged. "Okay." I looked out the window.

"But, then, you're no stranger to ugly stories." He paused. "She was an alcoholic, my mother. And she wasn't exactly normal—sane—during those rare times when she was sober. Doro says she was too sensitive. Anyway, when I was about three, I did something that made her mad. I don't remember what. But I remember very clearly what happened afterward. For punishment, she held my hand over the flame of our gas range. She held it there until it was completely charred. But I was lucky. Doro came to see her later that same day. I wasn't even aware of when he killed her. I remember, I wasn't aware of anything but alternating pain and exhaustion between the time she burned me and the time Doro's healer arrived. You might know the healer. She's one of Emma's granddaughters. Over a period of weeks, she regenerated the stump that I had left into a new hand. Even now, ten years after my transition, I don't understand how she did it. She does for other people the things Emma can only do for herself. When she had finished, Doro placed me with saner people."

I whistled. "So that's what Emma meant."

" Yes."

I moved uncomfortably in the seat. "As for the rest of what she said, Karl. . . . "

"She was right."

"I don't want anything from you."

He shrugged.

He didn't say much more to me that night. Doro was still at the house, paying a lot of attention to Vivian. I had dinner with them all, then went to bed. I could put up with them until my transition, surely. Then maybe for a change I'd be one of the owners instead of one of the owned.

I was almost asleep when Karl came up to my room. Neither of us put a light on but there was light enough from one of the windows for me to see him. He took off his robe, threw it into a chair and climbed into bed with me.

I didn't say anything. I had plenty to say and all of it was pretty caustic. I didn't doubt that I could have gotten rid of him if I had wanted to. But I didn't bother. I didn't want him but I was stuck with him. Why play games?

He was all right, though. Gentle and, thank God, silent. I didn't know whether he had come to me out of charity, or curiosity, and I didn't want to know. I knew he still resented me—at least resented me. Maybe that was why, when we were finished, he got up and went to get his robe. He was going back to his own room.

"Karl."

I could see him turn to look in my direction.

"Stay the night."

42

"You want me to?" I didn't blame him for sounding surprised. I was surprised.

"Yes. Come on back." I didn't want to be alone. I couldn't have put into words how much I suddenly didn't want to be alone, couldn't stand to be alone, how much it scared me. I found myself remembering how Rina would pace the floor at night sometimes. I would see her crying and pacing and holding her head. After a while, she would go out and come back with some bum who usually looked a little like her—like us. She'd keep him with her the rest of the night even if he didn't have a dime in his pocket, even if he was too drunk to do anything. And sometimes even if he knocked her around and called her names that trash like him didn't have the right to call anybody. I used to wonder how Rina could live with herself. Now, apparently, I was going to find out.

Karl came back to my bed without another word. I didn't know what he was thinking, but he could have really hurt me with just a few words. He didn't. I tried to thank him for that.

· Three ·

KARL

The warehouse was enormous. Whitten Coleman Service Building, serving thirty-three department stores over three states. Doro had begun the chain seventy years before, when he bought a store for a small, stable family of his people. The job of the family was simply to grow and prosper and eventually become one of Doro's sources of money. Descendants of the original family still held a controlling interest in the company. They were obedient and self-sufficient, and, for the most part, Doro let them alone. Through the years, their calls to him for help had become fewer. As they grew in size and experience, they became more able to handle their own problems. Doro still visited them from time to time, though. Sometimes he asked favors of them. Sometimes they asked favors of him. This was one of the latter times. Karl, Doro, the warehouse manager, and the chief of security walked through the warehouse toward the loading docks. Karl had never been inside the warehouse before, but now he led the way through the maze of dusty stock areas and busy marking rooms. In turn, he was led by the thoughts of several workers who were efficiently preparing to steal several thousand dollars' worth of Whitten Coleman merchandise. They had gotten away with several earlier thefts in spite of the security people who watched them, and the cameras trained on them.

Quietly, Karl pointed out the thieves—including two security men—and explained their methods to the security chief. And he told the chief where the group had hidden what they had left of the merchandise they had already stolen. He had almost finished when he realized that something was wrong with Mary.

He maintained a mental link with the girl now that he was married to her. And now that Doro had made clear what would happen to him if Mary died in transition.

Something about the girl's expanding ability had changed. Suddenly she was no longer passively absorbing the usual ambient mental noise. She was unwittingly reaching out for it, drawing it to her. The last fragments of what Doro called her childhood shield—the mental protection that served young actives until they were old enough to stand transition—was crumbling away. She was in transition.

Karl broke off what he was saying to the security chief. Suddenly he was caught up in the experience Mary was having. She was running, screaming. . . .

No. No, it wasn't Mary who was running. It was another woman—the woman Mary was receiving from. The two were one. One woman running down stark white corridors. A woman fleeing from men who were also dressed in white. She gibbered and babbled and wept. Suddenly she realized that her own body was covered with slimy yellow worms. She tore at the worms frantically to get them off. They changed their coloring from yellow to yellow streaked with red. They began to burrow into her flesh. The woman fell to the floor tearing at herself, vomiting, urinating.

She hardly felt the restraining hands of her pursuers, or the prick of the needle. She did not have even enough awareness of the world outside her own mind to be grateful for the eventual oblivion.

Karl snapped back to the reality of the warehouse with a jolt. He found himself holding on to the steel support of some overhead shelving. His hands hurt from grasping it so tightly. He shook his head, saw Doro and the two warehousemen staring at him. The warehousemen looked concerned. Doro looked expectant. Karl spoke to Doro. "I've got to get home. Now."

Doro nodded. "I'll drive you. Come on."

Karl followed him out of the building, then blindly, mechanically got in on the driver's side. Doro spoke to him sharply. Karl jumped, frowned, moved over. Doro was right. Karl was in no shape to drive. Karl was in no shape to do anything. It was as though he were plunging into his own transition again.

"You're too close to her," said Doro. "Pull back a little. See if you can sense what's happening to her without being caught up in it."

Pull back. How? How had he gotten so close, anyway? He had never been caught up in Mary's pretransition experiences.

"You know what to expect," Doro told him. "At this point she's going to be reaching for the worst possible stuff. That's what's familiar to her. That's what's going to attract her attention. She'll get an avalanche of it—violence, pain, fear, whatever. I don't want you caught up in it unless she obviously needs help."

Karl said nothing. He was already trying to separate himself from Mary. The mental link he had established with her had grown into something more than he had intended it to be. If two minds could be tangled together, his and Mary's were.

Then he realized that she had become aware of him, was watching him as he tried to untangle himself. He had never permitted her to be aware of his mental probing before. He stopped what he was doing now, concerned that he had frightened her. She would have enough fear to contend with within the next twelve hours without his adding to it.

But she was not afraid. She was glad to have him with her. She was relieved to discover that she was not facing the worst hours of her life alone.

Karl relaxed for a few minutes, less eager to leave her now. He could still remember how glad he had been to have Emma with him during his transition. Emma couldn't help mentally, but she was a human presence with him, drawing him back to sanity, reality. He could do at least that much for Mary.

"How is she?" Doro asked.

"All right. She understands what's happening."

"Something is liable to snatch her away again any minute."

"I know."

"When it happens, let it happen. Watch, but stay out of it. If you see a way to help her, don't."

"I thought that's what I was for. To help."

"You are, later, when she can't help herself. When she's ready to give up."

Karl glanced at Doro while keeping most of his attention on Mary. "Do you lose a lot of her kind?"

Doro smiled grimly. "She doesn't have a 'kind.' She's unique. So are you, though you aren't as unusual as I hope she'll be. I've been working toward both of you for a good many generations. But yes." The smile vanished. "Several of her unsuccessful predecessors have died in transition."

Karl nodded. "And I'll bet most of them took somebody with them. Somebody who was trying to help them."

Doro said nothing.

"I thought so," said Karl. "And I already know from Mary's thoughts that you killed the ones who managed to survive transition."

"If you know, why bring it up?"

Karl sighed. "I guess because it still surprises me that you can do things like that. Or maybe I'm just wondering whether she or I will still be alive this time tomorrow—even if we both survive her transition."

"Bring her through for me, Karl, and you'll be all right."

"And her?"

"She's a dangerous kind of experiment. Believe me, if she turns out to be another failure, you'll want her dead more than I will."

"I wish I knew what the hell you were doing. Aside from playing God, I mean."

"You know enough."

"I don't know anything."

"You know what I want of you. That's enough."

It never did any good to argue with Doro. Karl leaned back

and finished disentangling himself from Mary. He would be with her in person soon. And even without Doro's warning he would not have wanted to go through much more of her transition with her. Before he broke the connection, he let her know that he was on his way to her, that she wouldn't be alone long. It had been two weeks since their marriage, two weeks since she had called him back to her bed. he hadn't gone out of his way to hurt her since then.

He watched Doro maneuver the car into the right lane so that they could get on the Forsyth Freeway. Doro cut across the lanes, wove through the light traffic carelessly, speeding as usual. He had no more regard for traffic laws than he did for any other laws. Karl wondered how many accidents Doro had caused or been involved in. Not that it mattered to Doro. Had human life ever mattered to Doro beyond his interest in human husbandry? Could a creature who had to look upon ordinary people literally as food and shelter ever understand how strongly those people valued life? But yes, of course he could. He understood it well enough to use it to keep his people in line. He probably even understood it well enough to know how Karl and Mary both felt now. It just didn't make any difference. He didn't care.

Fifteen minutes later, Doro pulled into Karl's driveway. Karl was out of the car and heading for the house before Doro brought the car to a full stop. Karl knew that Mary was in the midst of another experience. He had felt it begin. He had kept her under carefully distant observation even after he had severed the link between them. Now, though, even without a deliberately established link, he was having trouble preventing himself from merging into her experience. Mary was trapped in the mind of a man who had to eventually burn to death. The man was trapped inside a burning house. Mary was experiencing his every sensation.

Karl went up the back stairs two at a time and ran through the servants' quarters toward the front of the house. He knew Mary was in her room, lying down, knew that, for some reason, Vivian was with her.

He walked into the room and looked first at Mary, who lay in the middle of her bed, her body rolled into a tight, fetal knot.

She made small noises in her throat like choked screams or moans, but she did not move. Karl sat down on the bed next to her and looked at Vivian.

"Is she going to be all right?" Vivian asked.

"I think so."

"Are *you* going to be all right?"

"If she is, I will be."

She got up, came to rest one hand on his shoulder. "You mean, if she comes through all right, Doro won't kill you."

He looked at her, surprised. One of the things he liked about her was that she could still surprise him. He left her enough mental privacy for that. He had read his previous women more than he read her and they had quickly become boring. He had hardly read Vivian at all until she had asked him to condition her and let her stay with him, help her stay, in spite of Mary. He had not wanted to do it, but he had not wanted to lose her, either. The conditioning he had imposed on her kept her from feeling jealousy or hatred toward Mary. But it did not prevent her from seeing things clearly and drawing her own conclusions.

"Don't worry," he told her. "Both Mary and I are going to make it all right."

She looked at Mary, who still lay knotted in the agony of her experience. "Is there anything I can do to help?"

"Nothing."

"Can I . . . can I stay. I'll keep out of the way. I just—"

"Vee, no."

"I just want to see what she has to go through. I want to see that the price she has to pay to . . . to be like you is too high."

"You can't stay. You know you can't."

She closed her eyes for a moment, dropped her hand to her side. "Then, let me go. Let me leave you."

He stared at her, surprised, stricken. "You know you're free to go if that's really what you want. But I'm asking you not to."

"I'll become an outsider if I don't leave you now." She shrugged hopelessly. "I'll be alone. You and Mary will be alike, and I'll be alone." There was no anger or resentment in her, he could see. Her conditioning was holding well enough. But she had been much more aware of Mary's loneliness than Karl had

49

realized. And when Karl began occasionally sleeping with Mary, Vivian had begun to see Mary's life as a preview of her own. "You won't need me," she said softly. "You'll only come to me now and then to be kind."

"Vee, will you stay until tomorrow?"

She said nothing.

"Stay at least until tomorrow. We've got to talk." He reinforced the request with a subtle mental command. She had no telepathic ability at all. She would not be consciously aware of the command, but she would respond to it. She would stay until the next day, as he had asked, and she would think her staying was her own decision. He promised himself that he would not coerce her further. Already it was getting too easy to treat her like just another pet.

She drew a deep breath. "I don't know what good it will do," she said. "But yes, I'll stay that long." She turned to go out of the room and ran into Doro. He caught her as she was stumbling blindly around him, and held her.

Doro looked at Mary, who had finally straightened herself out on the bed. She looked back at him wearily.

"Good luck," he said quietly.

She continued to watch him, not responding at all.

He turned and left with Vivian, still holding her as she cried.

Karl looked down at Mary.

She continued to stare after Doro and Vivian. She spoke softly. "Why is it Doro is always so kind to people after he messes up their lives?"

Karl took a tissue from the box on her night table and wiped her face. It was wet with perspiration.

She gave him a tired half smile. "You being 'kind' to me, man?"

"That wasn't my word," said Karl.

"No?"

"Look," he said, "you know how it's going to be from now on. One bad experience after another. Why don't you use this time to rest?"

"When it's over, if I'm still alive, I'll rest." And then explosively, "Shit!"

He felt her caught up in someone else's fear, stark terror. Then he was caught too. He was too close to her again.

For a moment, he let the alien terror roll over him, engulf him. He broke into an icy sweat. Abruptly he was elsewhere— standing outside in the back yard of a house built near the edge of one of the canyons. Coming up the slope from the canyon was the longest, thickest snake he had ever seen. It was coming toward him. He couldn't move. He was terrified of snakes. Abruptly he turned to run. He caught his foot on a lawn sprinkler, fell screaming, his body twisting, thrashing. He felt his own leg snap as he hit the ground. But the break registered less on him than the snake. And the snake was coming closer.

Karl had had enough. He drew back, screened out the man's terror. At that instant, Mary screamed.

As Karl watched, she turned on her side, curling up again, pressing her face into the pillow so that the sounds she made were muffled.

He watched her mentally as well, or watched the ophidiophobe whose mind held her. He thought he understood something now. Something he had wondered about. He knew how Mary's expanding talent, acting without control, was opening one pathway after another to other people's raw emotions. And now he realized that when he let himself be caught up in those emotions, he was standing in the middle of an open pathway. He was shielding her from the infant fumbling of her own ability by accepting the consequences of that fumbling himself. That was why Doro had told him to back off. When he was too close to Mary, he was helping her. He was preventing her from going through the suffering that was normal for a person in transition. And since the suffering was normal, perhaps it was in some way necessary. Perhaps an active could not mature without it. Perhaps that was why Doro had warned him to help Mary only when she could no longer help herself.

"Karl?"

He looked at her, realizing that he had let his attention wander. He didn't know what had finally happened to the frightened man. He didn't care.

"What did you do?" she asked. "I could feel myself getting caught up in something else. Then for a while it was gone."

He told her what he had learned, and what he had guessed. "So at least now I know how to help you," he finished. "That gives you a better chance."

"I thought Doro would tell you how to help me."

"No, I think half Doro's pleasure comes from watching us, running us through mazes like rats and seeing how well we figure things out."

"Sure," she said. "What are a few rat lives?" She took a deep breath. "And, speaking of lives, Karl, don't help me unless I'm about to lose mine. Let me try to get through this on my own."

"I'll do whatever seems necessary as you progress," he said. "You're going to have to trust my judgment. I've been through this already."

"Yeah, you've been through it," she said. He saw her hands tighten into fists as something clutched at her mind before she could finish. But she managed to get a few more words out. "And you went through it on your own. Alone."

She struggled all evening, all night, and well into the next morning. During her few lucid moments he tried to show her how to interpose her own mind shield between herself and the world outside, how to control her ability and regain the mental peace that she had not known for months. That was what he had had to learn to bring his own transition to an end. If she didn't want his protection, perhaps he could at least show her how to protect herself.

But she did not seem to be able to learn.

She was growing weaker and wearier. Dangerously weary. She seemed ready to sink into oblivion with the unfortunate people whose thoughts possessed her. She had passed out a few times, earlier. Now, though, he was afraid to let her go again. She was too weak. He was afraid she might never regain consciousness.

He lay beside her on the bed listening to her ragged breathing, knowing that she was with a fifteen-year-old boy somewhere in Los Angeles. The boy was being methodically beaten to death by three older boys—members of a rival gang.

Just watching the things she had to live through was sickening. Why couldn't she pick up the simple shielding technique?

She started to get up from the bed. Her self-control was all but gone. She was moving as the boy moved miles away. He was trying to get up from the ground. He didn't know what he was doing. Neither did she.

Karl caught her and held her down, thankful, not for the first time that night, that she was small. He managed to catch her hands before she could slash him again with her nails. The blood was hardly dry on his face where she had scratched him before. He held her, pinning her with his weight, waiting for it to end.

Then, abruptly, he was tired of waiting. He opened his mind to the experience and took the finish of the beating himself.

When it was over, he stayed with her, ready to take anything else that might sweep her away. Even now she was stubborn enough not to want him there, but he no longer cared what she wanted. He brushed aside her wordless protests and tried to show her again how to erect shielding of her own. Again he failed. She still couldn't do it.

But after a while, she seemed to be doing something.

Staying with her mentally, Karl opened his eyes and moved away from her body. Something was happening that he did not understand. She had not been able to learn from him, but she was using him somehow. She had ceased to protest his mental presence. In fact, her attention seemed to be on something else entirely. Her body was relaxed. Her thoughts were her own, but they were not coherent. He could make no sense of them. He sensed other people with her mentally, but he could not reach them even clearly enough to identify them.

"What are you doing?" he asked aloud. He didn't like having to ask.

She didn't seem to hear him.

I asked what you were doing! He gave her his annoyance with the thought.

Mary noticed him then, and somehow drew him closer to her. He seemed to see her arms reaching out, her hands grasping him, though her body did not move. Suddenly suspicious, he tried to break contact with her. Before he could complete the attempt, his universe exploded.

MARY

I couldn't have said what I was doing. I knew Karl was still with me. His mental voice was still reaching me. I didn't mean to grab him the way I did. I didn't realize until afterward that I had done it. And even then, it seemed a perfectly natural thing to do. It was what I had done to the others.

Others, yes. Five of them. They seemed to be far away from me, perhaps scattered around the country. Actives like Karl, like me. People I had noticed during the last minutes of my transition. People who had noticed me at the same time. Their thoughts told me what they were, but I became aware of them— "saw" them—as bright points of light, like stars. They formed a shifting pattern of light and color. I had brought them together somehow. Now I was holding them together—and they didn't want to be held.

Their pattern went through kaleidoscopic changes in design as they tried to break free of me. They were bright, darting fragments of fear and surprise, like insects beating themselves against glass. Then they were long strands of fire, stretching away from me, but somehow never stretching quite far enough to escape. They were writhing, shapeless things, merging into each other, breaking apart, rolling together again as a tidal wave of light, as a single clawing hand.

I was their target. They tore at me desperately with the hand they had formed. I didn't feel it. All I could feel was their emotions. Desperation, anger, fear, hatred. . . . They tore at me harmlessly, tore at each other in their confusion. Finally they wore themselves out.

They rested grouped around me, relaxed. They were threads of fire again, each thread touching me, linked with me. I was comfortable with them that way. I didn't understand how or why I was holding them, but I didn't mind doing it. It felt right.

I didn't want them frightened or angry or hating me. I wanted them the way they were now, at ease, comfortable with me.

I realized that there was something really proprietary about my feelings toward them. As though I was supposed to have charge over them and they were supposed to accept me. But I also realized that I had no idea how dangerous it might be for me to hold a group of experienced active telepaths on mental leashes. Not that it would have mattered if I had known, though, since I couldn't find a way to let them go. At least they were peaceful now. And I was so tired. I drifted off to sleep.

It was light out when Karl woke me by sitting up in bed and pulling the blankets off me. Late morning. Ten o'clock by the clock on my night table. It was a strange awakening for me. My head didn't hurt. For the first time in months, I didn't have even a slight headache. I didn't realize until I moved, though, that several other parts of my body hurt like hell. I had strained muscles, bruises, scratches—most of them self-inflicted, I guess. At least, none of them were very serious; they were just going to leave me sore for a while.

I moved, gasped, then groaned and kept still. Karl looked down at me without saying anything. I could see a set of deep, ugly scratches down the left side of his face, and I knew I had put them there. I reached up to touch his face, ignoring the way my arm and shoulder muscles protested. "Hey, I'm sorry. I hope that's all I did."

"It isn't."

"Oh, boy. What else?"

"This." He did something—tugged at the mental strand of himself that still connected him to me. That brought me fully awake. I had forgotten about my captives, my pattern. Karl's sudden tug was startling, but it didn't hurt me, or him. And I noticed that it didn't seem to bother the five others. Karl could tug only his own strand. The other strands remained relaxed. I knew what Karl wanted. I spoke to him softly.

"I'd let you go if I knew how. This isn't something I did on purpose."

"You're shielded against me," he said. "Open and let me see if there's anything I can do."

I hadn't realized I was shielded at all. He had tried so hard to teach me to form my own shield, and I hadn't been able to do it. Apparently I had finally picked up the technique without even realizing it—picked it up when I couldn't stand any more of the mental garbage I was getting.

So now I had a shield. I examined it curiously. It was a mental wall, a mental globe with me inside. Nothing was reaching me through it except the strands of the pattern. I wondered how I was supposed to open it for him. As I wondered, it began to disintegrate.

It surprised me, scared me. I wanted it back.

And it was back.

Well, that wasn't hard to understand. The shield kept me secure as long as I wanted it to. And there were degrees of security.

I began the disintegration process again, felt the shield grow thinner. I let it become a kind of screen—something I could receive other people's thoughts through. I experimented until I could hold it just heavy enough to keep out the kind of mental noise I had been picking up before and during my transition. It kept out the noise, but it didn't keep me in. I could reach out and sense whatever there was to be sensed. I swept my perception through the house experimentally.

I sensed Vivian still asleep in Doro's bed. And, in another way, I sensed Doro beside her. Actually, I only sensed a human shape beside her—a body. I was aware of it in the way I was aware of the lamp on the night table beside it. I could read Vivian's thoughts with no effort at all. But somehow, without realizing it, I had drawn back from trying to read the mind of that other body. Now, cautiously, I started to reach into Doro's mind. It was like stepping off a cliff.

I jerked back instantly, thickening my screen to a shield and struggling to regain my balance. As fast as I had moved to draw away, I had the feeling I had almost fallen. Safe as I knew I was in my own bed, I had the feeling that I had just come very near death.

"You see?" said Karl as I lay gasping. "I told you you'd find out why actives don't read his mind. Now open again."

"But what was it? What happened?"

"You almost committed suicide."

I stared at him.

"Telepaths are the people he kills most easily," he said. "Normally he can only kill the person physically nearest to him. But he can kill telepaths no matter where they are. Or, rather, he can if they help him by trying to read his mind. It's like begging him to take you."

"And you let me do it?"

"I could hardly have stopped you."

"You could have warned me! You were watching me, reading me. I could feel you with me. You knew what I was going to do before I did it."

"Your own senses warned you. You chose to ignore them."

He was colder than he had been on the day I met him. He was sitting there beside me in bed acting like I was his enemy. "Karl, what's the matter with you? You just worked your ass off trying to save my life. Now, for heaven's sake, you'd let me blunder to my death without saying a word."

He took a deep breath. "Just open again. I won't hurt you. But I've got to find a way out of whatever it is you've caught me in."

I opened. Obviously, he wasn't going to act human again until I did. I felt him reach into my mind, watched him review my memories—all those that had anything to do with the patterns. There wasn't much.

So, in a couple of seconds he knew how little I knew. He had already found out he couldn't break away from the pattern. Now he knew for sure that I couldn't let him go either. He knew there wasn't even a way for him to force me to let him go. I wondered why he thought he'd have to force me—why he thought I wouldn't have let him go if I could have. He answered my thought aloud.

"I just didn't believe anyone could create and maintain a trap like that without knowing what they were doing," he said. "You're holding six powerful people captive. How can you do that by accident or instinct or whatever?"

"I don't know."

He withdrew from my thoughts in disgust. "You also have some very Dorolike ideas," he said. "I don't know how the others feel about it, Mary, but you don't own me."

It took me a minute to realize what he was talking about. Then I remembered. My proprietary feelings. "Are you going to blame me for thoughts I had while I was in transition?" I asked. "You know I was out of my head."

"You were when you first started to think that way. But you aren't now, and you're still thinking that way."

That was true. I couldn't help the feeling of rightness that I had about the pattern—about the people of the pattern being my people. I felt it even more strongly than I had felt Doro's mental keep-out sign. But that didn't matter. I sighed. "Look, Karl, no matter what I feel, you find me a way to break this thing, free you and the others, and I'll co-operate in any way I can."

He had gotten up. He was standing by the bed watching me with what looked like hatred. "You'd better," he said quietly. He turned and left the room.

PART
TWO

· Four ·

SETH DANA

There was water. That was the important thing. There was a well covered by a tall, silver-colored tank. And beside it there was an electric pump housed in a small wooden shed. The electricity was shut off, but the power poles were all sturdily upright, and the wire that had been run in from the main road looked all right. Seth decided to have the electricity turned on as soon as possible. Otherwise he and Clay would either have to haul water from town or get it from some of the nearer houses.

Seth looked over at Clay, saw that his brother was examining the pump. Clay looked calm, relaxed. That alone made Seth's decision to buy him this desert property worthwhile. There were few neighbors, and those widely scattered. The nearest town was twenty miles away. Adamsville. And it wasn't much of a town. About twelve hundred dull, peaceful people. Clay had been reasonably comfortable even while they were passing through it. Seth wiped the sweat from his forehead and stepped into the shadow cast by the well's tank. Just morning and it was hot already.

"Pump look all right, Clay?"

Octavia E. Butler

"Looks fine. Just waiting for some electricity."

"How about you?" He knew exactly how Clay was, but he wanted to hear his brother say it aloud.

"I'm all right too." Clay shook his head. "Man, I better be. If I can't make it out here, I can't make it anywhere. I'm not picking up anything now."

"You will, sooner or later," said Seth. "But probably not much. Not even as much as if you were in Adamsville."

Clay nodded, wiped his brow, and went to look at the shack that had served to house the land's former occupant. An old man had lived there pretty much as a hermit. He had built the shack just as, several years before, he had built a real house—a home for his wife and children. A home that they had lived in for only a few days when the wind blew down the power lines and they had to resort to candles. One of the children had invented a game to play with the candles. In the resulting fire, the man had lost his wife, his two sons, and most of his sanity. He had lived on the property as a recluse until his death, a few months back. Seth had bought the property from his surviving daughter, now an adult. He had bought it in the hope that his latent brother might finally find peace there.

Clay shouldn't have been a latent. He was thirty, a year older than Seth, and he should have gone through transition at least a decade before. Even Doro had expected him to. Doro was father to both of them. He had actually worn one body long enough to father two children on the same woman with it. Their mother had been annoyed. She liked variety.

Well, she had variety in Clay and Seth. One son was not only a failure but a helpless failure. Clay was abnormally sensitive even for a latent. But as a latent, he had no control. Without Seth he would be insane or dead by now. Doro had suggested privately to Seth that a quick, easy death might be kindest. Seth had been able to listen to such talk calmly only because he had been through his own agonizing latent period before his transition. He knew what Clay would have to put up with for the rest of his life. And he knew Doro was doing something he had never done before. He was allowing Seth to make an important decision.

"No," Seth had said. "I'll take care of him." And he had done it. He had been nineteen then to Clay's twenty. Clay had not cared much for the idea of being taken care of by anyone, least of all his younger brother. But pain had dulled his pride.

They had traveled around the country together, content with no one place for long. Sometimes Seth worked—when he wanted to. Sometimes he stole. Often he shielded his brother and accepted punishment in his stead. Clay never asked it. He saved what was left of his pride by not asking. He was too unstable to work. He got jobs, but inevitably he lost them. Some violent event caught his mind and afterward he had to lie, tell people he was an epileptic. Employers seemed to accept his explanation, but afterward they found reason to fire him. Seth could have stopped them, could have seen to it that they considered Clay their most valuable employee. But Clay didn't want it that way. "What's the point?" he had said more than once. "I can't do the work. The hell with it."

Clay was slowly deciding to kill himself. It was slow because, in spite of everything, Clay did not want to die. He was just becoming less and less able to tolerate the pain of living.

So now a lonely piece of land. A so-called ranch in the middle of the Arizona desert. Clay could have a few animals, a garden, whatever he wanted. Whatever he could take care of in view of the fact that he would be incapacitated part of the time. He would be receiving money from some income property Seth had insisted on stealing for him in Phoenix, but in more personal ways he would be self-sufficient. He would be able to bear his own pain—now that there would be less of it. He would be able to make his land productive. He would be able to take care of himself. If he was to live at all, he would have to be able to do that.

"Hey, come on in here," Clay was calling from within the hermit's shack. "Take a look at this thing."

Seth went into the shack. Clay was in what had been a combination kitchen-bedroom-living room. The only other room was piled high with bales of newspapers and magazines and stacked with tools. A storage room, apparently. What Clay was looking at was a large cast-iron wood-burning stove.

Seth laughed. "Maybe we can sell that thing as an antique and use the money to buy an electric stove. We'll need one."

"What we?" demanded Clay.

"Well, you, then. You don't want to have to fight with that thing every time you want to eat, do you?"

"Never mind the stove. You're starting to sound like you changed your mind about leaving."

"No I haven't. I'm going as soon as you're settled in here. And—" He stopped, looked away from Clay. There was something he had not mentioned to his brother yet.

"And what?"

"And as soon as you get somebody to help you."

Clay stared at him. "You've got to be kidding."

"Man, you need somebody."

"The hell I do! Some crazy old man lived out here by himself, but me, I need somebody. No! No way!"

"You want to try to drive the van into town yourself?" Suddenly Seth was shouting. "How many people you figure you'll kill along the way? Aside from yourself, I mean." Clay had not dared to drive since his last accident, in which he had nearly killed three people. But obviously he had not been thinking about that. Seth spoke again, softly this time. "Man, you know you're going to have to go into town sooner or later."

"I'd rather hitch in with somebody who lives around here," muttered Clay. "I could go to that place we passed—the one with the windmill."

"Clay, you need somebody. You know you do."

"Another Goddamn baby sitter."

"How about a wife? Or at least a woman."

Now Clay looked outraged. "*You* want to find me a woman?"

"Hell no. Find your own woman. But I'm not leaving until you do."

Clay looked around the shack, looked out the open door. "No woman in her right mind would want to come out here and share this place with me."

"This place isn't bad. Hell, tell her what you're going to do with it. Tell her about the house you're going to build her. Tell her how good *you're* going to take care of *her*."

Clay stared at him.

"Well?"

"She's going to have to be some woman to look at these God-forsaken rocks and bushes and listen to me daydreaming."

"You'll do all right. I never knew you to have trouble finding a woman when you wanted one."

"Hell, that was different."

"I know. But you'll do all right." Seth would see that he did all right. When Clay found a woman he liked, Seth would fix things for him. Clay would never have to know. The woman would "fall in love" faster and harder and more permanently than she ever had before. Seth didn't usually manipulate Clay that way, but Clay really needed somebody around. What if something caught his mind while he was fixing food, and he fell across the stove? What if a lot of things! Best to get him a good woman and tie her to him tight. Best to tie Clay to her a little, too. Otherwise Clay might get mean enough to kick her out over nothing.

And it would be a good idea to see that a couple of Clay's nearest neighbors were friendly. Clay tended to make friends easily, then lose them just as easily because his violent "epileptic seizures" scared people. People decided that he was either crazy or going crazy, and they backed away. Seth would see that the neighbors here didn't back away.

"I think I'll go back to Adamsville and make one of the store owners open up," he told Clay. "You want to go along and start your hunt?" He could feel Clay cringe mentally at the thought.

"No thanks. I'm not in any hurry. Besides, I need a chance to look the place over myself before I think about bringing somebody else out here."

"Okay." Seth managed not to smile. He looked around the shack. There was an ancient electric refrigerator in one corner waiting for the electricity to be turned on. And in the storage room, he could see an old-fashioned icebox—the kind you had to put ice in. He decided to bring back some ice for it. The electricity couldn't be turned on until late tomorrow at the soonest, and he wanted to buy some food.

"Anything special you want me to bring back, Clay?"

Clay wiped his forehead on his sleeve and looked out into the bright sunlight. "Couple of six-packs."

Seth grunted. "Yeah. You didn't have to tell me that." He went out to the van and got in. The van was a big oven. He almost blistered his hand on the steering wheel. And he was getting a headache.

He hadn't had a headache since his transition. In fact, this one felt like the ones he used to get when he was approaching transition. But you only went through that once. The sun must have been affecting him. Best to get moving and let the wind cool him off.

He started down the winding dirt path that led to the edge of his property. The path crossed railroad tracks and met a gravel road. That road led to the main highway. The place was isolated, all right. It was a bad place to get sick. And Seth was getting sick. It wasn't the heat—or, if it was, the wind blowing through the van window wasn't helping. He felt worse than ever. He was just reaching the railroad tracks when he lost control of the van.

Something slammed into his thoughts as though his mental shield didn't exist. It was an explosion of mental static that blotted out everything else, left him able to do nothing other than endure it, and endure the fierce residue of pain and shock that followed it.

By some miracle, he did not wreck the van. He ran it into the sign that identified his property as the something-or-other ranch. But the dry wooden signpost snapped easily against the bumper and fell without damaging the van.

Seth lost consciousness for a moment. When he came to, he saw that he had managed to stop the van and that he had fallen across the horn. He sat up wondering whether he had made enough noise to alert Clay, back at the shack.

Several seconds later, he heard someone—it must have been Clay—running toward the van. Then all real sound was drowned by the "sound" within his head. Mental static welling up again agonizingly. It was not like transition. He received no individual violent incidents that he could distinguish. Instead he felt himself seized, held, and somehow divided against himself. When he tried to shield himself from whatever was attacking him, it was as though he had tried to close a door while his leg or arm was still in the doorway. He was being used against himself somehow.

He was vaguely aware of the van door opening, of Clay asking what had happened. He did not even try to answer. If he had opened his mouth, he would have screamed.

When he finally found the strength to try again to defend himself against whatever had attacked him, his defense was thrown back in his face. With it, he received his only comprehensible communication from his attacker. A one-word command that left him no opportunity for argument or disobedience.

Come.

He was being drawn westward, toward California, toward Los Angeles, toward Forsyth, one of the many suburbs of Los Angeles, toward. . . .

He could see the house he was to go to, a white stucco mansion. But he could not see who called him there, or why he had been called, or how his caller was able to exert such influence over him. Because he would definitely go to Forsyth. He had no choice. The pull was too strong.

The intensity of the call lessened to a bearable din and the shock of the attack passed.

He and Clay would go to California. He couldn't leave Clay here alone in the desert. And he couldn't stay to see Clay settled in. He couldn't stay for anything at all. Clay's independence would have to wait. Everything would have to wait.

RACHEL DAVIDSON

Rachel had made herself sick by following Eli's suggestion. Thus it seemed only reasonable that Eli take her place and preach the sermon today. And it was only reasonable that she stay at the hotel, relaxed, semiconscious, so that her body did not shake from this one illness that she was helpless against.

And since everything was so reasonable, she thought, why had she brought herself to full consciousness despite her shaking? Why was she now in a cab on her way to the church, hastily dressed, her hair barely combed, without a prepared sermon? Returning, Eli would say, like an addict to her heroin.

Well, let Eli say whatever he wanted to. Let him do whatever he wanted to. But when she reached the church, let him not stand in that pulpit one minute longer than it took him to introduce her. But he would know that. He would take one look at her face and get out of her way.

He and his ideas of how a healing should be performed! He had never performed one in his life. Never dared to try, because he knew that, even if he managed to succeed a time or two with great help from the sick person's own suggestibility, he would never equal Rachel. He could never perform one tenth of the healings she performed, because she never failed. What he would strain to do, what he would sweat over and call for divine assistance with, she could do easily. Easily, but not without cost. The power, the energy she used in a healing service had to come from somewhere. Eli had called her a parasite, a second Doro. He had talked her into forgoing her usual "price." She had tried, and that was why she was sick now. That was why the taxi driver, who was black too and who knew the church at the address she gave, asked her sympathetically whether she was going to see "that traveling faith healer."

"I'm going to see her, all right," said Rachel through her teeth. Her grimness must have surprised him. He asked no more questions. A few moments later, when he pulled up at the church, she threw him a few bills and ran in without waiting for her change.

She managed to remember her robe because wearing it had become such a habit with her. Eli, as much a showman as a minister, had insisted on it through all the six years that they had worked together. A flowing white robe.

The congregation was singing when she walked into the auditorium. Watery, pallid, uninspired singing. They were making unco-ordinated noises with their throats. And their number! In her tours, Rachel was used to people sitting in the aisles, pushing in from outside when there was no more room for them. She had filled circus-type tents when she appeared in them. But there were empty seats out there now.

Had her last performance been so bad? Had following Eli's stupid advice hurt her so much?

She needed more people. She took a deep breath and walked into view from one of the choir doors. Today, of all days, she needed more people.

"Sister Davidson! Praise the Lord, she's here!" The cry went up in the middle of the song, and the song would have died away had she not joined in and kept it going. Her voice was a strong, full contralto that her audiences loved. She could have moved them with her singing even if she had nothing else. But she had a great deal more to offer than singing. If only there were more of them!

Eli Torrey gave her a long, bitter look. She knew the expression on her own face as she looked back at him. She could see it as he saw it. She could see it through his eyes. The hungry, drawn look that so many mistook for religious fervor.

Eli started to step away from the pulpit as the song ended.

She stopped him with a thought. *Introduce me!*

Why? She had to pluck his thoughts from his mind. He was only a latent. He could not project in any controlled way. *You think there's one person out there who doesn't know who you are?*

Introduce me, Eli, or I'll control you and do it myself. I'll run you like a puppet! She did not bother to take his reply.

Furious as he was, he was too much of a showman not to give her the best introduction he could.

The service.

She could have preached to her people in Chinese and it literally would not have mattered. All that mattered was that she was there and she had them. From that first song, they were hers. Not one of them could have gotten up and walked out of the church. Not one of them would have wanted to. Her control of them was not usually so rigid, but, then, she was not usually so desperate in her need of them. Their minds were full of her. Their voices, the very swaying, hand-clapping movements of their bodies were for her. When their mouths said, "Yes, Jesus!" and "Preach it!" and "Amen!" they really meant "Rachel,

Rachel, Rachel!" She drank it in and loved them for it. She demanded more and more.

By the time the service was half over, they would have cut their own throats for her. They fed her, strengthened her, drove out her sickness, which was, after all, no more than a need for them, for their adoration.

Eli said she was playing God, perverting religion, turning good, Christian people into pagans who worshiped only her. Eli was right, of course. He should have been. He was one of her first and oldest worshipers. But his conscience bothered him, and, from time to time, he managed to infect her with some of his guilt.

Behind her was a childhood spent in a home that was Christian before it was anything else. Eli's home. Eli was a distant cousin of hers. Doro had had her adopted by Eli's minister parents. Both his father and his mother were ministers. But in spite of the pressure they had put on Rachel she had rejected much of their religious teaching. All she retained was enough to make her nervous sometimes. Nervous and vulnerable to Eli. But not now.

Now she drew all she dared from the small crowd, forcing herself to stop before she was satisfied, to avoid doing them any real harm. Then she prepared to repay them. The candidates for healing had already formed a line in the main aisle.

And the healing began.

Eyes closed, she would mouth a prayer and lay her hands on the candidate. Sometimes she shouted, imploring God to hear and answer her. Sometimes she seemed to have trouble and have to try a second time.

Showmanship! Eli and his parents had taught her some of it. The rest she had learned from watching real faith healers. It meant nothing, as far as the actual healing was concerned.

In her years of healing, she had learned enough to diagnose quickly just by allowing her perception to travel over the candidate's body once. That was useful in that many of the people who came to her did not really know what was wrong with them. Even some who came with doctors' diagnoses were mistaken. Thus she saved a few seconds of looking for a nonexistent problem and went right to work on whatever was really wrong. The work?

Stimulating the growth of new tissues—even brain and nerve tissues that were not supposed to regenerate. Destroying tissue that was useless and dangerous—cancer, for instance. Strengthening weak organs, "reprogramming" organs that malfunctioned. More. Much more. Psychological problems, injuries, birth defects, etc. Rachel could have been even more spectacular than she was. The totally deaf child gained hearing, but the one-armed man—he had come to get help in his fight against alcoholism—did not grow a new arm. He could have. It would have taken weeks, but Rachel could have handled it. To do so, though, she would have had to show herself to be more than a faith healer. She was afraid of what people might decide she was. Whether or not she accepted the story of Christ as fact, she realized that anyone with abilities like his—and hers—would get into trouble if he really put them to work.

Eli knew what she could do. And he knew all that she could make him understand about how she did it. Because she had to tell someone. Eli was her family now that his parents were dead. And he filled other functions. Doro had said he would. Cousin, business manager, lover, slave. She was a little ashamed of that last sometimes, but never ashamed enough to let him go.

Now, though, she was almost content. She had fed. It was not enough, but it would hold her until the next night, when, no doubt, a bigger crowd would gather. Soon she would send this small crowd home tired, weak, spent, but eager to return and feed her again. And eager to bring their friends and families out to see her.

She accepted only a limited number of candidates—again as a matter of self-protection—and that number was almost exhausted when the interruption came. Interruption. . . .

It was a mental explosion that, for uncounted seconds, blotted out her every other sense. She had been standing, one hand on a woman in a wheelchair, the other raised in apparent supplication. Now she froze there, blind, deaf, mute with shock. The only thing that kept her on her feet was her habit of strictness with herself. Minor theatrics she had always used. They were part of her show. Uncontrolled hysterics—especially of the kind that she could have—were absolutely forbidden.

Somehow when the din inside her head lessened she finished with the woman in the wheelchair, sent her away walking slowly, pushing her own chair, and crying.

Then, without explanation, Rachel handed the service back to Eli and walked away from her bewildered congregation. She shut herself in an empty Sunday-school classroom to be alone to fight the thing that was happening to her.

Sometime later, she heard Eli in the hall calling her. By then the battle was ended, lost. By then Rachel knew she had to go to Forsyth. Someone had called her in a way that she could not ignore. Someone had made a puppet of her. There was justice in that, she supposed. She reached out to Eli, called him to her to tell him that she was leaving.

JESSE BERNARR

Jesse and the girl, this one's name was Tara, slept late, then got up and drove into Donaldton. It was Sunday and Jesse's twenty-sixth birthday. He was feeling generous enough to ask the girl what she wanted to do instead of telling her.

She wanted to get a lunch and go to the park. There, though she did not say it, she wanted to show Jesse off. She would be the envy of the female population of Donaldton and she knew it. Best to show him off while she had him. She knew she could only have him until someone else caught his eye. When that happened, he would send her home to her husband and her turn might not come again for months—might not ever come again.

Jesse smiled to himself as he read her thoughts. Donaldton girls, even shy, undemanding ones like Tara, thought that way when they were with him. They worked as hard as they could to keep him and flaunt him—which was understandable and all right as far as Jesse was concerned. But sometimes Jesse went after girls from the surrounding towns. Girls who didn't know him even by reputation, and who weren't quite so eager.

He and Tara went to a little cafe and had a lunch prepared.

There was only one waitress on duty and there were two other customers waiting to be served when Jesse arrived. But they didn't mind waiting a little longer. They wished him a happy birthday.

Jesse wasn't carrying any cash. He rarely did. He never needed it in Donaldton. The waitress smiled at him as he and Tara took the lunch and went back to the car.

Tara drove to the lake as she had driven into Donaldton. Jesse had wrecked three cars and nearly killed himself before he gave up driving. There was just no future in it for someone who might at any time be hit by mental disturbances from other drivers, pedestrians, whatever. It wasn't as bad as it had been during his transition, but it still happened. Doro said his mental shielding was defective. Jesse didn't worry about it. The advantages of his sensitivity outweighed the disadvantages. And Tara was a good driver. All his girls were.

There were other Sunday picnickers in the park—old people sunning themselves and families with young children. And there was a scattering of young couples and teen-agers. Donaldton, Pennsylvania, was small and didn't offer much in the way of entertainment or recreation. People who would have preferred something more exciting wound up in the park.

The people were well spread out, though. There was plenty of room. There was so much room, in fact, that Tara was silently annoyed when Jesse chose a place only a few yards from another couple.

Jesse pretended not to notice her annoyance. "Want to go for a swim before we eat?"

"Oh, but . . . we don't have suits. I didn't know we were coming here when we left the house. . . . "

Jesse glanced around, seemingly casually. "That girl over there has a new one that will fit you," he said, nodding toward the female half of the nearby fully clothed couple.

"Oh." He was in one of his moods again, she was thinking. She was going to be humiliated. This wasn't like taking food from the cafe. That had been more like a gift. But this girl had brought her bathing suit for her own use.

73

Jesse smiled, reading her every thought. "Go on. Go get it. And while you're at it, get the guy's trunks for me."

She cringed inside but got up to do as he said. He watched her walk toward the couple.

The distance was too great for him to hear what she said to them clearly, so he picked up the conversation mentally.

"Could I borrow . . . I mean . . . Jesse wants your bathing suits." She could not have felt more completely foolish, but she expected nothing more than that the couple would hand her the suits and let her escape back to Jesse.

The girl took one look at Tara and at the watching Jesse and started to get her suit out. The man didn't move. It was his reaction that Jesse was waiting for. He didn't have to wait long.

"You want to borrow our *what?*"

"Bathing suits." Tara looked at the girl. "You're from town, aren't you? Tell him."

"You tell him." The girl didn't particularly resent the loss of the suit. Donaldton people never resented giving Jesse what he wanted. The girl resented Tara.

Tara didn't want to be there. She didn't even want the damned suits. If the girl couldn't realize that. . . . "Never mind. I'll have Jesse come over and tell him." She started away.

"All right, wait. Wait!" When Tara turned back to face the girl, the girl was holding out her own suit and the man's trunks. But before Tara could take them, the man snatched them away.

"What the hell are you doing?"

The girl was angry now, and the man was the only one she could take her anger out on safely. "He's Jesse Bernarr and he wants to borrow our suits. Will you please let me give them to him?"

"No! Why the hell should I?" He glanced at Tara. "Look, you go back and tell Jesse Bernarr, whoever he is. . . . " He stopped as Jesse's shadow fell across him. He looked up, confused, and by now angry. He was a big man, Jesse noticed. He would be tall when he stood up. Massive shoulders and chest. He looked a little bigger than Jesse, in fact. And he did not like not knowing what was going on.

"You've got to be Jesse Bernarr," he said. He paused as

though he expected confirmation from Jesse. He got only silence. "Look, I don't know what the joke is, mister, but it's not funny. Now, why don't you take your girl and go play your kid games somewhere else."

"I could." Jesse plucked the man's name from his mind. It was Tom. "I don't feel like swimming any more. But there are a couple of things I think you ought to learn."

And there was a simple, effortless way of teaching them to him. But sometimes Jesse liked to expend a little effort. Especially with characters like this Tom who took so much inner pride in their physical prowess. Sometimes Jesse liked to reassure himself that even without his extra abilities he would still be better than Tom's kind.

He said, "You visit a place for the first time, Tom, you ought to be more willing to listen when the natives try to warn you about local customs." He smiled at Tom's girl. She smiled back a little uncertainly. "It could save you a lot of trouble."

Tom got up, watching Jesse. "Man, you sure want to fight bad. I'd give a lot to know why." They faced each other, Tom looking down at Jesse from his slightly superior height.

Tom's girl stood up quickly and stepped between them, her back to Tom. "He'll listen to me, Jess. Let me talk to him."

Jesse pushed her out of the way gently, casually. If he hadn't, Tom would have. But Tom resented Jesse doing it for him. Resented it enough to take the first swing. Jesse, anticipating him, dodged easily.

A stray child saw them, yelled, and people began to take notice and gather around.

Only people from outside Donaldton who didn't know the odds against Tom came to watch a fight. Donaldton people came to see Jesse Bernarr having himself some fun. And they didn't mind. Even Tom's girl didn't mind Jesse having a little fun with Tom. What frightened her was that Tom didn't know what he was up against. He was liable to make Jesse angry enough to really hurt him. If she had been out with a Donaldton man, she wouldn't have worried.

As the two men fought, though, it was Tom whose anger grew, silently encouraged by Jesse. Jesse mentally goaded Tom to fight as though his life were at stake. Then an explosion went off in Jesse's head and Tom got his chance.

Jesse was only vaguely aware of the beating his body was taking as he struggled to close out the mental blast. But there was no way to close it out. No way to dull it as it screamed through him. Tom had a field day.

When the "noise" finally lessened, when it didn't fill every part of Jesse's mind, he realized that he was on the ground. He started groggily to get up, and the man whose anger he had mentally encouraged kicked him in the face.

His head snapped back—not as far as Tom would have liked—and he lost consciousness.

He didn't come to all at once. First he was aware only of the call drawing him, destroying any mental peace he might have had before he became aware of the condition of his body. He didn't seem to be hurt seriously, but he could feel a dozen places where his flesh was split and bruised. His face was lumpy and already swollen. Some of his teeth had been kicked in. And he hurt. He hurt all over. He spat out blood and broken teeth.

Damn that out-of-town bastard to hell!

The thought of Tom roused him to look around. Somebody from Donaldton was standing over him, thinking about moving him back into town to a bed.

Not far away, Tom struggled between two more Donaldton men and cursed steadily.

Jesse staggered to his feet. The crowd was still there. Probably some out-of-towner had gone for the police. Not that it mattered. The police were old friends of Jesse's.

Jesse refused to mute his own pain. It came as near as anything could to blocking out the call to Forsyth. And, although Jesse had not yet analyzed what had happened to him, the message of the call was clear—and clearly something he wanted no part of. Besides, he wanted to hurt. He wanted to look at Tom and hurt. He started to smile, had to spit more blood, then spoke softly. "Let him go."

Jesse moved in, anticipating Tom's swings, avoiding them. Tom couldn't surprise him. And as angry as Jesse was now, that meant Tom couldn't touch him. Slowly, methodically, he cut the bigger man to pieces.

Now Tom's strength betrayed him. It kept him on his feet when he should have fallen, kept him fighting, well after he was beaten. When he finally did collapse to the ground, it kept him conscious and aware—aware solely of pain.

Jesse walked away and left him lying there. Let his girl take care of him.

The townspeople drifted away, too. They had had a much better show than they had bargained for. To the out-of-towners, Tom seemed to have gotten no more than he deserved. They resumed their Sunday outing.

A few minutes later, Tara was shaking her head and wiping blood from Jesse's face with a cold, wet paper napkin. "Jess, why'd you let him beat you up like that? How are you going to go to your birthday party tonight, now?"

He glanced at her in annoyance and she fell silent. Party, hell! If he could just get rid of this damned buzzing in his head, he would be all right.

So, somewhere in California, there was a town called Forsyth, and there were other actives there—more of Doro's people. So what! Why should he run to them, come when they called? Nobody on the other end of that buzz could have anything to offer him that was better than what he had.

ADA DRAGAN

They were screaming at each other over some small thing—a party Ada would not attend. Yesterday the screaming had been over the neighbors whom Ada had interfered with. She had sensed them beating their six-year-old brutally, and she had stopped them. For once, she had accomplished something good with her ability. Foolish pride had made her tell Kenneth. Kenneth had decided that her interference had been wrong.

She could not tolerate large groups of people, and she could not tolerate child abuse. Kenneth called the first immature and the second none of her business. Everything she did either angered or humiliated him. Everything. Yet she stayed with him. Without him she would be totally alone.

She was an active. She had power. And all her power did, most of the time, was cut her off from other people, make it impossible for her ever to be one of them. Her power was more like a disease than a gift. Like a mental illness.

She had gone to a doctor once, secretly. A psychiatrist a few miles away, in Seattle. She had given him a false name and told him only a little. She had stopped when she realized that he was about to suggest a period of hospitalization. . . .

Now she wondered bitterly whether the doctor had been right. It was her "illness," after all, that had caused her to descend to this screaming. She said things to Kenneth that she had not thought herself capable of saying to anyone. He did not realize the degradation and despair this signified in her. Only one thought saved her from complete loss of control. The man was her husband.

She had married him out of desperation, not love. But he was her husband nonetheless, and he had served a purpose. If she had not married him, she might be saying these things to her parents—her stepparents—the only people besides Doro whom she could ever remember loving. It had been very important once—that she protect her parents from what she had become. She wondered if it was still important. If she still cared what she said, even to them.

Abruptly she was tired of the argument. Tired of the man's fury pounding at her mind and her ears. Tired of her own pointless anger. She turned and walked away.

Kenneth caught her shoulder and spun her around so quickly that she had no time to think. He slapped her hard, throwing all the weight of his big body against her. She fell back against the wall, then slipped silently to the floor to lie stunned, while, above her, he demanded that she learn to listen when he spoke. At that moment, violence, chaos convulsed her treacherous mind.

Ada was quick. She did not need time to wonder what was happening or to realize that there would finally be an end to her aloneness. She reacted immediately. She screamed.

Kenneth had hurt her, but suddenly the physical pain lost all meaning in the face of this new thing. This thing that brought her the pain of a hope roughly torn away.

Since her change, that terrible night three years before, when all the world had come flooding into her mind, she had treated her condition as a temporary thing. Something that would some-day end and let her be as she had been. This was a belief that Doro had tried to talk her out of. But she had been able to convince herself that he was lying. He had refused to introduce her to others who were like her, though he claimed there were others. He had said that it would be painful to her to meet them, that her kind tolerated each other badly. But she had looked for herself, had sifted through thousands of minds without finding even one like her own. Thus she had decided that Doro was lying. She had believed what she wanted to believe. She was good at that; it kept her alive. She had decided that Doro had told only part of the truth. That there had been others like her. It was unthinkable that she had been the only person to undergo this change. And that the others had recovered, changed back.

This hope had sustained her, given her a reason to go on living. Now she had to see it for the fallacy it was.

She lay on the floor crying, as she rarely did, in noisy, gasping sobs. Others. How had she searched for so long without finding them? It seemed that they had no trouble finding her. And the strength of the first attack, and even of the call that now pulled at her insistently, was far greater than anything she felt herself able to generate. Such power gave the unknown caller a terrible air of permanence.

Unexpectedly, Kenneth was lifting her to her feet, reassuring her that she was all right.

Steadying herself enough to sample his thoughts, she learned that he was a little frightened by her screaming. He had hit her before and gotten no reaction other than quiet tears.

The selfishness of his thoughts stabilized her. He was wondering what would happen to him if he had hurt her. He had long before ceased worrying about her for her own sake. And she had never forced him to do anything more than stay with her. She pulled away from him tiredly and went into the bedroom.

She would never be well again, never be able to go among people without being bombarded by their thoughts. And facing this, she could not possibly continue her present living arrangement. She could no longer force Kenneth to stay with her when he hated her as he did. Nor would she exert more control over him, to force an obscene, artificial love.

She would follow the call. Even if it had been less insistent, she would have followed it. Because it was all she had.

She would quarantine herself with others who were afflicted as she was. If she was alone with them, she would be less likely to hurt people who were well. How would it be, though? How much worse than anything she had yet known? A life among outcasts.

JAN SHOLTO

The neighborhood had changed little in the three years since Jan had seen it. New cars, new children. Two small boys ran past her; one of them was black. That was new too. She was glad her mind had not been open and vulnerable when the boy ran past. She had problems enough without *that* alienness. She looked back at the boy with distaste, then shrugged. She planned only a short visit. She didn't have to live there.

It occurred to her, not for the first time, that even visiting was foolish, pointless. She had placed her own children in a comfortable home where they would be well cared for, have better lives than she had had. There was nothing more that she could do for them. Nothing she could accomplish by visiting them. Yet for days she had felt a need to make this visit. Need, urge, premonition?

Thinking about it made her uncomfortable. She deliberately turned her attention to the street around her instead. The newness of it disgusted her. The unimaginative modern houses, the sapling trees. Even if the complexion of the neighborhood had not been changing, Jan could never have lived there. The place had no depth in time. She could touch things, a fence, a light standard, a signpost. Nothing went back further than a decade.

Nothing carried real historical memory. Everything was sterile and perilously unanchored to the past.

A little girl of no more than seven was standing in one of the yards watching Jan walk toward her. Jan examined the child curiously. Small, fine-boned and fair-haired, like Jan. Her eyes were blue, but not the pale, faded blue of Jan's eyes. The girl's eyes had the same deep, startling blue that had been one of her father's best features—or one of the best features of the body her father had been wearing.

Jan turned to walk down the pathway to the child's house.

As she came even with the girl, some sentimentality about the eyes made her stop and hold out her hand. "Will you walk to the house with me, Margaret?"

The child took the offered hand and walked solemnly beside Jan.

Jan automatically blocked any mental contact with her. She had learned painfully that children not only had no depth but that their unstable little animal minds could deliver one emotional outburst after another.

Margaret spoke as Jan opened the door. "Did you come to take me away?"

"No."

The child smiled at Jan in relief, then ran away, calling, "Mommy, Jan is here."

Jan raised an eyebrow at the irony of her daughter's words. Jan had once tried to condition the family here, the Westleys, to believe that they were the natural parents of Jan's children. She had had the power to do it, but she had not been skillful enough in her use of that power. She had failed. But time, combined with the simpler command that she had managed to instill in the Westleys—to care for the children and protect them—had turned her failure into success. Margaret knew that Jan was actually her mother. But it made no difference. Not to her; not to the Westleys.

In fact, the children were such a permanent part of the Westley household that Margaret's question seemed out of character. The question revived the feeling of foreboding that Jan had been trying to ignore.

Even the feel of the house was wrong. So wrong that she found herself being careful not to touch anything. Just being inside was uncomfortable.

The woman, Lea Westley, came in slowly, hesitantly, without Margaret or the boy, Vaughn. Jan resisted the temptation to reach into her thoughts and learn at once what was wrong. That part of her ability was still underdeveloped, because she did not like to use it. She enjoyed touching inanimate objects and winding back through the pasts of the people who had handled them before her. But she had never learned to enjoy direct mind-to-mind contact. Most people had vile minds anyway.

"I thought you might be coming, Jan." Lea Westley fumbled with her hands. "I was even afraid you might take Margaret."

Verbal confirmation of Jan's fears. Now she had to have the rest. "I don't know what's happened, Lea. Tell me."

Lea looked away for a moment, then spoke softly. "There was an accident. Vaughn is dead." Her voice broke on the last word and Jan had to wait until she could compose herself and go on.

"It was a hit-and-run. Vaughn was out with Hugh," her husband, "and someone ran a red light. . . . It happened last week. Hugh is still in the hospital."

The woman was genuinely upset. Even through layers of shielding, Jan could feel her suffering. But, more than anything else, Lea Westley was afraid. She was afraid of Jan, of what Jan might decide to do to the people who had failed in the responsibility she had given them.

Jan understood that fear, because she was feeling a slightly different version of it herself. Someday Doro would come back and ask to see his children. He had promised her he would, and he kept the few promises he made. He had also promised her what he would do to her if she was unable to produce two healthy children.

She shook her head thinking about it. "Oh, God."

Lea was instantly at her side, holding her, weeping over her, saying again and again, "I'm so sorry, Jan. So sorry."

Disgusted, Jan pushed her away. Sympathy and tears were the last things Jan needed. The boy was dead. That was that. He had been a burden to her before she placed him with the Westleys. Now, dead, he was again a burden in spite of all her efforts to see that he was safe. If only Doro had not insisted that she have children. She had been looking forward to his return for so long. Now, instead of waiting for it, she would have to flee from it. Another town, another state, another name—and the likelihood that none of it would do any good. Doro was a specialist at finding people who ran from him.

"Jan, please understand. . . . It wasn't our fault."

Stupid woman! Lea became an outlet for Jan's frustration. Jan seized control of her, spun her around, and propelled her puppetlike out of the living room.

Lea Westley's scream of terror when Jan finally released her was the last thing Jan was physically aware of for several minutes.

A mental explosion rocked her. Then came the forced mind-to-mind contact that she fought savagely and uselessly. Then the splitting away of part of herself, the call to Forsyth.

Jan regained consciousness on Lea Westley's sofa, with Lea herself sitting nearby, crying. The woman had come back despite Jan's heavy-handed treatment. She knew how foolish it would be to run from Jan even if she had known positively that Jan meant her harm. Perhaps, in that knowledge of her own limitations, she was more sensible than Jan herself. Lying still now with the call drawing her, Jan felt unusual pity for Lea.

"I don't care that he's dead, Lea." The words came out in a whisper even though Jan had intended to speak normally.

"Jan!" Lea was on her feet at once, probably not understanding, probably realizing only that Jan was again conscious.

"You don't have to worry, Lea. I'm not going to hurt you."

Lea heard this time, and she collapsed weeping with relief. Jan tried standing, and found herself weak but able to manage.

"Be good to Margaret for me, Lea. I might not be able to come to see her again."

She walked out, leaving Lea staring after her.

California.

Was it Doro calling her somehow with this thing in her mind? She knew he had other telepaths—better telepaths. He might be using one of them to reach her. It was possible that he had somehow learned of his son's death and struck at her through someone else. If he had, his efforts were paying off. She was going to California.

She felt all the terror that the controlled Lea must have known. She couldn't help herself. She had to go to Forsyth. And if Doro was there, she would be going to her death.

· Five ·

MARY

When Karl left my room, I lay in bed thinking, remembering. Karl and I had sort of accepted each other over the past two weeks. He had gotten a lot easier to talk to—and I suppose I had too. He had stopped trying to pretend I wasn't there, and I had stopped resenting him. In fact, I had probably come to depend on him more than I should have. And he really had just worked damned hard to keep me alive. Yet, only a few hours later, he had done enough emotional backsliding to sit by and let me almost kill myself—all because of this pattern thing. I wondered how big a mental leap it would be for him to go from a willingness to let me be killed to a willingness to kill me himself.

Or maybe I was overreacting. Maybe I was just disappointed because I had expected my transition to bring me closer to him. I had expected just what I knew Vivian was afraid of: that, after my transition, she would become excess baggage. If I had to be Karl's wife, I meant to be his only wife.

But now. . . . I had never felt anyone's hostility the way I felt Karl's just before he went out. That was part of what it meant to be in full control of my telepathic ability. Not a very comfort-

85

able part. I knew he had gone to see Doro—had gone to roust Doro out of bed and ask him what the hell had gone wrong. I wondered if anything really had gone wrong.

Doro wanted an empire. He didn't call it that, but that was what he meant. Maybe I was just one more tool he was using to get it. He needed tools, because an empire of ordinary people wasn't quite what he had in mind. That, to him, would be like an ordinary person making himself emperor over a lot of cattle. Doro thought a lot of himself, all right. But he didn't think much of the families of half-crazy latents he had scattered across the country. They were just his breeders—if they were lucky. He didn't want an empire of them either. He and I had talked about it off and on since I was thirteen. That first conversation said most of it, though.

He had taken me to Disneyland. He did things like that for me now and then while I was growing up. They helped me survive Rina and Emma.

We were sitting at an outdoor table of a cafe having lunch when I asked the key question.

"What are we for, Doro?"

He looked at me through deep blue eyes. He was wearing the body of a tall, thin white man. I knew he knew what I meant, but still he said, "For?"

"Yeah, for. You have so many of us. Rina said your newest wife just had a kid." He laughed for some reason. I went on. "Are you just keeping us for a hobby—so you'll have something to do, or what?"

"No doubt that's part of it."

"What's the other part?"

"I'm not sure you'd understand."

"I'm mixed up in it. I want to know about it whether I understand or not. And I want to know about you."

He was still smiling. "What about me?"

"Enough about you so that I'll have a chance to understand why you want us."

"Why does anyone want a family?"

"Oh, come on, Doro. Families! Dozens of them. Tell me, really. You can start by telling me about your name. How come you only have one, and one I never heard of at that."

"It's the name my parents gave me. It's the only thing they gave me that I still have."

"Who were your parents?"

"Farmers. They lived in a village along the Nile."

"Egypt!"

He shook his head. "No, not quite. A little farther south. The Egyptians were our enemies when I was born. They were our former rulers, seeking to become our rulers again."

"Who were your people?"

"They had another name then, but you would call them Nubians."

"Black people!"

"Yes."

"God! You're white so much of the time, I never thought you might have been born black."

"It doesn't matter."

"What do you mean, 'It doesn't matter'? It matters to me."

"It doesn't matter because I haven't been any color at all for about four thousand years. Or you could say I've been every color. But either way, I don't have anything more in common with black people—Nubian or otherwise—than I do with whites or Asians."

"You mean you don't want to admit you have anything in common with us. But if you were born black, you *are* black. Still black, no matter what color you take on."

He crooked his mouth a little in something that wasn't quite a smile. "You can believe that if it makes you feel better."

"It's true!"

He shrugged.

"Well, what race do you think you are?"

"None that I have a name for."

"That doesn't make any sense."

"It does when you think about it. I'm not black or white or yellow, because I'm not human, Mary."

That stopped me cold. He was serious. He couldn't have been more serious. I stared at him, chilled, scared, believing him even though I didn't want to believe. I looked down at my plate, slowly finished my hamburger. Then, finally, I asked my question. "If you're not human, what are you?"

And his seriousness broke. "A ghost?"

"That's not funny!"

"No. It may even be true. I'm the closest thing to a ghost that I've run into in all my years. But that's not important. What are you looking so frightened for? I'm no more likely to hurt you now than I ever was."

"What are you?"

"A mutation. A kind of parasite. A god. A devil. You'd be surprised at some of the things people have decided I was."

I didn't say anything.

He reached over and took my hand for a moment. "Relax. There's nothing for you to be afraid of."

"Am I human?"

He laughed. "Of course you are. Different, but certainly human."

I wondered whether that was good or bad. Would he have loved me more if I had been more like him? "Am I descended from your . . . from the Nubians, too?"

"No. Emma was an Ibo woman." He ate a piece of french fry and watched a couple with about seven yelling little kids troop by. "I don't know of any of my people who are descended from Nubians. Certainly none of them were descended from my parents."

"You were an only child?"

"I was one of twelve. I survived, the others didn't. They all died in infancy or early childhood. I was the youngest and I only survived until I was your age—thirteen."

"And they were too old to have more kids."

"Not only that. I died while I was going through something a lot like transition. I had flashes of telepathy, got caught in other people's thoughts. But of course I didn't know what it was. I was afraid, hurt. I thrashed around on the ground and made a lot of noise. Unfortunately, both my mother and my father came running. I died then for the first time, and I took them. First my mother, then my father. I didn't know what I was doing. I took a ot of other people too, all in panic. Finally I ran away from the village, wearing the body of one of my cousins—a young girl. I ran straight into the arms of some Egyptians on a slave raid. They were just about to attack the village. I assume they did attack."

"You don't know?"

"Not for sure, but there was no reason for them not to. I couldn't hurt them—or at least not deliberately. I was already half out of my mind over what I had done. I snapped. After that I don't know what happened. Not then, not for about fifty years after. I figured out much later that the span I didn't remember, still don't remember, was about fifty years. I never saw any of the people of my village again." He paused for a moment. "I came to, wearing the body of a middle-aged man. I was lying on a pallet of filthy, vermin-infested straw in a prison. I was in Egypt, but I didn't know it. I didn't know anything. I was a thirteen-year-old boy who had suddenly come awake in someone else's forty-five-year-old body. I almost snapped again.

"Then the jailer came in and said something to me in a language that, as far as I knew, I had never heard before. When I just lay there staring at him, he kicked me, started to beat me with a small whip he was carrying. I took him, of course. Automatic. Then I got out of there in his body and wandered through the streets of a strange city trying to figure out what a lot of other people have been trying to figure out ever since: Just what in the name of all gods was I?"

"I never thought you might wonder that."

"I didn't for long. I came to the conclusion that I was cursed, that I had offended the gods and was being punished. But after I had used my ability a few times deliberately and seen that I could have absolutely anything I wanted, I changed my mind. Decided that the gods had favored me by giving me power."

"When did you decide that it was okay for you to use that power to make people . . . make them. . . ."

"Breed them, you mean."

"Yeah," I muttered. *Breed* didn't sound like the kind of word that should be applied to people. The minute he said it, though, I realized it was the right word for what he was doing.

"It took time for me to get around to that," he said. "A century or two. I was busy first getting involved in Egyptian religion and politics, then traveling, trading with other peoples. I started to notice the way people bred animals. It stopped being just part of the background for me. I saw different breeds of dogs, of cattle, different ethnic groups of people—how they looked when they kept to themselves and were relatively pure, when there was crossbreeding."

"And you decided to experiment."

"In a way. I was able by then to recognize the people . . . the kinds of people that I would get the most pleasure from if I took them. I guess you could say, the kinds of people who tasted best."

I suddenly lost my appetite. "God! That's disgusting."

"It's also very basic. One kind of people gave me more pleasure than other kinds, so I tried to collect several of the kind I liked and keep them together. That way, they would breed and I would always have them available when I needed them."

"And that's how we began? As food?"

"That's right."

I was surprised, but I wasn't afraid. I didn't think for one minute that he was going to use me or anybody I knew for food. "What kind of people taste best?" I asked.

"People with a certain mental sensitivity. People who have the beginnings, at least, of some unusual abilities. I found them in every race I encountered, but I never found them in very large numbers."

I nodded. "Psis," I said. "There's the word you need. A word that sort of groups everybody's abilities together. I read it in a science-fiction magazine."

"I know about it."

"You know everything. So people with some psionic ability 'taste' better than others. But we're not still just food, are we?"

"Some of my latents are. But my actives and potential actives are part of another project. They have been for some time."

"What project?"

"To build a people, a race."

90

So that was it. I thought about it for a moment. "A race for you to be part of?" I asked. "Or a race for you to own?"

He smiled. "That's a good question."

"What's the answer?"

"Well . . . to get an active, I have to bring together people of two different latent families—people who repel each other so strongly that I have to take one of them to bring them together. That means all the actives of each generation are my children. So maybe the answer is . . . a little of both."

Maybe it was a lot of both. Maybe he hadn't told me just how experimental I was—just what different things I was supposed to do. And maybe he hadn't told Karl, either.

I got out of bed trying to ignore the parts of me that hurt. I took a long, hot bath, hoping to soak away some of the pain. It helped a little. By the time I finally dressed and went downstairs, nobody but Doro was still around.

"Tell me about it while you're having breakfast," he said.

"Hasn't Karl already told you?"

"Yes. Now I want to hear it from you."

I told him. I didn't add in any of my suspicions. I just told him and watched him. He didn't look happy.

"What can you tell me about the other actives you're holding?" he asked.

I almost said "nothing" before I realized it wasn't true. "I can tell where they are," I said. "And I can tell them apart. I know their names and I know—" I stopped, looked at him. "The more I concentrate on them, the more I find out about them. How much do you want to know?"

"Just tell me their names."

"A test? All right. Rachel Davidson, a healer. She's some relation to Emma. She works churches pretending to be a faith healer, but faith doesn't have anything to do with it. She—"

"Just their names, Mary."

"Okay. Jesse Bernarr, Jan Sholto, Ada Dragan, and Seth Dana. There's something strange about Seth."

"What?"

"Something wrong, painful. But no, wait a minute, it's not

Seth who has something wrong with him. It's Seth's brother, Clay. I see. Clay's a latent and Seth is protecting him."

"Doesn't it bother you that most of these people are shielded?"

"I didn't realize they were." I checked quickly. "You're right. Everyone but Seth is shielded. Hell, I'm still shielded. I forgot the shield was there, but it is. Not even thinned a little."

"But you don't have any trouble reading them through it?"

"No. It's one-way communication, though. I can read them, but none of them have managed to find out who I am. And none of them realize when I'm reading them. A while ago, when Karl was reading me, I could feel it. I knew when he started, when he stopped, and what he got."

"Can you tell whether any of the others are closer to you, closer to Forsyth now than they were when you first became aware of them?"

I checked. It was like turning my head to read a wall chart. That easy. And I noticed what I hadn't noticed before. "Two of them are a lot closer. Rachel and Seth. They're approached from slightly different directions, and Rachel's coming much faster, but, Doro, they're both on their way here."

"And the others?"

I checked again. "They'll be coming too. They can't help it. I see that now. My pattern is pulling them here."

Doro said something that I knew had to be a curse even though it was in a foreign language. He came over to me and put his hand on my shoulder. He looked worried. That was unusual for him. I sat there knowing damned well that he was thinking he was going to have to kill me. This pattern thing wasn't part of his plan, then. I was an experiment going bad before his eyes.

I looked up at him. I wasn't afraid. I realized that I should have been, but I wasn't. "Give it a chance," I said quietly. "Let the five of them get here, and let's see how they react."

"You don't know how badly my actives usually react to each other."

"Karl's reaction to me was bad enough. Why did you put us together if you didn't think we could get along?"

"You and Karl are more stable than the others; you come

from four of my best lines. You were supposed to get along fairly well together."

"Another experiment. All right, it can still work. Just give it a chance. After all, what have you got to lose?"

"Some very valuable people."

I stood up and faced him. "You want to throw me away before you see how valuable I might be?"

"Girl, I don't *want* to throw you away at all."

"Give me a chance, then."

"A chance to do what?"

"To find out whether this group of actives is different—or whether I can make them different. To find out whether I or my pattern can keep them from killing each other, or me. That's what we're talking about, isn't it?"

"Yes."

"Well?"

He looked at me. After a moment, he nodded. I didn't even feel relieved. But, then, I had never really felt threatened. I smiled at him. "You're curious, aren't you?"

He looked surprised.

"I know you. You really want to see what will happen—if it will be different from what's happened before. Because this has happened before, hasn't it?"

"Not quite."

"What was different before? I might be able to learn from my predecessors' mistakes."

"Do you think anything you could have learned before your transition could have helped you avoid trapping my actives in your pattern?"

I took a deep breath. "No. But tell me anyway. I want to know."

"No you don't. But I'll tell you. Your predecessors were parasites, Mary. Not quite the way I am, but parasites nevertheless. And so are you."

I thought about that, then shook my head slowly. "But I haven't hurt anybody. Karl was right next to me and I didn't—"

"I said you weren't like me. I'm fairly sure you could have killed Karl, though. I suspect Karl realizes that."

I sat down. He had finally said something that really hit me. I had kind of built Karl up as a superman in my mind. I could see how he owned Vivian and the servants. His house and his life style were clear evidence of his power. He wasn't Doro, but he was a good second. "I could have *killed* him? How?"

"Why? Want to try it?"

"Oh, shit, Doro, come on. I want to know how to avoid trying it. Or is that going to be impossible too?"

"That's the question I want an answer to. That's what I'm curious about. More than curious. Your predecessors never trapped more than one active at a time. Their first was always the one who had helped them through transition. They always needed help to get through transition. If I didn't provide it, they died. On the other hand, if I did provide it, sooner or later they killed the person who had helped them. They never wanted to kill, and especially they didn't want to kill that person. But they couldn't help themselves. They got . . . hungry, and they killed. Then they latched onto another active, drew him to them, and went through the feeding process again. Unfortunately, they always killed other actives. I can't afford that."

"Did they . . . trade bodies the way you do?"

"No. They took what they needed and left the husk."

I winced.

"And their patterns gave them an access to their victims that their victims couldn't close off—as you already know."

"Oh." I felt almost guilty—as though he were telling me about things that I had already done. As though I had already killed the people in my pattern. People who hadn't done anything to me.

"So you can see why I'm worried," he said.

"Yes. But I can't see why you'd want somebody like me around at all—why you'd breed somebody like me if all my kind can do is feed on other actives."

"Not your kind, Mary. Your predecessors."

"Right. They killed one at a time. I kill several at once. Progress."

"But do you kill several at once?"

"I hope I don't kill any at all—at least not unintentionally.

But you don't give me much to base that hope on. What am I for, Doro? What are you progressing toward?"

"You know the answer to that."

"Your race, your empire, yes, but what place is there in it for me?"

"I'll be able to tell you that after I've watched you for a while."

"But—"

"The thing for you to do now is rest so that you'll have a better chance of handling your people when they get here. Your transition was several hours longer than normal, so you're probably still tired."

I was tired. I had gotten only a couple of hours' sleep. I wanted answers, though, more than I wanted rest. But he'd made it pretty clear that I wasn't going to get them. Then I realized what he had just said. "My people?"

"Both you and Karl say you feel as though they're yours."

"And both Karl and I know that, if they really belong to anybody other than themselves, it's you."

"You belong to me," he said. "So I'm not giving up anything when I give you charge of them. They're yours as long as you can handle them without killing them."

I stared at him in surprise. "One of the owners," I muttered, remembering the bitter thoughts I'd had two weeks before. "How did I suddenly become one of the owners?"

"By surviving your transition. What you have to do now is to survive your new authority."

I leaned back in my chair. "Thanks. Any pointers?"

"A few."

"Speak up, then. I have the feeling I'm going to need all the help I can get."

"Very likely. First you should realize that I'm delegating authority to you only because you'll need it if you're to have any chance at all of staying alive among these people. You're going to have to accept your own proprietary feelings as legitimate and demand that your people accept you on your terms." He paused, looked hard at me. "Keep them out of your mind as

95

much as you can. Use your advantage. Always know more about them than they know about you. Intimidate them quietly."

"The way you do?"

"If you can."

"I have a feeling you're rooting for me."

"I am."

"Well . . . I wouldn't ask why, on a bet. I'd rather think it was because you really gave a damn about me."

He just smiled.

KARL

Karl had never wanted quite as much as he did now to hurt something, to kill something, someone. He looked at Vivian sitting next to him, her mind ablaze with fear, her face carefully expressionless.

The blast of a horn behind him let him know that he was sitting through a green light. He restrained an impulse to lash back at the impatient driver. He could kill with his ability. He had, twice, accidentally, not long after his transition. He wondered why he refrained from doing it again. What difference would it make?

"Are we going back home?" Vivian asked.

Karl glanced at her, then looked around. He realized that he was heading back toward Palo Verde. He had left home heading nowhere in particular except away from Mary and Doro. Now he had made a large U and was heading back to them. And it wasn't just an ordinary unconscious impulse driving him. It was Mary's pattern.

He pulled over to the curb, stopped under a NO PARKING sign. He leaned back in the seat, his eyes closed.

"Will you tell me what's the matter with you?" Vivian asked.

"No."

She was doing all she could to keep calm. It was his silence that frightened her. His silence and his obvious anger.

He wondered why he had brought her with him. Then he remembered. "You're not leaving me," he said.

"But if Mary came through transition all right—"

"I said you're not leaving!"

"All right." She was almost crying with fear. "What are you going to do with me?"

He turned to glare at her in disgust.

"Karl, for heaven's sake! Tell me what's wrong." Now she was crying.

"Be quiet." Had he ever loved her, really? Had she ever been more than a pet—like all the rest of his women? "How was Doro last night?" he asked.

She looked startled. By mutual agreement, they did not discuss her nights with Doro. Or they hadn't until now. "Doro?" she said.

"Doro."

"Oh, now—" She sniffed, tried to compose herself. "Now, just a minute—"

"How was he?"

She frowned at him, disbelieving. "That can't be what's bothering you. Not after all this time. Not as though it was my fault, either!"

"That's a pretty good body he's wearing," said Karl. "And I could see from the way you were hanging on him this morning that he must have given you a pretty good—"

"That's enough!" Outrage was fast replacing her fear.

A pet, he thought. What difference did it make what you said or did to a pet?

"I'll defy Doro when you do," she said icily. "The moment you refuse to do what he tells you and stick to your refusal, I'll stand with you!"

A pet. In pets, free will was tolerated only as long as the pet owner found it amusing.

"You've got your nerve complaining about Doro and me," she muttered. "You'd climb into bed with him yourself if he told you to."

Karl hit her. He had never done such a thing before, but it was easy.

She screamed, then foolishly tried to get out of the car. He caught her arm, pulled her back, hit her again, and again.

He was panting when he stopped. She was bloody and only half conscious, crumpled down on the seat, crying. He hadn't controlled her. He had wanted to use his hands. Just his hands. And he wasn't satisfied. He could have hurt her more. He could have killed her.

Yes, and then what? How many of his problems would her death erase? He would have to get rid of her body, and then still go back to his master, and now, by God, his mistress. Once he was there, at least Mary's pattern would stop pulling at him, dragging at him, subverting his will as easily as he subverted Vivian's. Nothing would be changed, though, except that Vivian would be gone.

Only a pet?

Who was he thinking about? Vivian or himself? Now that Doro had tricked him into putting on a leash, it could be either, or both.

He took Vivian by the shoulders and made her sit up. He had split her lip. That was where the blood came from. He took out a handkerchief and wiped away as much of it as he could. She looked at him first, vacillating between fear and anger; then she looked away.

Without a word, he drove her to Monroe Memorial Hospital. There he parked, took out his checkbook, and wrote a check. He tore it out and put it in her hands. "Go. Get away from me while you can."

"I don't need a doctor."

"All right, don't see one. But go!"

"This is a lot of money," she said, looking at the check. "What's it supposed to pay me for?"

"Not pay you," he said. "God, you know better than that."

"I know you don't want me to go. Whatever you're angry about, you still need me. I didn't think you would, but you do."

"For your own good, Vee, go!"

"I'll decide what's good for me." Calmly she tore the check into small pieces. She looked at him. "If you really wanted me to go—if you want me to go now—you know how to make it happen. You do know."

He looked at her for a long moment. "You're making a mistake."

"And you're letting me make it."

"If you stay, this might be the last time you'll have the freedom to make your own mistakes."

"You're wrong to try so hard to frighten me away when you want me to stay so badly."

He said nothing.

"And I am staying, as long as you let me. Will you tell me what was wrong now?"

"No."

She sighed. "All right," she said, trying not to look hurt. "All right."

· Six ·

DORO

It occurred to Doro when Rachel Davidson arrived that she was the most subtly dangerous of his seven actives. Mary was the most dangerous period, though he doubted that she understood this yet. But there was nothing subtle about Mary. Rachel was, as Mary had said, related to Emma. She was the daughter of Emma's most successful granddaughter, Catherine—a woman who could easily have outlived Emma if she had had better control of her mental shielding. As it was, she had spent too much of her time and energy trying to keep the mental noise of the rest of humanity out of her mind—as though she were a latent. But a latent would have been less sensitive. Catherine Davidson had simply decided at thirty-nine that she couldn't stand any more. She had lain down and died. Every one of Doro's previous healers had made similar decisions. But Rachel was only twenty-five, and her shielding was much better. Doro hoped that her decision, if she made it at all, was several years away. At any rate, she was very much alive now, and she would be more trouble than Mary could be expected to handle so quickly. But Doro decided to watch for a while before he warned Rachel. Before he gave Mary the help Mary did not know she needed. He sat by the fireplace and watched the two women meet.

Rachel was a full head taller, several shades darker, and from the look on her face, very puzzled. "Whoever you are," she said, "you're the one I'm looking for—the one who called me here."

"Yes."

"Why? Who are you? What do you want?"

"My name is Mary Larkin. Come on in and sit down." Then, when Rachel was seated, "I'm an active, like you. Or not quite like you. I'm an experiment." She looked at Doro. "One of his experiments that got out of hand."

Rachel and Doro found themselves staring at each other, Doro almost as surprised as Rachel. Clearly, Mary was not going to let him be the observer that he had intended to be.

"Doro?" said Rachel tentatively.

"Yes."

"Thank goodness. If you're here, this must make sense somehow. I just walked out in the middle of a service in New York. I was so desperate to get here that I had to steal some poor person's place on a plane."

"What did you do with Eli?" Doro asked.

"Left him to handle the rest of the day's services. No one will be healed, I know, but no doubt he'll entertain them. Doro, what's going on?"

"An experiment, as Mary said."

"But it obviously isn't out of hand yet. She's still alive. Or is that temporary?"

"If it is, it's none of your business," said Mary quickly.

"It wouldn't be if you hadn't dragged me here," said Rachel. "But since you did—"

"Since I did, Rachel, and since I am still alive, you'd better plan on my being around for a while."

"Either plan on it or do something about it myself," muttered Rachel. Then she frowned. "How do you know my name? I didn't tell you."

"Yes you did. This morning, when this whole damn thing started. When it was supposed to be ending for me." Suddenly, Mary seemed to sag. She looked more than tired, Doro thought.

She looked a little frightened. Doro had made her rest for a few hours before Rachel's arrival. But how much real rest could she get thinking about what was in store for her? Thinking about it but not really knowing?

"What are you talking about?" demanded Rachel.

"I finished my transition this morning," said Mary. "And then, as if that wasn't enough, this other thing, this pattern, just sort of snapped into existence. Suddenly I was holding six other actives in a way that I didn't understand. Holding them, and calling them here."

Rachel was watching her, still frowning. "I thought there were others, but this whole thing was so insane I didn't trust my own senses. Are the others coming here, then?"

"Yes. They're on their way now."

"Do you want us here?"

"No!" Mary's vehemence startled Doro. Had she already decided that being "one of the owners" was so bad?

"Then, why don't you let us go?" said Rachel.

"I've tried," said Mary. "Karl has tried. My husband. He's been an active for ten years and he couldn't find a way out. As far as I can see, the only person who might have any helpful ideas is Doro."

And both women looked at him. Mary's whole attitude had changed. Suddenly she was edging away from the chance she had all but begged for earlier. And she kept passing the buck to Doro—kept saying in one way or another, "It's his fault, not mine!" That was true enough, but it was going to hurt her if she didn't stop emphasizing it. Rachel had already all but dismissed her as having no real importance. She was an irritant. No more. And healers were very efficient at getting rid of irritants.

"What kind of call did you receive, Rae?" he asked. "Was it like a verbal command, or like—"

"It was like getting hit with a club at first," she said. "And the noise . . . mental static like the worst moments of transition. Maybe I was picking up the last of Mary's transition. Then I was drawn here. There may have been words. I was only aware of images that let me see where I was going. Images, and that terrible planted compulsion to go. So here I am. I had to come. I had no choice at all."

Doro nodded. "And now that you're here, do you think you could leave if you wanted to?"

"I want to."

"And you can't?"

"I could, yes. But I wouldn't be very comfortable. At the airport, I realized that I was only a few miles away from here. I wanted that to be enough. I wanted to get a hotel room and wait until whoever was calling me got tired and gave up. I went to a hotel and tried to register. My hand was shaking so much I couldn't write." She shrugged. "I had to come. Now that I'm here I have to stay—at least until someone figures out a way to make your little experiment let me go."

"You'll need a room here, then," said Doro. "Mary."

Mary looked at him, then at Rachel. "Upstairs," she said tonelessly. "Come on."

They were on their way out when Doro spoke again. "Just a moment, Rae." Both women stopped. "It's possible that in a few days you'll need my help more than Mary will, but right now she is just out of transition."

Rachel said nothing.

"She'd better not even catch a cold, healer."

"Are you going to warn the others away from her too when they get here?"

"Of course. But since you're here now, and since you've already made your feelings clear, I didn't think I should wait to speak to you."

She smiled a little in spite of herself. "All right, Doro, I won't hurt her. But get me out of this, please. I feel like I'm wearing a damned leash."

Doro said nothing to that. He spoke to Mary. "Come back when you've got Rachel settled. I want to talk to you."

"Okay." She must have read something of what he wanted to say in his tone. She looked apprehensive. It didn't matter. She was an adult now, and on the verge of being a success. The first success of her kind. He would push her. She could stand it, and right now she needed it.

She came back a few minutes later and he motioned her into a chair opposite him.

"Are you shielded?" he asked.

"Yes."

"Can you tell by your pattern whether anyone else is near here—about to arrive?" His own ability had told him that no one was.

"No one is," she said.

"Good. We won't be interrupted." He looked at her silently for a long moment. "What happened?"

Her eyes slid away from his. "I don't know. I was just nervous, I guess."

"Of course you were. The trick is not to tell everyone about it."

She looked at him again, frowning, her small, expressive face a mask of concern. "Doro, I saw them in my mind and they didn't scare me. I didn't feel a thing. I had to keep reminding myself that they were probably dangerous, that I should be careful. And even when I was reminding myself, I don't think I really believed it. But now . . . just meeting one of them. . . . "

"You're afraid of Rachel?"

"I sure as hell am."

It was an unusual thing for her to admit. Rachel must have thoroughly shaken her. "What is it about her that frightens you?"

"I don't know."

"You should know."

She thought for a moment. "It was just a feeling at first—like the feeling I ignored when I tried to read you this morning. A feeling of danger. A feeling that she could carry out those threats she kept not quite making." She stopped, looked at Doro. He said nothing. She went on. "I guess the dangerous thing about her is the one you hinted at just before we went up. That if she can heal the sick, she can probably make people sick too."

"I didn't say you should guess," said Doro. "I said you should *know*. You can read her every thought, every memory, without her being aware of it. Use your ability."

"Yeah." She took a deep breath. "I'm not used to that yet. I guess I'll be doing it automatically after a while."

"You'd better. And when I'm finished with you here, I want you to read them all. Including Karl. I want you to learn their weaknesses and their strengths. I want you to know them better than they know themselves. I don't want you to be uncertain or afraid with even one more of them."

She looked a little surprised. "Well, I can find out about them, all right. But as for not being afraid . . . if a person like Rachel wants to kill me, I'm not going to be able to stop her just because I know her." She paused for a moment. "Now I know— I just found out—that Rachel can give me a heart attack or a cerebral hemorrhage or any other deadly thing she wants to. So I know. So what?"

"What else did you find out about Rachel?"

"Junk. Nothing that does me any good. Stuff about her personal life, her work. I see she's a kind of parasite too. It must run in my family."

"Of course it does. But she's got nothing like your power. And you've seen a thing you don't realize you've seen, girl."

"What?"

"That you're at least as dangerous to Rachel as she is to you. Since you can read her through her shield, she won't be able to surprise you—unless you're just careless. And if you see her coming, you should be able to stop her."

"I don't see how, unless I kill her. But it doesn't matter. I was reading her again as you spoke. She's not about to come after me, now that you've ordered her not to."

"No, she wouldn't. But I won't always be standing between you and her. I'm giving you time—not very much time—to learn to handle yourself among these people. You'd better use it."

She swallowed, nodded.

"Do you understand what Rachel does? Do you see that you are to her, and to the others, what she is to her congregations?"

"A kind of mental vampire draining strength . . . or something from people. Strength? Life force? I don't know what to call it."

"It doesn't matter what you call it. She has to take it to do her healing, and healing is the only purpose she's found for her life. Can you see that what she sets up at each of her services is a kind of temporary pattern?"

"Yes. But at least she doesn't kill anybody."

"She could, very easily. Ordinarily people have no defense against what she does—the way she feeds. If she took too much from her crowds, she'd begin killing the very old, the very young, the weak, even the sick that she intended to heal."

"I see."

"See, too, that while you can take from her, she can't take from you."

"Because I can shield her out."

"You don't have to shield her out. Let her in if you like."

"What do you mean?" She looked at him in horror.

"Exactly what you think I mean."

She frowned. "Are you telling me it's all right for me to kill now when, just a few hours ago, you said—"

"I know what I said. And I still don't *want* anyone killed. But I'm gambling on you, Mary. If you survive among these people, I have a chance of winning."

"Winning your empire. Is there anybody whose life you wouldn't risk for your Goddamn empire?"

"No."

For a moment, she glared at him angrily. Then the anger faded as though she didn't have the energy to sustain it. Doro was accustomed to the look. All his people faced him with it at one time or another. It was a look of submission.

"What I've decided to do," said Doro, "is give you the life of one of the actives if you need it. If you have to make an example of someone, I'll let it pass as long as you keep control of yourself and don't go beyond that one."

She thought about that for a long moment. "Permission to kill," she said finally. "I don't know how I feel about that."

"I hope you won't have to use it. But I don't want you totally handicapped."

"Thanks. I think. God, I hope I'm like Rachel. I hope I don't have to kill."

"You won't find out until you get started on someone."

She sighed. "Since this is all your fault, will you stay around for a while? I won't have Karl. I'll need somebody."

"That's another thing."

"What?"

"Stop telling the actives that the one show of power you've given them, the one thing you've done that they can't resist or undo, is my fault."

"But it is. . . . "

"Of course it is. And the moment they realize I'm here, they'll know it is. They don't have to be told. Especially when your telling them sounds like whining for pity. There's no pity in them, girl. They're going to feel about as sorry for you as you do for Vivian, or for Rina."

That seemed to sober her.

"You're going to have to grow up, Mary," he said quietly. "You're going to have to grow up fast."

She studied her hands, large, frankly ugly, her worst feature. They lay locked together in her lap. "Just stay with me for a while, Doro. I'll do the best I can."

"I had intended to stay."

She didn't bother hiding her relief. He got up and went to her.

MARY

There were incidents as my actives straggled in. I had pried through their minds and gotten to know all of them except Rachel before I even met them—so that none of them surprised me much.

Doro beat the holy shit out of Jan almost as soon as she arrived, because she'd done something stupid. I don't think he would have touched her, otherwise. One of the two kids she'd had by him was dead and he wasn't happy about it. She said it was an accident. He knew she was telling the truth. But she panicked.

He was talking to her—not very gently—and he started toward her for some reason. She ran out the front door. That, he doesn't allow. Don't run from him. Never run. He called her back, warned her. But she kept going. He would have gone after her if I hadn't stopped him.

"She'll be back," I said quickly. "Give her a chance. The pattern will bring her back." I wondered why I bothered to try to help her. I shouldn't have cared what happened to her. She had taken one look at Rachel and me and thought, *Oh, God, niggers!* And she was the one Doro had chosen to have kids by. Surely Rachel and Ada would have been better parents.

Anyway, Doro waited—more out of curiosity than anything else, I think. Jan came back in about thirty minutes. She came back cursing herself for the coward she was and believing that Doro would surely kill her now. Instead, he took her up to his room and beat her. Beat her for God knows how long. We could hear her screaming at first. I read the others and found what I thought I'd find. That every one of them knew from personal experience how bad Doro's beatings could be. I knew myself, though, like the others, I hadn't had one for a few years.

Now we just sat around not looking at each other and waiting for it to be over. After a while things were quiet. Jan was in bed for three days. Doro ordered Rachel not to help her.

Rachel had enough to do helping Jesse when he came in. He was the last to arrive, because he wasted two days trying to fight the pattern. He came in mad and tired and still pretty cut up from a fight he'd gotten into on the day I called him. I had found out about that by reading his mind. And I knew about the little town he owned in Pennsylvania, and the things he did to the people there, and the way he made them love him for it. I was all ready to hate his guts. Meeting him in person didn't give me any reason to change my mind.

He said, "You green-eyed bitch, I don't know how you dragged me here, but you damned well better let me go. Fast."

I was in a bad mood. I had been hearing slightly different versions of that same song from everybody for two days. I said, "Man, if you don't find something better to call me, I'm going to knock the rest of your teeth out."

He stared at me as though he wasn't quite sure he'd heard right. I guess he wasn't very used to people talking back to him and making it stick. He started toward me. The two words he managed to get out were, "Listen, bitch—"

I picked up a heavy little stone horse statuette from the end table next to me and tried to break his jaw with it. My thoughts were shielded so that he couldn't anticipate what I was going to do the way he did with the guy he beat up back in Donaldton. I left him lying on the floor bleeding and went up to Rachel's room.

She answered my knock and stood in her doorway glaring down at me. "Well?"

"Come downstairs," I said. "I have a patient for you."

She frowned. "Someone is hurt?"

"Yeah, Jesse Bernarr. He's the last member of our 'family' to come in. He came in a little madder than the rest of you."

I could feel Rachel sweep the downstairs portion of the house with her perception. She found Jesse and focused in tight on him. "Oh, fine," she muttered after a moment. "And me with nothing to draw on."

But she went right down to him. I followed, because I wanted to see her heal him. I hadn't seen anything so far but her memories.

She knelt beside him and touched his face. Suddenly she was viewing the damage from the inside, first coming to understand it, then stimulating healing. I couldn't find words to describe how she did it. I could see. I could understand, I thought. I could even show somebody else mentally. But I couldn't have talked about it. I began wondering if I could do it.

Rachel was still busy over Jesse when I left. I went into the kitchen, sort of in a daze. I was mentally going over a lot of Rachel's other healings—the ones I'd gotten from her memory. What I had learned from her just now made everything clearer. I felt as though I had just begun to understand a foreign language—as though I had been hearing it and hearing it, and suddenly a little of it was getting through to me. And that little was opening more to me.

I pulled open a drawer and took out a paring knife. I put it to my left arm, pressed down, cut quickly. Not deep. Not too deep. It hurt like hell, anyway. I made a cut about three inches long, then threw the knife into the sink. I held my arm over the sink too, because it started to bleed. I stopped the pain, just to find out whether or not I could. It was easy. Then I let it hurt again. I wanted to feel everything I did in every way I could feel it. I stopped the bleeding. I closed my eyes and let the fingers of my right hand move over the wound. Somehow that was better. I could concentrate my perception on the wound, view it from the inside, without being distracted by what my eyes were seeing. My arm began to feel warm as I began the healing, and it grew warmer, hot. It wasn't really an uncomfortable feeling, though, and I didn't try to shut it out. After a while it cooled, and I could feel that my arm was completely healed.

I opened my eyes and looked at it. Part of the arm was still wet with blood, where it had run down. But where the cut had been, I couldn't see much more than a fine scar. I rinsed my arm under the faucet and looked again. Nothing. Just that little scar that nobody would even see unless they were looking for it.

"Well," said Rachel's voice behind me. "Doro said you were related to me."

I turned to face her, smiling, a little prouder of myself than I should have been in the presence of a woman who could all but raise the dead. "I just wanted to see if I could do it."

"It took you about five times longer than it should have for a little cut like that."

"Shit, how long did it take you the first time you tried it?" Then I thought I saw a chance to make peace with her. I had been in one argument after another with the actives since they arrived. It was time to stop. It really was. "Never mind," I said. "You're right. I did take a long time, compared to you. Maybe you could help me learn to speed it up. Maybe you could teach me a little more about healing, too."

"Either you learn on your own or you don't learn," she said. "No one taught me."

"Was there anybody around who could have?"

She didn't say anything.

"Look, you'd be a good teacher, and I'd like to learn."

"Good luck."

"The hell with you, then." I turned away from her, disgusted, and went to the refrigerator to make myself a ham-and-cheese sandwich. I was skinny at least partly because I didn't usually snack on things like that, but I felt hungry now. I figured Rachel would leave, but she didn't.

"Where's the cook?" she asked.

"In her room watching soap operas, I guess. That's usually where she is when she isn't in here."

"Would you call her down?"

"Why?"

"I made Jesse sleep when I finished with him, but I could feel then how hungry he was."

I froze with my sandwich halfway to my mouth. "Is he? And how do *you* feel?" I didn't have to ask. I could read it from her faster than she could say it.

"Fine. Not drained at all. I—" She looked at me, suddenly accusing. "You know how I should be feeling, don't you?"

"Yes."

"How do you know?"

I was surprised to realize how much I didn't want to tell her. None of them knew that I could read them through their shields, that nothing they could do would keep me out. They hated me enough already. But I had already decided not to hide my ability. Not to act as though I were ashamed of it or afraid of them. "I read it in your mind," I said.

"When?" She was beginning to look outraged.

"That doesn't matter. Hell, I don't even remember exactly when."

"I've been shielded most of the time. Unless you read it just now while I was healing . . . you were reading me then, weren't you?"

"Yes."

"You watched what I did, then came in here to try it on yourself."

"That's right. Doesn't it seem strange to you that you don't feel drained?"

"We'll get back to that. I want to find out more about your snooping. I didn't feel you reading me just now."

I took a deep breath. "I could say that was because you were so busy with Jesse, but I won't bother. Rachel, you'll never feel me reading you unless I want you to."

She looked at me silently for several seconds. "It's part of your special ability, then. You can read people without their being aware of it. And . . . you can read people without thinning your shield enough to have them read you. Because you weren't open just now. I would have noticed." She stopped as though waiting for me to say something. I didn't. She went on, "And you can read people right through their shields. Can't you!" It was a demand or an accusation. Like she was daring me to admit it.

"Yes," I said. "I can."

"So you've taken our mental privacy as well as our freedom."

"It looks like I've given you something, too."

"Given me what?"

"Freedom from the parasitic need you feel so guilty about sometimes."

"If you weren't hiding behind Doro, I'd show you how much I appreciate your gift."

"No doubt you'd try. But since Doro is on my side, shouldn't we at least try to get along?"

She turned and walked away from me.

Nothing was settled and I had one more strike against me. But at least I was starting to learn to heal. I had a feeling I should learn as much as I could about that as quickly as I could. In case Rachel tried something desperate.

Nobody tried anything for a while, though. There was only the usual arguing. Jesse promised me he was going to "get" me. He was a big, dumb, stocky guy, blond, good-looking, mean—a troublemaker. But, somehow, he was the one active that I was never afraid of. And he was wary of me. He told himself I was crazy, and he kept away from me in spite of his threat.

People began to get together in the house to do something besides argue.

Seth started sleeping in Ada's room, and Ada, our mouse, started to look a little more alive.

Jesse went to Rachel's room one night to thank her for healing him. His gratitude must have pleased her. He went back the next night to thank her again.

Karl said "Good morning" to me once. I think it just slipped out.

Rachel told Doro—not me—that I had been right. That she could heal now without taking strength from a crowd. In fact, she said she wasn't sure she still could draw strength from crowds. She said the pattern had changed her, limited her somehow. Now she seemed to be using her patients' own strength to heal them—which sounded as though it would be dangerous if her patient was in bad shape to start with. Jesse had merely eaten a couple of steaks when she let him wake up. Steaks, a lot of fries, salad, and about a quart of milk. But Jesse was such a big guy that I suspected that was the way he usually ate. I found out later that I was right. So, evidently, the healing hadn't weakened him that much.

I kept to myself during those first days. I watched everybody—read everybody, that is. I found that Rachel had spread the word about my abilities and everybody figured I was watching them. They didn't like it. They thought a lot of shit at me when I was in a room with them. But I almost never read them steadily when I was with them, talking to them. I had to keep my attention on what they were saying. So it took me a while to realize that I was being cursed out on two levels.

I was settling in, though. I was learning not to be afraid of any of them. Not even Karl. They were all older than I was and they were all physically bigger. For a while, I had to keep telling myself I couldn't afford to let that matter. If I went on letting them scare me, I'd never be able to handle them. After a while, I started to convince myself. Maybe I was influenced by the kind of thoughts I picked up from them when they were off guard. Sometimes, even while they were complaining or arguing or cursing at me, they were aware of being very comfortable within the pattern. Jesse wasn't getting any of the mental static that had used to prevent him from driving a car, and Jan didn't have to always be careful what she touched—bothered by the latent mental images she had used to absorb from everything. And, of course, Rachel didn't need her crowds. And Clay Dana didn't need as much help from Seth as he had before he came to us. Clay seemed to be getting some benefit from the pattern even though he wasn't a member of it. And that left Seth with more time for Ada.

Everybody was settling in. But the others didn't like it. It scared them that they were not only getting used to their leashes but starting to see benefits in them. It scared hell out of them that maybe they were giving in the way ordinary people gave in to them. That they were getting to be happy slaves like Karl's servants. Their fear made them fight harder than ever against me. I could understand their feelings, but that wasn't enough. I had to do something about them. I was fed up with hearing about them. I thought for a while, then went to talk to Doro.

I had come to depend on Doro more now than I ever had before. He was the only person in the house that I could talk to without getting blamed, cursed, or threatened. I had all but moved into his room. So, one night, about two weeks after my transition, I walked into his room, fell across his bed, and said, "Well, I guess this has gone on long enough."

"What?" he asked. He was at his desk scribbling something that looked like ancient Egyptian hieroglyphics in a notebook.

"Everybody sitting around waiting for something that isn't going to happen," I said. "Waiting for the pattern to just disappear."

"What are you going to do?"

"Get them all together and make them face a few facts. And then, after they stop screaming, get them thinking about what they can do with themselves in spite of the pattern." I sat up and looked at him. "Hell, they're all telepaths. They don't have to be able to go miles from home to get work done. And God knows they need something to do!"

"Work?"

"Right. Jobs, interests, goals." I had been thinking about it for days now. "They can make their own jobs. It will give them less time to bitch at me. Rachel can have a church if she wants one. The others can look around, find out what they want."

"If they're reasonable. They might not be, you know."

"Yeah."

"They might not stop screaming, as you put it, until they've tried to lynch you."

"Yeah," I repeated. I took a deep breath. "Want to sit in and see the blood?"

He smiled. "There might not be any blood if I'm there."

"Then, by all means, sit in."

"Oh, I will. But it will only be to let them know I'm acknowledging your authority over them. I'm going to turn them loose, Mary."

I swallowed. "Already, huh?"

"They're yours. It's time you jumped in among them."

"I guess so." I really wasn't surprised. I had seen him working up to this. He couldn't read my mind, but he watched me as closely as I watched everybody else. He questioned me. I didn't mind. He let the others complain to him about me, but he didn't question them about me or make them promises. That, I appreciated. So now it was time for me to be kicked out of the nest.

"You'll be leaving if this works, won't you?" I asked.

"For a while. I'll be back. I have a suggestion that might help you both before and after I leave, though."

"What?"

"Let Karl in on what you're going to do before you do it. Let him get over some of his anger with you and see the sense in what you're saying. Then, if I understand him as well as I think I do, he'll stand with you if any of the others threaten you."

"Isn't that just trading one protector for another? I'm supposed to be able to protect myself."

"Oh, you can. But, chances are, you'll have to do it by killing someone. I was trying to help you avoid that."

I nodded. I knew he was still worried that my killing might be a chain-reaction thing. That if I took one of the actives, then, sooner or later, I'd have to take another. And another. I had a feeling that, when he left, he wouldn't go any farther than Emma's house. And from there, he'd keep whatever special senses he had trained on me.

"Is Karl alone now?" he asked.

I checked. "Yes, for a change." Karl had been screwing

around with Jan, of all people. He couldn't have found a better way to disgust me.

"Then, go to him now. Talk to him."

I gave Doro a dirty look. It was late, and I was in no mood to hear the things Karl would probably say to me. I just wanted to go to bed. But I got up and went to see Karl.

He was lying on his back interfering with the thoughts of some sleeping local politician. I hesitated for a moment to find out what he was doing. He was just making sure that a company he and Doro controlled got a zone variance it needed to erect a building. He had a job, anyway. I knocked at his door.

He listened silently to what I had to tell him, his face expressionless.

"So we're here, we belong to you, and that's that," he said quietly.

"That wasn't my point."

"Yes it was. Along with the fact that we might as well find some way to live our lives this way and make the best of it."

"All I want us to do is settle down and start acting like human beings again."

"If that's still what we are. What do you want from me?"

"Help, if you can give it. If you will."

"Me, help you?"

"You're my husband."

"That wasn't my idea."

I opened my mouth, then closed it again. This wasn't the time to fight with him.

"Doro will back you up," he said. "He's all you need."

"He's putting me on my own. He's putting *us* on *our* own."

"Why? What have you done?"

"Nothing, so far. It's not punishment. He just thinks it's time we found out whether we can survive without him—as a group."

"Whether you can survive."

"No, us, really. Because, if things go bad, I'm not about to let the others get me without taking as many of them as I can with me." I took a deep breath. "That's why I want your help. I'd like to get through this without killing anybody."

116

He looked a little surprised. "Are you so sure you can kill?"

"Positive."

"How can you know? You've never tried."

"You don't want to hear how I know, believe me."

"Don't be stupid. If you want my help at all, you'd better tell me everything."

I looked at him. I made myself just look at him until I could answer quietly. "I know the same way you know how to eat when you're hungry. I'm that kind of parasite, Karl. I suppose you and the others might as well face it the way I have."

"You . . . you're saying you're a female Doro?"

"Not exactly, but that's close enough."

"I don't believe you."

"Oh yes you do."

He stared at me silently for a moment. "I didn't want to believe you could read me through my shield either."

"I can. That's part of my ability, too."

"You have enough abilities not to need my help."

"I told you why I need you."

"Yes. You don't want to kill."

"Not unless somebody is stupid enough to attack me."

"But if hunger is what you feel, how can you avoid doing something about it eventually? You'll have to kill."

"It's more like having an appetite—like being able to eat but not really being hungry."

"But you will get hungry. It seems to me that's why we're here. We're your food supply. You're gathering people the way Doro does. It just isn't as much work for you as it is for him."

"Yeah," I said softly. "I've been thinking things like that myself. They might be all wrong. But even if they aren't, I don't know what to do about it."

He turned his head, stared at a bookcase. "Short of committing suicide, there's not much you can do."

"And I'm not about to do that. But I'll tell you, as mad as these people make me sometimes, it would be almost as hard for me to kill one of them as it would be for me to commit suicide. I don't want their lives."

"For now."

"And I don't want anybody forcing me to change my mind. Because, if I do, I'm not sure I'll be able to control myself. I might kill more of you than I mean to." I got up to leave. "Karl, I'm not asking you to make up your mind now, or promise me anything. I just wanted you to know there was a choice to make." I started for the door.

"Wait a minute."

I stopped, waited.

"You're closed, shielded all the time," he said. "I don't think you've unshielded once since you did it for me after your transition."

"Would you if you were living with people who wanted to kill you?"

"What if I asked you to open for me? Just for me. Now."

"Why?"

"Because you need me. And because I need to see the truth of what you're telling me."

"I thought that was settled."

"I've got to see it for myself, Mary. I've got to be certain. I can't . . . do what you're asking until I've seen for myself that it's necessary."

I read him, saw that he was telling the truth. He was angry and bitter and he didn't like himself much for even thinking about siding with me. But he knew it was his best chance for survival—for a while, at least.

I opened. I was more worried about accidentally taking him than I was about what he might find out. I was a little touchier about his rummaging through my memories than I had been before, but I put up with it. He didn't go after anything more than verification of what I had told him. That was all he cared about.

"All right," he said after a moment.

I shielded, looked at him.

"I'll do what I can to help you," he said. "And heaven help both of us."

· Seven ·

MARY

Winning Karl over gave me the courage to get right to work on the others. I called everybody together in the living room at around ten the next morning. Karl came in with Vivian, and Seth Dana came with Ada and Clay. Vivian and Clay didn't really have to be there, of course, but it didn't matter to me that they were.

Karl had to go and get Jan. She said she wasn't about to take orders from me. I figured we'd have this meeting and then, if she still felt that way, I'd show her how gentle Doro had been with her.

And Doro had to get Jesse and Rachel. They were shacked up in Jesse's room now, like they meant to stay together for a while. They were sure as hell together in their opinion of me. In fact, they were so close together and they hated me so much that I knew if I had to take anybody, it would probably be one of them. And the way they had been acting for the past few days, I didn't see how I could get away with taking just one. Neither of them was going to sit by and watch the other killed.

That bothered me. I realized that their feelings for each other could be used against them—that, for a while at least, I could control one by threatening the other. But, somehow, I didn't want to do that. I'd try it if I had to, rather than kill them both and make myself a liability to Doro, but I hoped they wouldn't push me that far.

Once they were all in the room, with Doro sitting by himself off to one side, I made my speech. Doro told me later that I was too blunt, too eager to threaten and challenge. He was probably right.

I told everybody that the pattern was a permanent fixture binding them to me. It wasn't going anywhere, I wasn't going anywhere, and they weren't going to do anything to me. I told them I could kill them, would kill them if they pushed me, but that I didn't want to kill them if I could avoid it. I told them to follow the feelings I knew they were suppressing and accept the pattern. Get themselves some new interests or revive some old ones, get jobs if they wanted them, stop sitting around bitching like kids. I spoke quietly to them. I didn't rant and rave. But they still didn't like what I had to say.

And, of course, except for Karl, they didn't want to believe me. I had to open to them. I had thought that might be necessary. I hadn't been looking forward to it but I was ready to do it. First, though, I did what I could to throw a scare into them.

"Look," I said quietly. "You all know me. You know I'll do whatever I have to to defend myself. Try anything more than reading me now, and you've had it. That's all."

I opened. I could see that they were moving cautiously, trying to find out whether I had the power I claimed before they made any move against me—which was intelligent of them.

I had never opened my mind to anyone but Karl before. I had only the memories of the others to tell me what it was like to open to more than one person at a time. They had never done it deliberately. It was just that they couldn't stay shielded all the time, the way I could. Their shields cut off their mental perception totally. In a way, for them, shielding was like wandering around wearing a gag, a blindfold, and earplugs. None of them could put up with it for long. So sometimes they picked up things from each other. Sometimes two or three of them picked up something from one. They didn't like it, but they were learning to live with it. Doro had said that in itself was more than he had dared to hope for. Actives had never been able to live with it before. He said it seemed much easier for my actives to keep out of each other's minds than it had been for earlier generations. He gave my pattern the credit for that. Maybe my pattern deserved the credit for the way I was able to accept them all into my mind, too. Like them, I didn't enjoy it. But I wasn't nervous or afraid, because I knew I could defend myself if I had to, and I knew none of them meant to try anything—yet. I was just uncomfortable. Like I'd suddenly found myself stark naked in front of a lot of strangers, all of whom were taking a good look.

At least it was easy to keep track of them and know who was getting what. I hadn't been sure it would be with so many. But I spotted Jesse the moment he decided to do a little snooping into matters other than the truth of what I had told them.

I reached out and contracted the muscle of his lower leg into a tight, hard knot.

I had taken Rachel's advice and been working on my own to develop whatever healing ability I had. I was still a long way from being ready to call myself a healer, but I had learned a few things from viewing my body and other people's bodies from the inside. And I had read medical books and I had read Rachel. I found that I learned best, though, by watching people who had things wrong with them—seeing how their bodies healed, understanding what had gone wrong in the first place. If I could understand it, I could make it happen.

A few days before, I had gotten a bad cramp in my leg.

So now Jesse had a bad cramp in his leg. He yelled, more surprised than hurt—although it did hurt. And, of course, he snapped his attention away from me like a released rubber band.

It was a very quick, very easy thing, to cause a cramp. By the time the others realized I had done it, I was finished and paying attention to them again. They dropped away from me almost all at once. Almost. Rachel hung on, shaped her thoughts into words for me.

Don't think you can ever handle me that way!

Of course not, I sent back. *Unfortunately for you, the only way I can handle you is by killing you.*

She dropped away from me mad and scared and ashamed of herself for being scared.

As she broke contact, Jesse stood up. His cramp had faded away normally, since I hadn't done anything to prolong it or make it worse. I could have used his own muscle to break his leg. He didn't seem to realize that. He started toward me.

Karl got up quickly, stepped in front of Jesse. A distance runner facing a football player. They made a contrast. Karl spoke just as Jesse was about to knock him out of the way.

"A question, Jess," he said quietly. "Only a question. What do you imagine you'll do when you reach her—aside from letting her make an example of you, I mean." And he stepped out of Jesse's path and sat down again. Jesse stayed where he was, glaring first at Karl, then at me.

"One woman," he said bitterly. "A woman, for Godsake! The biggest damn thing about her is her mouth! And you're all going to let her tell you you're serving a life sentence in this place." He looked around the room, his eyes accusing. "She couldn't kill more than one or two of us if we all hit her at once. Don't you see? Her only hold on us is that the rest of you are so afraid of being the one she gets that you'd rather stay on her Goddamn leash than stand up to her!"

He looked around the room again, this time challengingly. "I'm willing to take a chance. Who'll stand with me? Who's as sick of being in jail as I am?"

I was watching Rachel. She looked at me and I glanced from her to Jesse, then back to her. The threat was delivered that simply, for what it was worth. Rachel understood. She kept quiet. Jesse was turning toward her when Seth spoke up.

"Jess, it seems to me you're forgetting about Doro."

Jesse looked over at Doro. Doro looked back expressionlessly. "I'm not forgetting." Jesse spoke to Seth, but kept his eyes on Doro. "I may have read a little more from Mary than you did—than any of the rest of you did. Maybe nobody but me noticed that Doro was about to dump her—put her on her own with us and let her sink or swim as best she could."

Nobody said anything.

"Well?" said Jesse to Doro. "Weren't you?"

"I was," said Doro. "But I hadn't done it yet."

"As long as you were going to, what difference does it make?"

Doro leaned back in his chair. "You tell me."

"You didn't say anything," said Jesse, frowning. "You weren't going to stop me."

"No."

"What were you going to do? Let me go through with it, and then kill me if she hadn't managed to?"

"Yes."

Jesse stared at him as though he was finally realizing that it was Doro he was talking to, not one of us. Without another word, he turned and went back to his chair.

Doro got up, came closer in to join the group. He sat down beside me, spoke to me softly.

"I warned you."

"I know," I said.

He looked around at the others. "You're all powerful people," he said. "I wish you weren't in such a hurry to kill yourselves. Alive, you could grow into something impressive and worthwhile."

"All seven of us," said Rachel bitterly.

"If you survive as a group, you won't be only seven long. Your numbers are small because I've deliberately kept them small. If you can work together now, you can begin to grow slowly through your own children and through the latents scattered around the country who are capable of producing telepathically active children. Latents who need only the right mates to produce actives. The seven of you can be the founders and the leaders of a new race." He paused, glanced at Jesse. "For any of you who don't realize it, that's what I want. That's what I've been trying to achieve for thousands of years. It's what I'll be on my way to achieving if the seven of you can stay together on your own without killing each other. I think you can. I think that, in spite of the way you've been acting, your own lives are still of some importance to you. Of course, if they aren't, I want to know that, too. So I'm withdrawing my protection from Mary. And, incidentally, I'm releasing her from the restriction I put on her." He glanced at me. "The rest of you don't know about that. You don't have to. You're free now to behave as intelligently or as stupidly as you like."

"You want us to spend the rest of our lives here?" demanded Rachel.

"If that's what turns out to be necessary," said Doro. "I doubt that it will be, though. You're a very young group. If you survive to grow older, I think you'll work out a comfortable arrangement."

"What arrangement!"

"I don't know, Rae. You're also a new kind of group. You'll have to find your own way. Perhaps pairs of you will take over other houses in this neighborhood. Perhaps, in time, you'll even find a way to travel long distances from Mary without discomfort."

"I wish I could show you what it feels like to go just a few miles from her," muttered Jesse. "Compare it to straining against a choke chain."

Doro looked over at him. "It's easier to take now, though, than it was when you first got here, isn't it?" He knew it was. I had read Jesse and told him so days before.

Jesse opened his mouth, probably to lie. But he knew he had about as much chance of getting a lie past Doro as he did of getting one past me. He closed his mouth for a moment, then said, "Easier or not, I don't like it any more now than I ever did. None of us do!"

"That's at least partly because all of you are trying so hard not to."

"I'm not trying," said Jan. "I'm just slowly going out of my mind from being cooped up in this place. I can't stand it!"

"You'll find a way to stand it," said Doro coldly.

"But why should I? Why should any of us? Why should we all suffer because of _her?_"

There was loud agreement all around.

"You needn't suffer at all," he said. "You know better than I do how easily you could slip into your new roles here if you wanted to." That was something else I had told him—how they were fighting not only me but their own inclinations. He took a deep breath. "But you're on your own. It would be wise of you to look for ways to live with your new situation, but if you choose not to, go ahead and kill each other."

"What if we just kill Mary?" said Rachel. She was looking at me as she spoke.

Doro gave her a look of disgust. Then he got up and left me sitting alone, went back to his place. Rachel looked at Jesse. Jesse picked it right up.

"Who's with us?" he said. "Who wants out of this jail now? Jan?"

"You want to . . . to kill her?" asked Jan.

"You know any other way out?"

"No. All right. I'm with you."

"Seth?"

"How many people you figure you need to kill one woman, Jess?"

"As many as I can get, man, and you're a damned fool if you can't see why. You've read her. You've seen what kind of parasite she is. We either get together and kill her, or we wait, and maybe she kills us off one by one."

I sat there watching, listening to all this, wondering why I was waiting. Jesse was getting people together to kill me and I was waiting. The only intelligent thing I was doing was keeping part of my attention on Rachel. She was the only one of them who might try something on her own. She could damage my body, and she could do it very quickly, I knew. But she couldn't do it without thinking about it first, deciding to do it. She was dead when she made that decision.

Seth turned to face me, stared at me for several seconds. "You know," he said, "in the two weeks I've been here, I don't think you and I have done much more than pop off at each other a couple of times. I don't know you."

"You've been busy," I said. I glanced at Ada, who sat close to him, looking scared.

"You're not afraid," said Seth.

I shrugged.

"Or, if you are, you hide it pretty good."

And Jesse. "Are you in or out, Dana?"

"Out," said Seth quietly.

"You're with her?" Jesse gestured sharply at me. "You like being a Goddamn slave?"

"No, not with her. Not against her, either. She hasn't done anything to me, man. At least, not anything that was her fault."

"What the hell does 'fault' have to do with it? You're going to be stuck with her for the rest of your life unless we get rid of her now."

Seth looked at Ada, then at Clay on his other side. I knew already that Ada wanted no part of this. Jesse, Jan, and Rachel were confirming Ada's worst fears; were, in her opinion, acting like people who deserved to be quarantined. Clay had been bitter about being dragged away from the fresh start he was going to make in Arizona. And when he heard I was the one who had done the dragging, he decided I was the one to hate. Then, like Seth, he had started to see me as just another of Doro's creations, no more to blame for what I was than anyone else in the house. Ironically, he felt sorry for me. He didn't want Seth involved in killing me.

"Well?" demanded Jesse. He glared at Seth.

"I've said what I had to say," said Seth.

Jesse turned away from him in disgust. "Well, Karl, I don't suppose you want to change sides."

Karl smiled a little. "I would if you had a chance, Jess. You don't, you know."

"Karl, please." Jan. Sweet Jan. Maybe I could get her, too. "Karl, with you helping us, we would have a chance."

Karl ignored her, glanced at me. "You are going to try to talk them out of this, aren't you?"

I nodded, turned to face Jesse. "Man, with three people insisting that they're going to attack me, I won't have time to be gentle. No more little cramps. You jump me, and you and Rachel are dead. I might not be able to get Jan, but you two don't have a chance."

"Let's make it even stronger than that," said Karl. "I don't want fighting. There's a possibility that Mary might lose control

126

and do a lot more damage than she intends to do. I've read her more thoroughly than you have. I think there's a real danger that, once she got started, she might take us all. If the three of you are foolish enough to attack her in spite of that possibility, you'd better attack me too."

The words were goads to Jesse. Abruptly, he dove at me through his strand of the pattern. I had no warning. He acted on impulse, without thinking. And using the pattern that way. . . . Until now, nobody had really used the pattern except me. His strand of the pattern struck at me snakelike. Fast. Blindingly fast.

I didn't have time to think about reacting. What happened, happened automatically. And it happened even faster than Jesse had moved.

He was mine. His strength was mine. His body was worthless to me, but the force that animated it was literally my ambrosia—power, sustenance, life itself.

By the time Jesse realized what was happening and tried to twist away, there was almost nothing left of him. His strand of the pattern thrashed feebly, uselessly.

I realized that I could leave him that way. I watched him with a kind of detached interest, and it occurred to me that if I let him go he would grow strong again. He was terrified now, and weak, but he wasn't getting any weaker on his own. He could live, if I let him, if I wasn't too greedy. He could live and grow strong and feed me again.

I opened my eyes, wondering when I had shut them. I felt higher than I ever had before. I held out my hand and looked at it. It was shaking. I was shaking all over, but, God, I felt good.

Everybody was looking at Jesse slumped in his chair. The surprise they were all radiating told me that he had just lost consciousness. They were not quite aware yet of what had happened. Rachel began to realize it first. She began turning toward me—in slow motion, it seemed—meaning to get her revenge. She thought Jesse was dead. She, a healer, thought he was dead, but I knew he was alive.

She finished turning. She was going to rupture a good-sized blood vessel in my brain.

I took her.

She didn't hand herself to me the way Jesse had. She fought me briefly. But somehow her struggles only helped me drain her strength. I was more conscious of what I was doing with her. I could see how my mental image of her shrank in proportion to the amount of strength I took. I took less from her than I had from Jesse. I didn't need anything at all from her—except peace. I wanted her to stop her useless struggling. I wanted her not to be able to do what she wanted to do to me. That was all. I let her know it.

Jesse! Her thought was full of bitterness and anger and grief. I tried to soothe her wordlessly the way I might have handled a frightened child. She struggled harder, terrified, hysterical, giving me more of her strength by her struggles.

Finally, she stopped, exhausted. *Jesse.* Grief now. Only grief.

He's alive, I sent.

He's dead! I saw him die.

I tell you he's alive. You took too quick a look. I pressed through her grief so that she could see that I was giving her truth. *He is alive. I didn't want his life. I don't want yours. Will you make me take yours anyway?*

You aren't going to kill me?

Not unless you make me.

Then, let me go. Let me see Jesse.

I let her go, opened my eyes again. Evidently, closing them was some kind of reflex. Now the others were looking at Rachel, were turning to look at me. I felt better than ever. But steadier now. No more shaking. I felt in control. Before, I'd felt ready to take off and fly across the room. Everybody was staring at me.

"They're both all right," I said. "Weak, I guess. Put them to bed. They'll regain their strength." Like Rachel's crowds going away to regain their strength. I remembered Jan suddenly and looked at her.

She stared back, round-eyed.

"How about you?" I said.

"No!" I thought she was going to get up and run out the door again. "No."

I laughed at her. I don't think I would have done that if I hadn't been so high. I might have had a lot more to say to her, but I wouldn't have laughed.

"What did you do?" asked Karl.

I looked at him, and I could have hugged him for no reason at all. No. There was a reason. A big one. "I found out something," I said. "I just found out that I don't have to kill."

"But what did you do to them?"

Abruptly I was annoyed, almost angry at him for wanting details now, when it was all so new, when I just wanted to sit back and savor what I was feeling. Doro came up behind me, put his hands on my shoulders, and massaged gently.

"Calm down a little," he said. "I know you feel good, but calm down."

"High," I said. I grinned at him. "I feel high. You know."

"Yes. See if you can rein yourself in enough to tell us what you did."

"You know."

"Tell us anyway."

"Took some of their strength." I leaned back, relaxed against the couch, pulling my thoughts together. "Only some. I'm not a monster. At least not the kind you made me think I was." Then, as an afterthought. "I took more from Jesse. I didn't know what I was doing when he jumped me."

"Seth, check Jesse," Doro ordered.

Apparently Seth did. I didn't pay any attention. "He's still breathing," Seth said after a moment.

"Rae," Doro said, "how do you feel?" Rachel was conscious then. But she didn't say anything. Curiosity reached me through my private haze. I looked at her.

She was crying. She wasn't making any noise at all, but her whole body shook. She made a sound of pain as we all turned to look at her, and hid her face in her hands. She was shielded to the others. But to me she radiated shame and defeat. Humiliation.

That reached me and cleared the nonsense out of my head. I stood up, half expecting to find myself staggering. I was steady enough, though. Good.

I went to her and took her arm. I knew she wanted to be away from us. Tears, especially tears of defeat, were private things. She looked up, saw that it was me, and tried to pull her arm away.

"Stop acting stupid," I told her. "Get up and come on."

She stared at me. I still had hold of her arm. She started to get up, then realized how weak she was. She was glad enough to lean on me then.

She swallowed, whispered, "What about Jesse?"

What in the name of heaven did she see in him? "The others will see that he gets upstairs," I said. I glanced back at Doro. "She'll be okay."

He nodded, went over and draped Jesse's big body over one shoulder, then followed Rachel and me upstairs.

· Eight ·

MARY

The meeting just dissolved. Nobody made me any promises. Nobody bowed or scraped. Nobody even looked scared—or felt scared. I checked. Once they got over their surprise, they were even reassured. They could see that Jesse and Rachel were going to be all right. They could see that all I wanted from them was a little co-operation. And now they knew they would be better off if they co-operated. The atmosphere of the house was more relaxed than it had been since the day of my transition.

Seth Dana came up and grinned at me. "Don't you get the feeling you should have done this two weeks ago?"

I smiled back and shook my head. "I don't think so. Two weeks ago, I would have had to kill somebody."

He frowned. "I don't see why."

"Everything was too new. You were all on short fuses. You and Ada hadn't gotten together and mellowed each other, so one or both of you would have been against me. If you had, Karl probably would have, too. He was about ready to strangle me anyway, then." I shrugged. "This is better. People have had time to cool off."

He gave me an odd look. "What do you think might have happened if you'd waited a little longer than two weeks, then, let Jesse and Rachel do some mellowing?"

"Jesse and Rachel weren't mellowing. They were feeding on each other's hatred, building each other up to jump me."

"You know," he said, "I got the impression at first that you just threw this meeting together on the spur of the moment."

"I did."

"Yeah. After two weeks of watching everybody and making sure your timing was as right as you could make it."

Clay Dana came over to where Seth and I were talking. Close up, he looked sort of gray and sick. I thought he must have just had a bad bout of mental interference. "Congratulations," he said to me. "Now that we all know the new pecking order, do either of you have any aspirins?"

Seth looked at him with concern. "Another headache?"

"Another, hell. It's the same one I've had for three days."

"From mental interference?" I asked.

"What else?"

"I thought you weren't getting as much of that now as you used to."

"I wasn't," he said. "It stopped altogether for a few days. That never happened in the middle of a city before. Then, three days ago, it started to come back worse than ever."

That bothered me. I hadn't paid much attention to Clay since he arrived, but I knew that anything new and different that went wrong with him, with his out-of-control mental ability, would eventually get blamed on me, on my pattern.

Seth spoke up as though on cue. "Look, Mary, I've been meaning to ask you if you could figure out what was happening to Clay. He's been in really bad shape, and it just about has to have something to do with the pattern."

"First the aspirins," said Clay. "Find out what you want after— Hey!"

That "Hey!" was almost a shout. I had gotten rid of his headache for him fast—like switching off a light.

"Okay?" I asked, knowing it was.

"Sure." He looked at me as though he suddenly wanted to get away from me.

I stayed with him mentally for a few moments longer, trying to find out just what was wrong with him. I didn't really know what to look for. I just assumed that it had something to do with the pattern. I took a quick look through his memories, thinking that that uncontrolled ability of his might have tuned in on the pattern somehow. But it hadn't in any way that I could see.

I scanned all the way back to the day he and Seth had arrived at the house. It was quick work but frustrating. I couldn't find a damned thing. Nothing. I switched my attention to the pattern. I had no idea at all of what to look for there and I was getting mad. I checked the pattern strand that stretched from Seth to me. Seth was in mental contact with Clay sometimes to protect him. Maybe, without realizing it, he had done something more than protect.

He hadn't.

I had nowhere else to go. There was something especially galling about suffering a defeat now, just minutes after I had won my biggest victory. But what could I do?

I shifted my attention back to Clay. There was a glimmer of something just as I shifted—like the glimmer of a fine spider web that catches the light just for a second and then seems to vanish again. I froze. I shifted back to the pattern, bringing it into focus very slowly. At first there was nothing. Then, just before I would have had a strong, clear focus on the pattern strands of my six actives, there was that glimmer again. I managed to keep it, this time, by not trying to sharpen my focus on it. Like looking at something out of the corner of your eye.

It was a pattern strand. A slender, fragile-seeming thread, like a shadow of one of the comparatively substantial strands of my actives. But it was a pattern strand. Somehow, Clay had become a member of the pattern. How?

I could think of only one answer. The pattern was made up of actives. Just actives, no latents until now. No latents period. Clay was on his way to transition.

The moment the thought hit me, I knew it was right. After a ten-year delay, Clay was going to make it. I tried to tell myself that I wasn't sure. After all, I had never seen anyone who was about to go into transition before. But I couldn't even make myself doubt. Clay was going to come through. He would belong to me, like the others. I knew it.

I brought my attention back to Seth and Clay, who stood waiting.

"That took long enough," said Seth. "What did you find out?"

"That your brother's not a latent any more," I said. "That he's headed toward transition."

There was a moment of complete silence. Then came quick, bitter disappointment radiating from both men. They didn't believe me.

Seth spoke quietly. "Mary, Doro himself gave up on Clay years ago, said he wouldn't ever reach transition."

"I know it. But there was no pattern back then."

"But Doro explained that—"

"Damnit, Seth, I'm explaining that Doro was wrong. He might know a hell of a lot, but he can't foretell the future. And he can't use my pattern to see what I can see!"

Karl came up as I was talking. When I finished, he asked, "What are you shouting about now?"

I told him and he just shrugged.

"Doro wants to see us both in the library," he said. "Now."

"Wait a minute," said Seth. "She can't leave now." He looked at me. "You've got to tell us how you know . . . how after all these years this could happen." So they were beginning to believe me.

"I'll have to talk to you after I see what Doro wants," I said. "It probably won't take long."

I followed Karl away from them, hoping I could get back to them soon. I wanted to learn more about what was happening to Clay myself. I was excited about it. But now, Doro and the Dana brothers aside, there was something else I had to do.

"Karl."

We had almost reached the library door. He stopped, looked at me.

"Thanks for your help."

"You didn't need it."

"Yes I did. I might not have been able to stop myself from killing if they had pushed me harder."

Karl nodded disinterestedly, turned to go into the library.

"Wait a minute."

He gave me a look of annoyance.

"I have a feeling that, even though you sided with me, you're the only one in the house that I haven't really won over."

"You didn't win anyone over," he said. "You bludgeoned the others into submission. I had already submitted."

"The hell with that," I said. I lowered my gaze a little, stared at his chest instead of his face. He was wearing a blue shirt open at the neck so that a little of his mat of brown chest hair showed. "I did what I had to do," I said. "What I was evidently born to do. I'm not fighting it any more, for the same reason Jesse and Rachel probably won't fight me any more. It doesn't do any good."

"Don't you think I understand that?"

"If you understand it, why are you still holding it against me?"

"Because Jesse was right about one thing. It doesn't really matter whether what you're doing to us is your fault or not. You're doing it. I'm not fighting you, but you shouldn't expect me to thank you, either."

"I don't."

He looked a little wary. "Just what do you want from me?"

"You know damn well what I want."

"Do I?" He stared at me for a long moment. "I suppose I do. Doro must be leaving." He turned and walked away.

I let him go this time. I felt like throwing something at him, but I let him go. The son of a bitch had Jan and Vivian both, and he had the nerve to talk about Doro and me. Or, rather, he had the nerve to use Doro to try to hurt me. If he couldn't get away from me, he'd hurt me. He shouldn't have been able to hurt me. But he was.

In the library, Doro was sitting at the reading table leafing through a book, and probably reading it. He read fast. Karl and I sat opposite him with an empty chair between us.

"I'll be leaving tomorrow," said Doro.

I felt rather than saw Karl's glance at me. I ignored him. Doro went on.

"Mary, it looks as though you've established yourself fairly well. I don't think anyone will bother you again."

"No."

"You're just going to leave?" said Karl. "Don't you have any plans for us now that Mary has become what you seemed to want her to become?"

"Mary's plan sounded all right to me," said Doro. "It might be harder for the group of you to organize your lives, held together as you are. But I'd rather give you a chance to try it. Let you find out whether you can build something of your own."

"Or at least of Mary's own," said Karl bitterly.

Doro looked from one of us to the other.

"He's still holding the pattern against me," I said. "But he might be right, anyway. I might have something we can start working on together." I told him about Clay Dana. He sat there listening, and looking more and more as though he didn't believe me.

"Clay lost any chance he had for becoming an active over ten years ago," he said.

"Ten years ago he didn't have the pattern to help him along."

"I find it hard to believe the pattern is helping him now. How could it? What did you do?"

"I don't know, exactly. But it must be the pattern. What other new thing has there been in his life in the past two weeks? He was a latent before he came here. And if I can push one latent toward transition, why can't I push others?"

"Oh, my God," muttered Karl. I ignored him.

"Look," I said, "we actives were all latents once. We moved up. Why can't others?"

"The others weren't bred for it. Clay was, and I can see now that you were right about him. But that doesn't mean—"

"*You* can see?"

"Of course. How could I have raised generations of actives if I wasn't able to judge my people's potential?"

"Oh, yeah." The ones who *tasted good*, yes. "Doro, I want to try bringing other latents to transition."

"How?"

"By doing to them the only thing I'd ever done to Clay before today. By reading them. Just reading them."

Doro shook his head. "Go ahead. It won't work."

Yes, it would. I felt sure that it would. And I could try it without even leaving the room. I thought of two of my cousins, a brother and sister—Jamie and Christine Hanson. We used to get into trouble together when we were little. As we grew older and started to receive mental interference, we got more antisocial. We abandoned each other and started to get into trouble separately. Doro didn't pay any attention to Jamie and Christine, and their parents had given up on them years ago. No transition was supposed to come along and put them back in control of their lives, so, let alone, they'd probably wind up in prison or in the morgue before they were a lot older. But I wasn't going to let them alone.

I reached out to the old neighborhood, got a bird's-eye view of it all at once. Dell Street and Forsyth Avenue. Emma's house. I could have focused in tight and read Rina or Emma. Instead, I followed Forsyth Avenue south past Piedras Altas, where heaven knew how many of my relatives lived, and on to Cooper Street, where I had even more family. On Cooper I recognized the Hanson house and focused in on it.

Christine was inside screaming at her mother. I noticed that she had shaved her head—probably more to get on her mother's nerves than for any other reason. I didn't pay any attention to what they were fighting about. I read her the way you skim pages of a phone book looking for a number. Only, I wasn't looking for anything. I noticed that she'd been pregnant three times—one miscarriage and two abortions. And she was only nineteen. And she'd been with some idiot friends when they decided to rob a liquor store. Some other things. I didn't care. I just read her. Then I went after Jamie.

I found him sitting on an old sofa in the garage, fooling around with a guitar. I read him and learned, among other things, that he had just gotten out of jail a few days before. He had been driving drunk, smashed into a parked car, backed up, drove away. But somebody got his license number. Ninety days.

Now that he was out, he couldn't take the running battle that was usually going on inside the house. So he was living in the garage until some money came his way and he could get his own place.

I shifted my attention to the pattern. I knew what to look for now. My experience with Clay had taught me. Slender threads, fragile, tentative, soon to grow into the real thing. I found them stretching between me and both Hansons. Both of them. They were mine.

I snapped back to the library, excited, elated. "I did it!"

I'm not quite sure what expression I was wearing, but Doro frowned and drew back from me a little.

"I did it! I got two more! You're going to have your damn empire sooner than you thought."

"Which two?" He spoke very quietly.

"Hanson. Christine and Jamie. They live over on Cooper Street. You used to see them around Emma's house sometimes when I was little."

"I remember." He stared down at the table for several seconds, still frowning. I assumed he was doing his own checking.

Karl reached over and touched my arm. "Show me," he said.

Not tell him, show him. Just like that. And just minutes after our little conversation in the hall. If he had caught me in any other mood I would have told him to go to hell. But I felt good. I opened to him.

He looked at the way I had brought the Hansons in, and he looked at my memories on Clay. That was all.

"You want to build an empire, all right," he said when he was finished. "But Doro isn't the one you want to build it for."

"Does it matter?" I asked.

And Doro answered. "No, it doesn't. All that matters is that you obey me." There was something frightening, something too intense about the way he was looking at me.

It was my turn to draw back a little. "I've always obeyed you."

"More or less. It could get harder now, though. Sometimes it's harder for a leader to obey. And sometimes it's harder to be lenient with a disobedient leader."

"I understand."

"No you don't. Not yet. But I think you're capable of understanding. That's why I'm willing to let you go ahead with what you're planning."

"It isn't exactly a plan yet," I said. "I haven't had time to think. . . . I just want to start bringing in latents, letting the pattern push them through transition—you were satisfied that the Hansons were on their way, I guess."

"Yes."

"Good. The houses in this neighborhood have room for a lot more people. All our neighbors can be persuaded to take in house guests."

"All of them?" said Karl sarcastically. "How many latents are you planning to enslave?"

"None," I said. "But I mean to have as many of them brought through transition as I can."

"Why?" Doro asked. "I mean aside from the fact that you've suddenly discovered you enjoy power."

"You should talk."

"Is there a reason?"

I thought about it. I needed a few hours of solitude to think and nose around other people's heads and decide what I was doing myself. "They're latents," I said. "And if Rina and the Hanson family and just about all the rest of my relatives are any indication, latents live like dogs. They spend most of their lives sharing other people's pain and slowly going crazy. Why should they have to go through that if I can give them a better way?"

"Are you so sure it is better?" asked Karl.

"You're damn right I am. How many latents do you imagine burn the hands off their kids like your mother did—or worse? And you know Doro doesn't pay attention to those kids. How could he? God knows how many thousands of them there are. So they get shitted on, and if they live to grow up, they shit on their own kids."

"And you're going to save them all." Karl radiated sarcasm.

I turned to look at him.

"You're not exactly vicious, Mary," he said. "But you're not altruistic, either. Why pretend to be?"

"Wait a minute, Karl," said Doro. And then to me, "Mary, as angry as he's just made you, I think he's right. I think there's a reason for what you want to do that you haven't faced yet. Think about it."

I had been just about to explode at Karl. Somehow, though, when Doro said the same thing in different words, it didn't bother me as much. Well, why did I want to see as many latents as possible brought through transition? So I could be an empress? I wouldn't even say that out loud. It sounded too stupid. But, whatever I called myself, I was definitely going to wind up with a lot of people taking orders from me, and that really didn't sound like such a bad thing. And as for altruism, whether it was my real motive or not, every latent we brought into the pattern would benefit from being there. He would regain control of his life and be able to use his energy for something besides fighting to stay sane. But, honestly, as bad as it sounds, I had known that latents were suffering for most of my life. I grew up watching one of them suffer. Rina. Of course I couldn't have done anything about it until now, but I hadn't really wanted to do anything. I hadn't cared. Not even during the time, just before my transition, when I found out just how much latents suffered. After all, I knew I wasn't going to be one much longer.

Altruism, ambition—what else was there?

Need?

Did I need those latents, somehow? Was that why I was so enthusiastic, so happy that I was going to get them? I knew I wanted them in the pattern. They belonged to me and I wanted them. The only way to find out for sure whether or not I *needed* them was to leave them alone and see how I fared without them. I didn't want to do that.

"I'm not sure what you want me to say," I told him. "You're right. I want to bring latents through for my own satisfaction. I admit that. I want them here around me. But as for why. . . . " I shook my head.

"You don't have to kill," said Doro quietly. "But you do have to feed. And six people aren't enough."

Karl looked startled. "Wait a minute, are you saying she's

going to have to keep doing what she did to Jesse and Rachel? That she'll have to choose one or two of us regularly and—"

"I don't know," said Doro. "It's possible, of course. And if it turns out to be true, I would think you'd want her to fill the neighborhood with other actives. But, on the other hand, she didn't take Rachel and Jesse because she wanted them. She took them in self-defense." He looked at me. "You haven't been an active long enough for this to mean much, but in the two weeks since your transition, have you felt any need, any inclination to take anyone?"

"No," I said. "Never. The idea disgusted me until I did it. Then I felt . . . well, you probably know."

"He might know," said Karl. "But I don't."

I opened and projected the sensation.

He jumped, whispered, "Jesus Christ." From him it sounded more like praying than cursing. "If that's what you felt, I'm surprised you didn't go ahead and take the rest of us."

"It's possible that she was only saving the rest of you for another time," said Doro. "But I don't think so. Somehow, her ability reminds me more of Rachel's. Rachel could have left her congregations unconscious or dead, but she never did. Never felt inclined to. It was easy for her to be careful, easy for her not to really take anyone. But, to a lesser degree, she took everyone. She gained what she needed, and her congregations lost nothing more than they could afford. Nothing that they couldn't easily replace. Nothing that they even noticed was gone."

Karl sat frowning at Doro for several seconds after Doro had finished. Then he turned to look at me. "Open to me again."

I sighed and did it. He would be easier to live with if he knew whether Doro was right or wrong—or at least knew he couldn't find out. I watched him, not really caring what he found. I stopped him just as he was about to break contact.

You and I are going to have to talk later.

About what?

About making some kind of truce before you manage to goad me into hitting back at you.

He changed the subject. *Do you realize you're exactly the*

kind of parasite he's described? Except, of course, you prey on actives instead of ordinary people.

I can see what you've found. I do seem to be taking a tiny amount of strength from you and from the others. But it's so small it's not bothering any of you.

That's not the point.

The point is, you don't want me taking anything. Do you have to be told that I don't know how to stop it any more than I know how it got started?

I know. The thought carried overtones of weary frustration. He broke contact, spoke to Doro. "You're right about her. She's like Rachel."

Doro nodded. "That's best for all of you. Are you going to help her with her cousins?"

"Help her?"

"I've never seen a person born to be a latent suddenly pushed into transition. I'm assuming they'll have their problems and need help."

Karl looked at me. "Do you want my help again?"

"Of course I do."

"You'll need at least one other person."

"Seth."

"Yes." He looked at Doro. "Are you finished with us?"

Doro nodded.

"All right." He got up. "Come on, Mary. We may as well have that talk before you get back to Seth and Clay."

DORO

Doro did not leave the Larkin house, as he had planned. Suddenly there was too much going on. Suddenly things were getting out of hand—or at least out of his hands.

Mary was doing very well. She was driven by her own need to enlarge the pattern and aided not only by Doro's advice but by the experience of the six other actives. From the probing Doro had made her do and the snooping she had done on her own, she now had detailed mental outlines of the other actives' lives. Knowing what they had done in the past helped her decide what she could reasonably ask them to do now. Knowing Seth, for instance, made her decide to take Clay from him, take charge of Clay herself.

"How necessary is the pain of transition?" she asked Doro before making her decision. "Karl said you told him to hold off helping me until I was desperate. Why?"

"Because, in earlier generations of actives, the more help the person in transition received, the longer it took him to form his own shield." Doro grimaced remembering. "Before I understood that, I had several potentially good people die of injuries that wouldn't have happened if their transitions had ended when they should have. And I had others who died of sheer exhaustion."

Mary shuddered. "Sounds like it would be best to leave them alone completely." She glanced at Doro. "Which is probably why I'm the only one out of the seven of us who had any help."

"You were also the only one of the seven to have a seventeen-hour transition. Ten to twelve hours is more normal. Seventeen isn't that bad, though, and since your predecessors died whenever I left them alone in transition, I decided that you needed someone. Actually, Karl did a good job."

"I think I'll pass on the favor," she said, "by doing a good job for Clay Dana before his brother helps him to death." She went to Seth, told him what Doro had just told her, then told him that she, not Seth, would attend Clay at Clay's transition. Later she repeated the conversation to Doro.

"You've got to be kidding," Seth had said. "No. No way."

"You're too close to Clay," she had told him. "You've spent more than ten years shielding him from pain."

"That doesn't make any difference."

"The hell it doesn't! What's your judgment going to be like when you have to hold off shielding him—when you have to decide whether he's in enough trouble for you to risk helping him? How objective do you think you're going to be when he's lying in front of you screaming?"

"Objective . . . !"

"His life is going to depend on what you decide to do, man—

or decide not to do." She looked at Clay. "How objective do you think he can be? It's your life."

Clay looked uncomfortable, spoke to his brother. "Could she be right, Seth? Could this be something you should leave to somebody else?"

"No!" said Seth instantly. And then again, with a little less certainty, "No."

"Seth?"

"Look, I can handle it. Have I ever let you down?"

And Mary broke in. "You probably never have, Seth, and I'm not going to give you a chance to ruin your record."

Seth turned to look at her. "Are you saying you're going to force me to stand aside?" His tone made the words more a challenge than a question.

"Yes," said Mary.

Seth stared at her in surprise. Then, slowly, he relaxed. "You could do it," he said quietly. "You could knock me cold when the time came. But, Mary, if anything happens to my brother, you'd better not let me come to."

"Clay will be all right," she said. "I plan to see to it. And I'm really not interested in knocking you out. I hope you won't make me do it."

"Then, tell me why. Make me understand why you're interfering in something that shouldn't even be any of your business."

"I started it, man. I'm the reason for it. If it's anybody's business, it's mine. Now, Clay has a better chance with me than he has with you because I can see what's happening to him both mentally and physically. I'm going to know if he really needs help. I'm not going to have to guess."

"What can you do but guess? You're barely out of transition yourself."

"I've got seven transition experiences to draw on. And you can believe I've studied all of them. Now it's settled, Seth."

Seth took it. Doro watched him with interest after Mary reported the conversation. And Doro caught Seth watching Mary. Seth did not seem angry or vindictive. It was more as though he was waiting for something to happen. He had accepted Mary's authority as, years before, he had accepted Doro's. Now he watched to see how she handled it. He seemed surprised when, days later, she gave him charge of her cousin Jamie, but he accepted the responsibility. After that, he seemed to relax a little.

Rachel was on her feet again two days after her attack on Mary. Jesse, more severely weakened, was in bed a day longer. Both became quieter, more cautious people. They, too, watched Mary—warily.

Mary sent Rachel to kidnap the Hansons. Forsyth was a small city; Rachel could go across town without much discomfort. She wouldn't be staying long, anyway.

"Make their parents believe they've left home for good," Mary told her. "Because, one way or another, they have. You shouldn't have much tampering to do, though. The parents aren't going to be sorry to lose them."

Rachel frowned. "Even so, it seems wrong to just go in and take them—people's children. . . ."

"They're not children. Hell, Jamie's a year older than I am. And if we don't take them, they probably won't make it through transition. If they don't manage to kill themselves by losing control at a bad time, somebody else will kill them by taking them to a hospital. You can imagine what it would be like to be a mental sponge picking up everything in a hospital."

Rachel shuddered, nodded, turned to go. Then she stopped and faced Mary again. "I was talking to Karl about what you're trying to do the community of actives that you want to put together."

"Yes?"

"Well, if I have to stay here, I'd rather live in a community of actives—if such a thing is possible. I'd like us to stop hiding so much and start finding out what we're really capable of."

"You've been thinking about it," said Mary.

"I had time," said Rachel dryly. "What I'm working up to is that I'm willing to help you. Help more than just going after these kids, I mean."

Mary smiled, looked pleased but not surprised. "I would have asked you," she said. "I'm glad I didn't have to. I didn't ask you to help anybody through transition because I wanted you standing by for all three transitions in case some medical problem comes up. Jan broke her arm during her transition and you probably know Jesse did some kind of damage to his back that could have been serious. It will be best if you're sort of on call."

"I will be," said Rachel. She left to get the Hansons.

Mary looked after her for a moment, then walked over to the sofa nearest to the fireplace, where Doro was sitting with a closed book on his lap.

"You're always around," she said. "My shadow."

"You don't mind."

"No. I'm used to you. In fact, I'm really going to miss you when you leave. But, then, you won't be leaving soon. You're hooked. You've got to see what happens here."

She couldn't have been more right. And it wasn't just the three coming transitions that he wanted to see. They were important, but Mary herself was more important. Her people were submitting now, all but Karl. And she would overcome Karl's resistance slowly.

Doro had wondered what Mary would do with her people once she had subdued them. Before she discovered Clay's potential, she had probably wondered herself. Now, though. . . . Doro had reworded Karl's question. How many latents did she think she wanted to bring through? "All of them, of course," she had said.

Now Doro was waiting. He didn't want to put limits on her, yet. He was hoping that she would not like the responsibility she was creating for herself. He was hoping that, before too long, she would begin to limit herself. If she didn't, he would have to step in. Success—his and hers—was coming too quickly. Worse, all of it depended on her. If anything happened to her, the pattern would die with her. It was possible that her actives, new and old, would revert to their old, deadly incompatibility without it. Doro would lose a large percentage of his best breeding stock. This quick success could set him back several hundred years.

Mary gave Karl charge of her bald girl cousin, Christine, and then probably wished she hadn't. Surprisingly, Christine's shaved head did not make her ugly. And, unfortunately, her inferior position in the house did not make her cautious. Fortunately, Karl wasn't interested. Christine just didn't have the judgment yet to realize how totally vulnerable she was. Mary had a private talk with her.

Mary gave Christine and Jamie a single, intensive session of telepathic indoctrination. They learned what they were, learned their history, learned about Doro, who had neglected their branch of Emma's family for two generations. They learned what was going to happen to them, what they were becoming part of. They learned that every other active in the house had gone through what they were facing and that, while it wasn't pleasant, they could stand it. The double rewards of peace of mind and power made it worthwhile.

The Hansons learned, and they believed. It wouldn't have been easy for them to disbelieve information force-fed directly into their minds. Once the indoctrination was over, though, they were let alone mentally. They became part of the house, accepting Mary's authority and their own pain with uncharacteristic docility.

Jamie went into transition first, about a month after he moved to Larkin House. He was young, strong, and surprisingly healthy in spite of having tried every pill or powder he could get his hands on.

He came through. He had sprained his wrist, blackened one of Seth's eyes, and broken the bed he was lying on, but he came through. He became an active. Seth was as proud as though he had just become a father.

Clay, who should have been first, was next. He came through in a short, intense transition that almost killed him. He actually suffered heart failure, but Mary got his heart started again and kept it going until Rachel arrived. Clay's transition was over in only five hours. It left him with none of the usual bruises and strains, because Mary did not try to restrain him with her own body or tie him down. She simply paralyzed his voluntary muscles and he lay motionless while his mind writhed through chaos.

Clay became an active, but not a telepathic active. His budding telepathic ability vanished with the end of his transition. But he was compensated for it, as he soon learned.

When his transition ended and he was at peace, he saw that a tray of food had been left beside his bed. He could just see it out of the corner of his eye. He was still paralyzed and could not reach it, but in his confusion and hunger, he did not realize this. He reached for it anyway.

In particular, he reached for the bowl of soup that he could see steaming so near him. It was not until he lifted the soup and drew it to him that he realized that he was not using his hands. The soup hovered without visible support a few inches above his chest. Startled, Clay let it fall. At the same instant, he moved to get away from it. He shot about three feet to one side and into the air. And stayed suspended there, terrified.

Slowly, the terror in his eyes was replaced by understanding. He looked around his bedroom at Rachel, at Doro, and, finally, at Mary. Mary apparently released him then from his paralysis, because he began to move his arms and legs now like a human spider hanging in mid-air from an invisible web. Slowly, deliberately, Clay lowered himself to the bed. Then he drifted upward again, apparently finding it an easy thing to do. He looked at Mary, spoke apparently in answer to some thought she had projected to him.

"Are you kidding? I can fly! This is good enough for me."

"You're not a member of the pattern any more," she said. She seemed saddened, subdued.

"That means I'm free to go, doesn't it?"

"Yes. If you want to."

"And I won't be getting any more mental interference?"

"No. You can't pull it in any more. You're not even an out-of-control telepath. You're not a telepath at all."

"Lady, you read my mind. You'll see that's no tragedy to me. All that so-called power ever brought me was grief. Now that I'm free of it, I think I'll go back to Arizona—raise myself a few cows, maybe a few kids."

"Good luck," said Mary softly.

He drifted close to her, grinned at her. "You wouldn't believe how easy this is." He lifted her clear of the floor, brought her up to eye level with him. She gazed at him, unafraid. "What I've got is better than what you've got," he joked.

She smiled at him finally. "No it isn't, man. But I'm glad you think it is. Put me down."

He lowered both her and himself to the floor as though he had been doing it all his life. Then he looked at Doro. "Is this something brand-new, or have you seen it before?"

"Psychokinesis," said Doro. "I've seen it before. Seen it several times in your father's family, in fact, although I've never seen it come about this smoothly before."

"You call that transition smooth?" said Mary.

"Well, with the heart problem, no, I guess not. But it could have been worse. Believe me, this room could be a shambles, with everyone in it injured or dead. I've seen it happen."

"My kind throw things," guessed Clay.

"They throw everything," said Doro. "Including some things that are nailed down securely. Instead of doing that, I think you might have turned your ability inward a little and caused your own heart to stop."

Clay shook himself. "I could have. I didn't know what I was doing, most of the time."

"A psychokinetic always has a good chance of killing himself before he learns to control his ability."

"That may be the way it was," said Mary. "But it won't be that way any more."

Doro heard the determination in her voice and sighed to himself. She had just shared a good portion of Clay's agony as she worked to keep him alive, and immediately she was committing herself to do it again. She had found her work. She was some sort of mental queen bee, gathering her workers to her instead of giving birth to them. She would be totally dedicated, and difficult to reason with or limit. Difficult, or perhaps impossible.

Christine Hanson came through in an ordinary transition, perhaps a little easier than most. She made more noise than either of the men because pain, even slight pain, terrified her. She had had a harder time than the others during the pretransition period, too. Finally, hoarse but otherwise unhurt, Christine completed her transition. She remained a telepath, like her brother. It was possible that one or both of them might learn to heal, and it was possible that they, Rachel, and Mary might be very long-lived.

Whatever potential Jamie and Christine had, they accepted their places in the pattern easily. They were Mary's first grateful pattern members. And their membership brought an unexpected benefit that Jesse accidentally discovered. Now all the members could move farther from Mary without discomfort. Suddenly, more people meant more freedom.

Doro watched and worried silently. The day after Christine's transition, Mary began pulling in more of her cousins. And Ada, who knew a few of her relatives, began trying to reach them in Washington. Doro could have helped. He knew the locations of all his important latent families But as far as he was concerned, things were moving too quickly even without his help. He said nothing.

He had decided to give Mary two years to make what she could of her people. That was enough time for her to begin building the society she envisioned—what she was already calling a Patternist society. But two years should still leave Doro time to cut his losses—if it became necessary—without sacrificing too large a percentage of his breeding stock.

He had admitted to himself that he didn't want to kill Mary. She was easily controllable in most matters, because she loved him; and she was a success. Or a partial success. She was giving him a united people, a group finally recognizable as the seeds of the race he had been working to create. They were a people who belonged to him, since Mary belonged to him. But they were not a people he could be part of. As Mary's pattern brought them together, it shut him out. Together, the "Patternists" were growing into something that he could observe, hamper, or destroy but not something he could join. They were his goal, half accomplished. He watched them with carefully concealed emotions of suspicion and envy.

PART THREE

· Nine ·

EMMA

Emma was at the typewriter in her dining room when Doro arrived. He had not called to say he was coming, but at least when he walked in without knocking, he was wearing a body she had seen him in before: the body of a small man, black-haired, green-eyed, like Mary. But the hair was straight and this body was white. He threw himself down on Emma's sofa and waited silently until she finished the page that she was working on.

"What is it?" he asked her when she got up. "Another book?"

She nodded. She was young. She was young most of the time now, because he was around so much. "I've discovered that I like writing," she said. "I should have tried it years earlier than I did." She sat down in a chair, because he was sprawled over the length of the sofa. He lay there frowning.

"What's the matter?" she asked.

"Mary's the matter."

Emma grimaced. "I'm not surprised. What's she done?"

"Nothing yet. It's what she's going to do after I talk to her. I'm going to put on the brakes, Em. The Patternist section of

Forsyth is as big as a small town already. She has enough people."

"If you ask me, she had enough two years ago. But now that you're ready to stop her, what are you going to do with all those actives—all those Patternists—when she's not around any more to maintain the Pattern?"

"I'm not out to kill Mary, Em. The Pattern will still be there."

"Will it?"

He hesitated. "You think she'll make me kill her?"

"Yes. And if you're realistic about it, you'll think so too."

He sighed, sat up. "Yes. I don't expect to salvage many of her people, either. Most of them were animals before she found them. Without her, they'll revert."

"Animals . . . with such power, though."

"I'll have to destroy the worst of them."

Emma winced.

"I thought you'd be more concerned about Mary."

"I was concerned about her. But it's too late for her now. You helped her turn herself into something too dangerous to live."

He stared at her.

"She's got too much power, Doro. She terrifies me. She's doing exactly what you always said you wanted to do. But she's doing it, not you. All those people, those fifteen hundred people in the section, are hers, not yours."

"But she's mine."

"You wouldn't be thinking about killing her if you believed that was enough."

"Em. . . . " He got up and went to sit on the arm of her chair. "What are you afraid of?"

"Your Mary." She leaned against him. "Your ruthless, egotistical, power-hungry little Mary."

"Your grandchild."

"Your creation! Fifteen hundred actives in two years. They bring each other through on an assembly line. And how many conscripted servants—ordinary people unfortunate enough to be taken over by those actives. People forced now to be servants in their own houses. Servants and worse!"

Her outburst seemed to startle him. He looked down at her silently.

"You're not in control," she said more softly. "You've let them run wild. How many years do you think it will take at this rate for them to take over the city? How long before they begin tampering with the state and federal government?"

"They're very provincial people, Em. They honestly don't care what's happening in Washington or Sacramento or anywhere else as long as they can prevent it from hurting them. They pay attention to what's going on, but they don't influence it very often."

"I wonder how long that will last."

"Quite a while, even if the Pattern survives. They honestly don't want the burden of running a whole country full of people. Not when those people can run themselves reasonably well and the Patternists can reap the benefits of their labor."

"That, they have to have learned from you."

"Of course."

"You mentioned Washington and Sacramento. What about here in Forsyth?"

"This is their home territory, Em. They're interfering too much here to avoid being noticed by Forsyth city government, half asleep as it is. To avoid trouble, they took over the city about a year and a half ago."

Emma stared at him, aghast.

"They've completely taken over the best section of town. They did it quietly, but still Mary thought it safest for them to control key mutes in city hall, in the police department, in—"

"Mutes!"

He looked annoyed, probably with himself. "It's a convenient term. People without telepathic voices. Ordinary people."

"I know what it means, Doro. I knew the first time I heard Mary use it. It means niggers!"

"Em—"

"I tell you, you're out of control, Doro. You're not one of them. You're not a telepath. And if you don't think they look down on us non-telepaths, us niggers, the whole rest of humanity, you're not paying attention."

"They don't look down on me."

"They don't look up to you, either. They used to. They used to respect you. Damnit, they used to love you, the originals. The 'First Family.'" Her tone ridiculed the name that the original seven actives had adopted.

"Obviously this has been bothering you for a long time," said Doro. "Why haven't you said anything about it before?"

"It wasn't necessary."

He frowned.

"You knew." Her tone became accusing. "I haven't told you a single thing that you haven't been aware of for at least as long as I have."

He moved uncomfortably. "Sometimes I wonder if you aren't a little telepathic yourself."

"I don't have to be. I know you. And I knew you'd reach a point when no matter how fascinated you were with what Mary was doing, no matter how much you loved the girl, she'd have to go. I just wish you'd made up your mind sooner."

"Back when she brought her first latents through, I decided to give her two years. I'd like to give her a good many more if she'll co-operate."

"She won't. How willing would you be to give up all that power?"

"I'm not asking her to give up anything but this recruitment drive of hers. She's got a good many of my best latents now. I don't dare let her go on as she has been."

"You want the section to grow now by births only?"

"By births, and through the five hundred or so children they've collected. Children who'll eventually go through transition. Have you seen the private school they've taken over for the children?"

"No. I keep away from the section as much as I can. I assume Mary knows how I feel about her already. I don't want to keep reminding her until she decides to change my mind for me."

Doro started to say something, then stopped.

"What is it?" asked Emma.

For a moment, she thought he wasn't going to answer. Then, "I mentioned you to her once. I said I didn't want you bothered by any of her people. She gave me a strange look and said she'd already taken care of that. She said, 'Don't worry about her. Bitchy old woman that she is, she's wearing my brand. If anybody even tries to read her, the first thing they'll see is that she's my private property.'"

"Her what!"

"She means you're under her protection, Em. It might not sound like much, but, with it, none of the others are going to touch you. And, apparently, she isn't interested in controlling you herself."

Emma shuddered. "How generous of her! She must feel awfully secure in her power. You trained her too well. She's too much like you."

"Yes," said Doro. "I know."

She looked at him sharply. "Did I hear pride in your voice?"

Doro smiled faintly. "She's shown me a lot, Em. She's shown me something I've been trying to find out for most of my life."

"All I can see that she's shown you is what you'd be like as a young woman. I recall warning you about underestimating young women."

"Not what I'd be like as a woman. I already know that. I've been a woman I-don't-know-how-many times. No. What I'd be like as a complete entity. What I'd be like if I hadn't died that first time—died before I was fully formed."

"Before you were. . . . " Emma frowned. "I don't understand. How do you know you weren't fully formed when you died?"

"I know. I've seen enough almost-Doros, enough near successes to know. I should be telepathic, like Mary. If I were, I would have created a pattern and fed off live hosts instead of killing. As it is, the only time I can feel mind-to-mind contact with another person is when I kill. She and I kill in very much the same way."

"That's it?" said Emma. "That's all you've been reaching for, for so long—someone who kills in the same way you do?"

"All?" There was bitterness in his voice. "Does it seem such a small thing, Em, for me to want to know what I am—what I should have been?"

"Not a small thing, no. Not a wise thing, either. Your curiosity—and your loneliness, I think—have driven you to make a mistake."

"Perhaps. I've made mistakes before."

"And survived them. I hope you survive this one. I can see now why you kept your purpose secret for so long."

"Yes."

"Does Mary know?"

"Yes. I never told her, but she knows. She saw it herself after a while."

"No wonder you love her. No wonder she's still alive. She's you—the closest thing you've ever had to a true daughter."

"I never told her any of that, either."

"She knows. You can depend on it." She paused for a moment. "Doro, is there any way she could. . . . I mean, if she's complete and you're not, she might be able to. . . . "

"To take me?"

Emma nodded.

"No. If she could, she would never have lived past the morning of her transition. She tried to read me then. If she hadn't, I would have ordered her to try as soon as I saw her. I wanted to look at her in the only way that would tell me whether she could possibly become a danger to me. I looked, and what I saw told me she couldn't. She's like a scaled-down model of me. I could have taken her then, and I can now."

"It's been a long time since you've seen someone you thought could be dangerous. I hope your judgment is still as good as you think it is."

"It is. In my life, I've met only five people I considered potentially dangerous."

"And they all died young."

Doro shrugged.

"I assume you're not forgetting that Mary can increase her strength by robbing her people."

"No. It doesn't make any difference. I watched her very carefully back when she took Rachel and Jess. I could have taken her then. In fact, the extra strength she had acquired made her seem a more attractive victim. Strength alone isn't enough to beat me. And she has a weakness I don't have. She doesn't move. She has just that one body, and when it dies, she dies." He thought about that and shook his head sadly. "And she will almost certainly die."

"When?"

"When she— If she disobeys me. I'm going to tell her my decision when I go there today. No more latents. She'll decide what she wants to do after that."

SETH

Seth Dana came out the back door of Larkin House thinking about the assignment Mary had just given him. The same old thing. Recruit more seconds—more people to help latents through transition. Patternists liked the way their numbers were increasing. Expansion was exciting. It was their own kind growing up, coming of age at last. But seconding was hard work. You were mother, father, friend, and, if your charge needed it, lover to an erratic, frightened, dependent person. People volunteered to be seconds when they were shamed into it. They accepted it as their duty, but they evaded that duty as long as they could. It was Seth's job to prompt them and then present them with sullen, frightened charges.

He was a kind of matchmaker, sensing easily and accurately which seconds would be compatible with which latents. His worst mistake had been his first, his decision to second Clay. Mary had stopped him then. She had not had to stop him again. He had no more close relatives to warp his judgment.

He got into his car, preoccupied, deciding which Patternists to draft this time. He started the car automatically, then froze, his hand poised halfway to the emergency brake. Someone had shoved the cold steel barrel of a gun against the base of his skull.

Startled from his thoughts, Seth knew a moment of fear.

"Turn off the ignition, Dana," said a man's voice.

Reacting finally, Seth read the man. Then he turned off the ignition. With equal ease, he turned off the gunman. He gave the man a mental command, then reached back and took the gun from his suddenly limp hand. He shut the gun in the glove compartment and looked around at the intruder. The man was a mute and a stranger, but Seth had seen him before, in the thoughts of a woman Seth had seconded. A woman named Barbara Landry, who had once been this man's wife.

"Palmer Landry," said Seth quietly. "You've gone to a lot of trouble for nothing."

The man stared at Seth, then at his own empty hand. "Why did I give you . . . ? How could you make me . . . ? What's going on here?"

Seth shrugged. "Nothing now."

"How do you know who I am? Why did I hand you . . . ?"

"You're a man who deserted his wife nearly a year ago," said Seth. "Then suddenly decided he wanted her back. The gun wasn't necessary."

"Where is she? Where's Barbara?"

"Probably at her house." Seth had personally brought Barbara Landry from New York two months before. A month and a half later, she had come through transition. Almost immediately, she had discovered that Bartholomew House—and Caleb Bartholomew—suited her perfectly. Seth hadn't bothered to erase her from the memories of the people she knew in New York. None of them had been friends. None of them had really cared what happened to her. But, apparently, she had told a couple of them where she was going, and with whom. And when Landry came back looking for her, he had found the information waiting. Seth had been careless. And Palmer Landry had been lucky. No one had noticed him watching Larkin House, and the person he had asked to point out Seth Dana had been an unsuspecting mute.

"You mean to tell me you've gotten rid of Barbara already?" Landry demanded.

"I never had her," said Seth. "Never wanted her, for that matter, nor she me. I just helped her when she happened to need help."

"Sure. You're Santa Claus. Just tell me where she's living."

"I'll take you there if you want." He had intended to draft

Bartholomew into some seconding anyway. But later. Bartholomew House was right across the street.

"Who's she living with?" asked Landry.

"Her family," said Seth. "She found a house she fit into quicker than most of us do."

"House?" The man frowned. "Whorehouse?"

"Hell no!" Seth looked around at him. Landry had a justifiably low opinion of his wife. Latents were hard people to live with. But Seth had not realized that it was that low. "We live communally here, several of us to a house. So when we say house, we don't just mean the building. We mean household. We mean people."

"What the hell are you? Some kind of religious nuts or something?"

Seth was about to answer him when Barbara Landry herself came out the back door of Larkin House.

The sound of her footsteps caused Landry to turn. He saw her, shouted her name once, then was out of the car, running toward her.

Barbara Landry was weak, as Patternists went, and she was inexperienced at handling her new abilities. That last made her a possible danger to her husband. Seth reached out to warn her, but he was a second too late.

Recoiling in surprise from Landry's sudden rush, Barbara instinctively used her new defenses. Instead of controlling him gently, she stopped him solidly, suddenly, as though she had hit him, as though she had clubbed him down. He fell, unconscious, without ever having touched her.

"My God," Barbara whispered horrified. "I didn't mean to hurt him. I had come to see you. Then I sensed him out here threatening you. I came to ask you not to hurt him."

"He'll be all right," said Seth. "No thanks to you. You're going to kill somebody if you don't learn to be careful."

"I know. I'm sorry."

He lectured her as though she were still his charge. "I've warned you. No matter how weak you are as a Patternist, you're a powerhouse as far as any ordinary mute is concerned."

She nodded solemnly. "I'll be careful. But, Seth, would you

help him for me? I mean, after he comes to. He probably needs money, and I know he needs even more to forget about me. I don't even like to think about what I put him through when we were together."

"He wants to be with you."

"No!"

"He could be programmed to live very comfortably here, Barbara. Matter of fact, he'd be happier here than anywhere else."

"I don't want him enslaved! I've done enough to him. Seth, please. Help him and let him go."

Seth smiled finally. "All right, honey, in exchange for a promise from you."

"What?"

"That you'll go back to Bart and make him give you a few more lessons on how to handle mutes without killing them."

She nodded, embarrassed.

"Oh, yeah, and tell him he's going to second a couple of people for me. I'm bringing the first one over tomorrow."

"Oh, but—"

"No excuses. Save me the trouble of arguing with him and I'll do a good job for you here." He gestured toward Landry.

She smiled at him. "You would anyway. But, all right, I'll do your dirty work for you." She turned and went down the driveway. She was a rare Patternist. Like Seth, she cared what happened to the people she had left behind in the mute world. Seth had always liked her. Now he would see that her husband got as good a start as Clay had gotten.

RACHEL

Rachel's newest assignment had bothered her from the moment Mary gave it to her. It was still bothering her now, as she stood at the entrance of a long communal driveway that led back into a court of dilapidated, dirty, green stucco houses. The houses were small—no more than three or four rooms each. The yards were littered with beer cans and wine bottles, and they were overgrown with weeds and shrubs gone wild. The look of the place seemed to confirm Rachel's suspicions.

Farther up the driveway, a group of teen-age boys tossed around a pair of dice and a surprisingly large amount of money. Intent on their game, they paid no attention to Rachel. She let her perception sweep over them and found three that she would have to come back for. Three latents who lived in the court, but who were not as bad off as those Mary had sent Rachel after.

This was a pocket of Emma's descendants hidden away in a corner of Los Angeles, suffering without knowing why, without knowing who they were. The women in three of the houses were sisters. They hated each other, usually spoke only to trade obscenities. Yet they continued to live near each other, satisfying a need they did not realize they had. One of them still had a husband. All three had children. Rachel had come for the youngest sister—the one whose husband was still with her. This one lived in the third house back, with her husband and their two young children. Rachel looked at the house and realized that she had been unconsciously refraining from probing it. She was going entirely on what Mary had told her. That meant that there were surely things inside that she would not want to see. Mary swept the areas she checked so quickly that she received nothing more than a momentary feeling of anxiety from the latents who were in serious trouble. She was like a machine, sweeping, detecting latents here and there mixed in with the mute population. And the worst ones, she gave to Rachel.

"Come on, Rae," she would say. "You know they're going to die if I send anybody else."

And she was right. Only Rachel could handle the most pathetic of Doro's discards. Or only she had been able to until now. Now her students were beginning to come into their own. The one she had with her now was just about ready to work alone. Miguela Daniels. Her father had married a Mexican woman, a mute. But he traced his own lineage back to Emma through both his parents. And Miguela was turning out to be a very good healer. Miguela came up beside her.

"What are you waiting for?" she asked.

"You," Rachel told her. "All right, let's go in. You won't like it, though."

"I can already feel that."

As they went to the door, Rachel finally swept the house with her perception and moaned to herself. She did not knock. The door was locked, but the people inside were beyond answering her knock.

The top portion of the door had once been a window, but the glass had long ago been broken. The hole had been covered by an oversized piece of plywood.

"Keep your attention on the boys in the back," Rachel told Miguela. "They can't see us from here, but this might be noisy."

"You could get one of them to break in."

"No, I can do it. Just watch."

Miguela nodded.

Rachel took hold of the overhanging edge of plywood, braced herself, and pulled. The wood was dry and old and thin. Rachel had hardly begun to put pressure on it when it gave along its line of nails and part of it came away in her hands. She broke off more of it until she could push the rest in and unlock the door. The smell that greeted them made Rachel hold her breath for a few seconds. Miguela breathed it and gagged.

"What's that Goddamn stink!"

Rachel said nothing. She pushed the door open and went in. Miguela grimaced and followed.

Just inside the door lay a young man, the husband, half propped up against the wall. Around him were the many bottles he had already managed to empty. In his hand was one he had not quite emptied yet. He tried to get up as the two women came in, but he was too drunk or too sick or too weak from hunger. Probably all three. "Hey," he said, his voice slurred and low. "What you think you're doing? Get out of my house."

Rachel scanned him quickly while Miguela went through the kitchen, into the bedroom. The man was a latent, like his wife. That was why the two of them had so much trouble. They had not only the usual mental interference to contend with, but they unwitttingly interfered with each other. They were both of Emma's family and they would make good Patternists, but, as latents, they were killing each other. The man on the floor was of no use to himself or anyone else as he was now.

He was filthy—not only unwashed but incontinent. He wallowed in his own feces and vomit, contributing his share to the strong evil smell of the place.

From the bedroom, Miguela cried out, "Mother of God! Rachel, come in here quickly."

Rachel turned from the man, intending to go to her. But, as she turned, there was a sound, a weak, thin cry from the sofa. Rachel realized abruptly that what she had thought were only bundles of rags were actually the two children she had sensed in the house. She went to them quickly.

They were skin and bones, both breathing shallowly, unevenly, making small sounds from time to time. Malnourished, dehydrated, bruised, beaten, and filthy, they lay unconscious. Mercifully unconscious.

"Rachel—" Miguela seemed to choke. "Rachel, come here. Please!"

Rachel left the children reluctantly, went to the bedroom. In the bedroom there was another child, an infant who was beyond even Rachel's ability. It had been dead for at least a few days. Neither Rachel nor Mary had sensed it before, because both had scanned for life, touching the living minds in the house and skimming over everything else.

The baby's starved body was crawling with maggots, but it still showed the marks of its parents' abuse. The head was a ruin. It had been hit with something or slammed into something. The legs were twisted as no infant's legs would have twisted normally. The child had been tortured to death. The man and the woman had fed on each other's insanity until they murdered one child and left the others dying. Rachel had stolen enough latents from prisons and insane asylums to know how often such things happened. Sometimes the best a latent could do was realize that the mental interference, the madness, was not going to stop, and then end their own lives before they killed others.

Staring down at the dead child in its ancient, peeling crib, Rachel wondered how even Doro had managed to keep so many latents alive for so long. How had he done it, and how had he been able to stand himself for doing it? But, then, Doro had nothing even faintly resembling a conscience.

The crib was at the foot of an old, steel-frame bed. On the bed lay the mother, semiconscious, muttering drunkenly from time to time. "Johnny, the baby's crying again." And then, "Johnny, make the baby stop crying! I can't stand to hear him crying all the time." She wept a little herself now, her eyes open, unseeing.

Miguela and Rachel looked at each other, Miguela in horror, Rachel in weariness and disgust.

"You were right," said Miguela. "I don't like this one damn bit. And this is the kind of thing you want me to handle?"

"There are too many of them for me," said Rachel. "The more help I get, the fewer of these bad ones will die."

"They deserve to die for what they did to that baby—" She choked again and Rachel saw that she was holding back tears.

"You're the last person I'd expect to hold latents responsible for what they do," Rachel told her. "Do I have to remind you what you did?" Miguela, unstable and violent, had set fire to the house of a woman whose testimony had caused her to spend some time in Juvenile Hall. The woman had burned to death.

Miguela closed her eyes, not crying but not casting any more stones, either. "You know," she said after a moment, "I was glad I turned out to be a healer, because I thought I could make up for that, somehow. And here I am bitching."

"Bitch all you want to," said Rachel. "As long as you do your work. You're going to handle these people."

"All of them? By myself?"

"I'll be standing by—not that you'll need me. You're ready. Why don't you back the van in and I'll draft a couple of the boys out back to help us carry bodies."

Miguela started to go, then stopped. "You know, sometimes I wish we could make Doro pay for scenes like this. He's the one who deserves all the blame."

"He's also the one who'll never pay. Only his victims pay."

Miguela shook her head and went out after the van.

JESSE

Jesse pulled his car up sharply in front of a handsome, red-brick, Georgian mansion. He got out, strode down the pathway and through the front door without bothering to knock. He went straight to the stairs and up them to the second floor. There, in a back bedroom, he found Stephen Gilroy, the Patternist owner of the house, sitting beside the bed of a young mute woman. The woman's face was covered with blood. It had been slashed and hacked to pieces. She was unconscious.

"My God," muttered Jesse as he crossed the room to the bed. "Did you send for a healer?"

Gilroy nodded. "Rachel wasn't around, so I—"

"I know. She's on an assignment."

"I called one of her kids. I just wish he'd get here."

One of her students, he meant. Even Jesse found himself referring to Rachel's students as "her kids."

There was the sound of the front door opening and slamming again. Someone else ran up the bare, wooden stairs, and, a moment later, a breathless young man hurried into the room. He was one of Rachel's relatives, of course, and as Rachel would have in a healing situation, he took over immediately.

"You'll have to leave me alone with her," he said. "I can handle the injuries, but I work best when I'm alone with my patient."

"Her eyes are hurt, too, I think," said Gilroy. "Are you sure you—"

The healer unshielded to show them that his self-confidence was real and based on experience. "Don't worry about her. She'll be all right."

Jesse and Stephen Gilroy left the room, went down to Gilroy's study.

Jesse spoke with quiet fury. "The main reason I got here so fast was so I could see the damage through my own eyes instead of somebody's memory. I want to remember it when I go after Hannibal."

"I should go after him," said Gilroy softly, bitterly. He was a slender, dark-haired man with very pale skin. "I would go after

167

him if he hadn't already proved to me how little good that does." His voice was full of self-disgust.

"People who abuse mutes are my responsibility," said Jesse. "Because mutes are my responsibility. Hannibal is even a relative of mine. I'll take care of him."

Gilroy shrugged. "You gave her to me; he took her from me. You ordered him to send her back; he sent her back in pieces. Now you'll punish him. What will that inspire him to do to her?"

"Nothing," said Jesse. "I promise you. I've talked to Mary and Karl about him. This isn't the first time he's sliced somebody up. He's still the animal he was when he was a latent."

"That's what's bothering me. He'd think nothing of killing Arlene when you're finished with him. I'm surprised he hasn't killed her already. He knows I can't stop him."

"There's no sense beating yourself with that, Gil. Except for the members of the First Family, nobody can stop him. He's the strongest telepath we've ever brought through transition. And the first thing he did, once he was through, was to smash his way through the shielding of his second and nearly kill her. For no reason. He just discovered that he could do it, so he did it."

"Somebody should have smashed him then and there."

"That's what Doro said. He claims he used to cull out people like Hannibal as soon as he spotted them."

"Well, I hate to find myself agreeing with Doro but—"

"So do I. But he made us. He knows just how far wrong we can go. Hannibal is too strong for Rachel or her kids to help him. Especially since he doesn't really want help. And he's too dangerous for us to tolerate any longer."

Gilroy's eyes widened. "You are going to kill him, then?"

Jesse nodded. "That's why I had to talk to Karl and Mary. We don't like to give up on one of our own, but Hannibal is a Goddamn cancer."

"You're going to do it yourself?"

"As soon as I leave here."

"With his strength . . . are you sure you can?"

"I'm First Family, Gil."

"But still—"

"Nobody who needed the Pattern to push him into transition can stand against one of us—not when we mean to kill." Jesse shrugged. "Doro had to breed us to be strong enough to come through without being prodded. After all, when the time came for us, there was nobody who could prod us without killing us." He stood up. "Look, contact me when that healer finishes with Arlene, will you? I just want to be sure she's all right."

GIlroy nodded, stood up. They walked to the door together and Jesse noticed that there were three Patternists in the living room. Two women and a man.

"Your house is growing," he said to Gilroy. "How many now?"

"Five. Five Patternists."

"The best of the people you've seconded, I'll bet."

Gilroy smiled, said nothing.

"You know," said Jesse as they reached the door. "That Hannibal . . . he even looks like me. Reminds me a little of myself a couple of years ago. There, but for the grace of Doro, go I. Shit."

JAN

Holding a smooth, rectangular block of wood between her hands, Jan Sholto closed her eyes and reached back in her disorderly memory. She reached back two years, to the creation of the Pattern. She had not only her own memories of that event but the memories of each of the original Patternists. They had unshielded and let her read them—not that they could have stopped her by refusing to open. Mary wasn't the only one who could read people through their shields. No one except Doro could come into physical contact with Jan without showing her some portion of his thoughts and memories. In this case, though, physical contact hadn't been necessary. The others had shown their approval of what she was doing by co-operating with her. She was creating another learning block—assembling their memories into a work that would not only tell the new Patternists of their beginnings but show them.

She was teacher to all the new Patternists as they came through. For over a year now, seconds had used her learning blocks to give their charges quick, complete knowledge of the section's rules and regulations. Other learning blocks offered them choices, showed them the opportunities available to them for making their own place within the section.

Abruptly, Jan reached Mary's memories. They jarred her with their raw intensity, overwhelmed her as other people's memories rarely did any more. They were good material, but Jan knew she would have to modify them. Left as they were, they would dominate everything else Jan was trying to record.

Sighing, Jan put her block aside. Of course it would be Mary's thoughts that gave trouble. Mary was trouble. That small body of hers was deceptive. Yet it had been Mary who saw possible use for Jan's psychometry. A few months after Mary had begun drawing in latents, she had decided to learn as much as she could about the special abilities of the rest of the First Family. In investigating Jan's psychometry, she had discovered that she could read some objects herself in a fragmented, blurred way, but that she could read much more clearly anything that Jan had handled.

"You read impressions from the things you touch," she had said to Jan. "But I think you put impressions into things, too."

"Of course I do," Jan had said impatiently. "Everyone does, every time they touch something."

"No, I mean . . . you kind of amplify what's already there."

"Not deliberately."

"Nobody ever noticed it before?"

"No one pays any attention to my psychometry. It's just something I do to amuse myself."

Mary was silent for a long moment, thinking. Then, "Have you ever liked the impressions that you got from something enough to keep them? Not just keep them in your memory but in the thing, the object itself—like keeping a film or a tape recording."

"I have some very old things that I've kept. They have ancient memories stored in them."

"Get them."

"*Please* get them," mimicked Jan. "May I see them, *please?*" Mary had taken to her new power too easily. She loved to order people around.

"The hell with you," said Mary. "Get them."

"They're my property!"

"Your property." The green eyes glittered. "I'll trade you last night for them."

Jan froze, staring at her. The night before, Jan had been with Karl. It was not the first time, but Mary had never mentioned it before. Jan had tried to convince herself that Mary did not know. Now, confronted with proof that she was wrong, she managed to control her fear. She wanted to ask what Mary traded Vivian for all the mute woman's nights with Karl, but she said nothing. She got up and went to get her collection of ancient artifacts stolen from various museums.

Mary handled one piece after another, first frowning, then slowly taking on a look of amazement. "This is fantastic," she said. She was holding just a fragment of what had been an intricately painted jar. A jar that held the story of the woman whose hands shaped it 6,500 years ago. A woman of a Neolithic village that had existed somewhere in what was now Iran. "Why is it so pure?" asked Mary. "God knows how many people have touched it since this woman owned it. But she's all I can sense."

"She was all I ever wanted to sense," said Jan. "The fragment has been buried for most of the time between our lives and hers. That's the only reason there was any of her left in it at all."

"Now there's nothing but her. How did you get rid of the others?"

Jan frowned. "There were archaeologists and some other people at first, but I didn't want them. I just didn't want them."

Mary handed her the fragment. "Am I in it now?"

"No, it's set. I had to learn to freeze them so that I didn't disturb them myself every time I handled them. I never tried letting another telepath handle them, but you haven't disturbed this one."

"Or the others, most likely. You like seconding, Jan?"

Jan looked at her through narrowed eyes. "You know I hate it. But what does that have to do with my artifacts?"

"Your artifacts just might stop you from ever having to second anybody else. If you can get to know your own abilities a little better and use them for more than your own amusement, they can open another way for you to contribute to the Pattern."

"What way?"

"A new art. A new form of education and entertainment— better than the movies, because you really live it, and you absorb it quicker and more completely than you do books. Maybe." She snatched up the jar fragment and a small Sumerian clay tablet and ran out to try them on someone. Minutes later, she was back, grinning.

"I tried them on Seth and Ada. All I told them to do was hold these things and unshield. They picked up everything. Look, you show me you can use what you've got for more than a toy and you're off seconding for good." The rush of words stopped for a moment, and when Mary spoke again, her tone had changed. "And, Jan, guess what else you're off of for good."

Jan had wanted to kill her. Instead, she had thrown her energy into refining her talent and finding uses for it. Instead, she had begun to create a new art.

ADA

Ada Dragan waited patiently in the principal's office of what was finally her school. A mute guardian who was programmed to notice such things had reported that one of her latent foster children—a fifteen-year-old girl—was having serious pretransition difficulties.

From the office, Ada looked out at the walled grounds of the school. It had been a private school, situated right there in the Palo Verde neighborhood. A school where people who were dissatisfied with the Forsyth Unified School District, and who could afford an alternative, sent their children. Now those people had been persuaded to send their children elsewhere.

This fall semester, only a month old, was the beginning of the first all-Patternist year. Ada welcomed it with relief. She had been working gradually toward the takeover, feeling her way for almost two years. Finally it was done. She had learned the needs of the children and overcome her own shyness enough to meet those needs. On paper, mutes still owned the school. But Ada and her Patternist assistants owned the mutes. And Ada herself was in full charge, responsible only to Mary.

It was a responsibility that had chosen Ada more than she had chosen it. She had discovered that she worked easily with children, enjoyed them, while most Patternists could not work with them at all. Only some of her relatives were able to assist her. Other Patternists found the emotional noise of children's minds intolerable. Children's emotional noise penetrated not only the general protection of the Pattern but the individual mental shields of the Patternists. It frayed their nerves, chipped away their tempers, and put the children in real danger. It made Patternists potentially even worse parents than latents.

Thus, no matter how much Patternists wanted to insure their future as a race—and they did want it now—they could not care for the children who were that future. They had to draft mutes to do it for them. First Doro, and now Mary, was creating a race that could not tolerate its own young.

Ada turned away from the window just as the mute guardian brought the girl in. The mute was Helen Dietrich, an elementary-school teacher who, with her husband, also cared for four latent children. Jan had moved the Dietrichs and several other teachers into the section, where they could do both jobs.

This girl, Ada recalled, had been a particularly unfortunate case—one of Rachel's assignments. Her life with the pair of latents who were her parents had left both her body and her mind a mass of scar tissue. Rachel had worked hard to right the damage. Now Ada wondered just how good a job she had done.

"Page," said Helen Dietrich nervously, "this is Ada Dragan. She's here to help you."

The girl stared at Ada through dark, sullen eyes. "I've already seen the school psychologist," she volunteered. "It didn't do any good."

Ada nodded. The school psychologist was a kind of experiment. He was completely ignorant of the fact that the Patternists now owned him. He was being allowed to learn as much as he could on his own. Nothing was hidden from him. But, on the other hand, nothing was handed to him. He, and a few others like him scattered around the section, were being used to calculate just how much information ordinary mutes needed to come to understand their situation.

"I'm not a psychologist," said Ada. "Nor a psychiatrist."

"Why not?" asked the girl. She extended her arms, which she had been holding behind her. Both wrists were bandaged. "I'm crazy, aren't I?"

Ada only glanced at the bandages. Helen Dietrich had told her about the suicide attempt. Ada spoke to the mute. "Helen, it might be easier on you if you left now."

The woman met Ada's eyes and realized that she was really being offered a choice. "I'd rather stay," she said. "I'll have to handle this again."

"All right." Ada faced the girl again. Very carefully, she read her. It was difficult here at the school, where so many other child minds intruded. This was one time when they became a nuisance. But, in spite of the nuisance, Ada had to handle the girl gently. At fifteen, Page was not too young to be nearing transition. Children who lived in the section, surrounded by Patternists and thus by the Pattern, did not need direct contact with Mary to push them into transition. The Pattern pushed them as soon as their bodies and minds could tolerate the shock. And this girl seemed ready—unless Rachel had just missed some mental problem and the girl was suffering needlessly. That was what Ada had to find out. She maintained contact with Page as she questioned her.

"Why did you try to kill yourself?"

The young mind made an effort to hold itself emotionless, but failed. The thought broke through, *To keep from killing others*. Aloud, the girl spoke harshly. "Because I wanted to die! It's my life. If I want to end it, it's my business."

She had not been told what she was. Children were told when they were about her age. They spent a few days with Ada or, more likely, with one of Ada's assistants, and they learned a little of their history and got some idea what their future would be like. Ada had dubbed these sessions "orientation classes." Page was scheduled for one next month, but apparently, nature had decided to rush things.

"You won't be allowed to kill yourself, Page. You realize that, don't you?" Deftly, Ada planted the mental command as she spoke so that even as the girl opened her mouth to insist that she would try again, she realized that she could not—or, rather, realized that she no longer wanted to. That she had changed her mind.

Page stood still for a moment, her mouth open, then backed away from Ada in horror. "You did that! I felt it. It was you!"

Ada stared at her in surprise. No nontelepath, no latent should have known—

"You're one of them," the girl accused shrilly.

Mrs. Dietrich stood frowning at her. "I don't understand. What's wrong with the girl?"

Page faced her. "Nothing!" Then, more softly, "Oh, God, everything. Everything." She looked down at her arms. "I'm not sick. I'm not crazy, either. But if I tell you what . . . what *she* is," she gestured sharply toward Ada, "you'd let me be locked up. You wouldn't believe—"

"Tell her what I am, Page," said Ada quietly. She could feel the girl's terror bleating against her mind.

"You read people's minds! You make them do things they don't want to do. You're not human!" She raised a hand to her mouth, muffling her next words slightly. "Oh, God, you're not human . . . and neither am I!" She was crying now, working herself into hysterics. "Now go ahead and lock me up," she said. "At least then I won't be able to hurt anyone."

Ada looked over at Helen Dietrich. "That's it, really. She knows just enough about what's happening to her to be frightened by it. She thinks she's becoming something that will hurt you or your husband or one of the other children."

"Oh, Page." The mute woman tried to put her arms around the girl, but Page twisted away.

"You already knew! You brought me to her even though you knew what she was!"

"Be still, Page," said Ada quietly. And the girl lapsed into terrified silence. To the mute, Ada said, "Leave now, Helen.

She'll be all right." This time, no choice was offered and Helen Dietrich left obediently. The girl, attempting to flee with her, found herself seemingly rooted to the floor. Realizing that she was trapped, she collapsed, crying in helpless panic. Ada went to her, knelt beside her.

"Page. . . . " She laid a hand on the girl's shoulder and felt the shoulder trembling. "Listen to me."

The girl continued to cry.

"You're not going to be hurt. You're certainly not going to be locked up. Now, listen."

After a moment the words seemed to penetrate. Page looked up at her. Clearly still frightened, she allowed Ada to help her from the floor onto one of the chairs. Her tears slowed, stopped, and she wiped her face with tissue from a box on the principal's desk.

"You should ask questions," said Ada softly. "You could have saved yourself a lot of needless worrying."

Page breathed deeply, trying to still her trembling. "I don't even know what to ask. Except . . . what's going to happen to me?"

"You're going to grow up. You're going to become the kind of adult your parents should have been but couldn't become alone."

"My parents," said Page with quiet loathing. "I hope you locked them up. They're animals."

"They were. They aren't now, though. We were able to help them—just as we've helped you, as we'll go on helping you." The girl should not have remembered enough about her parents to hate them. Rachel was always especially careful about that. But there was no mistaking the emotion behind the girl's words.

"You should have killed them," she said. "You should have cut their filthy throats!" She fell silent and stared down at her left arm. She touched the arm with her right hand, frowned at it. Ada knew then that the conditioning Rachel had imposed on the girl was still breaking down. From Page's mind Ada took the memory of a twisted, useless left arm permanently bent at the elbow, the hand hanging from it rag-limp, dead. The whole arm had been dead, thanks to an early violent beating that Page had received from her father. A beating and no medical attention. But Rachel had repaired the damage. Page's arm was normal now, but she was just remembering that it should not have been. And she was remembering more about her parents. Ada had to try to ease the knowledge.

"Our healers were able to do as much for your parents' minds as they were for your body," she said. "Your parents are different people now, living different lives. They're . . . sane people now. They aren't responsible for what they did when you knew them."

"You're afraid I'll try to get even."

"We can't let you do that."

"You can't make me forgive them, either." She stopped, frightened, suddenly realizing that Ada could probably do just that. "I hate them! I'd . . . I'd kill them myself if you sent me back to them." But she spoke without conviction.

"You won't be sent back to them," said Ada. "And I think, once you find out for yourself what made them the way they were, you'll know why we helped them instead of punishing them."

"They're . . . like you now?"

"They're both telepaths, yes." At thirty-seven, they were the oldest people to come through transition successfully. They had almost died in spite of everything Rachel could do. And they and three others who did die made Mary realize that most latents who hadn't been brought through by the time they were thirty-five shouldn't be brought through at all. To make their lives more comfortable, Mary had worked out a way of destroying their uncontrollable ability without harming them otherwise. At least then they could live the rest of their lives as normal mutes. But Page's parents had made it. They were strong Patternists, as Page would be strong.

"I'll be like you, too, then, won't I?" the girl asked.

"You will, yes. Soon."

"What will I be then to the Dietrichs?"

"You'll be the first of their foster children to grow up. They'll remember you."

"But . . . they're not like you. I can tell that much. I can feel a difference."

"They're not telepaths."

"They're slaves!" Her tone was accusing.

"Yes."

Page was silent for a moment, startled by Ada's willingness to admit such a thing. "Just like that? Yes, you make slaves of people? I'm going to be part of a group that makes slaves of people?"

"Page—"

"Why do you think I tried to die?"

"Because you didn't understand. You still don't."

"I know about being a slave! My parents taught me. My father used to strip me naked, tie me to the bed, and beat me, and then—"

"I know about that, Page."

"And I know about being a slave." The girl's voice was leaden. "I don't want to be a part of anything that makes people slaves."

"You have no choice. Neither do we."

"You could stop doing it."

"You'd still be with your parents if we didn't do it. We couldn't have cared for you." She took a deep breath. "We don't harm people like the Dietrichs in any way. In fact they're healthier and more comfortable now than they were before we found them. And the work they're doing for us is work they enjoy."

"If they didn't enjoy it, you'd change their minds for them."

"We might, but they wouldn't be aware of it. They would be content."

The girl stared at her. "Do you think that makes it better?"

"Not better. Kinder, in a frightening sort of way, I know. I'm not pretending that theirs is the best possible way of life, Page—although they think it is. They're slaves and I wouldn't trade places with them. But we, our kind, couldn't exist long without them."

"Then maybe we shouldn't exist! If our way is to enslave

good people like the Dietrichs and let animals like my parents go free, the world would be better without us."

Ada looked away from her for a moment, then faced her sadly. "You haven't understood me. Perhaps you don't want to; I wouldn't blame you. The Dietrichs, Page, those good people who took you in, cared for you, loved you. Why, do you imagine, they did all that?"

And abruptly, Page understood. "No!" she shouted. "No. They wanted me. They told me so."

Ada said nothing.

"They might have been taking in foster children, anyway."

"You know better."

"No." The girl glared at Ada furiously, still trying to make herself believe the lie. Then something in her expression crumbled. How did it feel, after all, to learn that the foster parents you adored, the only parents who had ever shown you love, loved you only because they had been programmed to?

Ada watched her, fully aware of what she was going through, but choosing for a moment to ignore it. "We call ourselves Patternists," she said quietly. "This is our school. You and the others here are our children. We want the best for you even though we're not capable of giving it to you personally. It isn't possible for us to take you into our homes and give you the care you need. It just isn't possible. You'll understand why soon. So we make other arrangements."

The girl was crying silently, her head bowed, her face wet with tears and twisted with pain. Now Ada went to her, put an arm around her. She continued to speak, now offering comfort in her words. The girl was going to be too strong to be soothed with lies or partial amnesia. She had already proved that. Nothing would do for her but the truth. But that truth was not entirely disillusioning.

"The Dietrichs deserve the love and respect you feel for them, Page, because you're right about them. They are good people. They love children naturally. All we did was focus that love on you, on the others. In your case we didn't even have to focus it much. I didn't think we would. That's why I chose them for you—and you for them."

Finally Page looked up. "You did? You?"

"Yes."

She thought about that, then leaned her head to one side, against Ada's arm. "Then I guess it's only right that you be the one to take me away from them."

Ada said nothing.

Page lifted her head, met Ada's eyes. "You are going to take me away, aren't you?"

"Yes."

"I don't want to go."

"I know. But it's time."

Page nodded, lowered her head again to rest it against Ada's arm.

· Ten ·

MARY

A few months into our first year, the original group of actives broke up. Rachel and Jesse moved out first—moved down the street to a house almost as big as ours. Then Jan moved alone. I had had a talk with her about using her psychometry as a kind of educational tool, or even as an art. At the same time, I told her to keep her hands off Karl. I didn't have that good a grip on him myself at the time, but I had already decided that, whether I got him or not, she wasn't going to. She left the next day.

Our new Patternists had been leaving us right along, taking over nearby houses, with Jesse preparing the way for them with the mutes who already lived there. They all had to learn to handle mutes—learn not to smash them and not to make robots of them. That was something Jesse had been able to do easily since his transition.

Seth and Ada moved to a house around the corner and across the street from us. Suddenly Karl and I were the only Patternists in Larkin House. We weren't back where we'd started or anything. Doro had finally left us, and we had a pair of latents with us. Everybody except Jan and Rachel was seconding somebody then.

New Patternists too, as soon as they could be trusted to handle it. But Karl and I were more alone together than we had ever been before. Even Vivian didn't matter much any more. She should have left Karl when he gave her the chance. Now she was a placid, bovine little pet. Karl controlled her without even thinking about it.

I was a predator and, frankly, not a very good one. But that was all right, because Karl wasn't as sure as he had once been that he minded being the prey. He was a little wary, a little amused. He had never really hated me, though. Hell, he and I would have gotten along fine together from back when he first climbed into my bed if it hadn't been for the Pattern and what the Pattern represented. It represented power. Power that I had and that he would never have. And while that wasn't something I threw at him, ever, it wasn't something I denied either.

The Pattern was growing because I searched out latents, had them brought in, and gave them their push toward transition. It was growing because of me. And nobody was better equipped to run it than I was. I hoped Karl could accept that and be comfortable enough with it to accept me. If he couldn't . . . well, I wanted him, but I wanted the thing I was building too. If I couldn't have both, Karl could go his way. I'd move out like the others and let him have his house back. Maybe he knew that.

"You know," he said one night, "for a while I thought you'd leave, like the others. There isn't really anything holding you here." We were in the study listening to the rain outside and not looking at a variety show on the television. Neither of us liked television. I don't know why we had bothered to turn it on that night.

"I didn't want to go," I said. "And since you weren't absolutely sure you wanted me to, I thought I'd hang around at least a while longer."

"I thought you might be afraid to leave—afraid that when Doro found out, he'd just order us back together."

"He might. But I doubt it. He's already gotten more than he bargained for from us."

"From you."

I shrugged.

"Why did you stay?"

"You know why. I wanted to be with you."

"The husband he chose for you."

"Yeah." I turned to face him. "Stupid me, falling in love with my own husband."

He didn't look away from me, didn't even change expression.

After a moment I grinned at him. "Not so stupid. We're a match."

He smiled thinly, almost grimly. "You're changing. I've been watching you change, wondering how far you would go."

"Changing how?"

"Growing up perhaps. I can remember when it was easier to intimidate you."

"Oh." I glanced at the television for a moment, listened as some woman tortured a song. "I'm a lot easier to get along with when I don't feel intimidated."

"So am I."

"Yeah." I listened to a few more bars of the woman's screaming, then shook my head. "You aren't paying any attention to this noise, are you?"

"No."

I got up and turned off the television. Now there was only the soft, rustling sound of the rain outside. "So, what are we going to do?" I asked him.

"We don't really have to do anything," he said. "Just let things progress as they have been."

I stared at him in silent frustration. That "silent" part was an effort. He laughed and moved over next to me.

"You don't read me very much any more, do you?"

"I don't want to read you all the time," I said. "Talk to me."

He winced and drew back, muttering something I didn't quite catch.

"What?" I asked.

"I said how generous of you."

I frowned. "Generous, hell. You can say whatever you've got to say to me."

"I suppose so. After all, if you read me all the time, I'll begin to bore you very quickly."

So that was it! He was afraid he was going to get paid for some of the things he'd done to his women. He was afraid I was going to try to make a male Vivian of him. Not likely. "Keep that up," I said, "and I won't have to read you to be bored. You're not pitiful, Karl, so, coming from you, self-pity is kind of disgusting."

I thought he would hit me. I'm sure he thought about it. After a moment, though, he just sort of froze over. He stood up. "Find yourself a place tomorrow and get out of here."

"Better," I said. "There's nothing boring about you when you get mad."

He started to walk away from me in disgust. I got up quickly and caught him by the hand. He could have pulled away easily, but he didn't. I took that to be significant and moved closer to him.

"You ought to trust me," I said. "By now you ought to trust me."

"I'm not sure trust is an issue here."

"It is." I reached up and touched his face. "A very basic issue. You know it."

He began to look harassed, as though I was really getting on his nerves. Or maybe as though I was really getting to him in another way. I slipped my arms around him hopefully. It had been a long time. Too long.

"Come on, Karl, humor me. What's it going to cost you?" Plenty. And he knew it.

We stood together for a long moment, my head against his chest. Finally he sighed and steered us back to the sofa. We lay down together, just touching, holding each other.

"Will you unshield?" he asked.

I was surprised but I didn't mind. I unshielded. And he lowered his shield so that there were no mental barriers between us. We seemed to flow together—frighteningly at first. I felt as though I were losing myself, combining so thoroughly with him that I wouldn't be able to free myself again. If he hadn't been so calm, I would have tried to reshield after the first couple of seconds. But I could see that he wasn't afraid, that he wanted me to stay as I was, that nothing irreversible was happening. I realized that he had done this with Jan. I could see the experience in his memory. It was something like the blending that he did naturally with the shieldless, mute women he had had. Jan hadn't liked it. She didn't much like any kind of direct mind-to-mind contact. But she had been so lonely among us, and so without purpose, that she had endured this mental blending just to keep Karl interested in her. But the blending wasn't an act that one person could enjoy while the other grimly endured.

I closed my eyes and explored the thing that Karl and I had become. A unit. I was aware of the sensations of his body and my own. I could feel my own desire for him exciting him and his excitement circling back to me.

We lost control. The spiral of our own emotions got out of hand. We hurt each other a little. I wound up with bruises and he had nail marks and bites. Later I took one look at what was left of the dress I had been wearing and threw it away.

But, my God, it was worth it.

"We're going to have to be more careful when we do that again," he said, examining some of his scratches.

I laughed and moved his hands away. The wounds were small. I healed them quickly. I found others and healed them too. He watched me with interest.

"Very efficient," he said. He met my eyes. "It seems you've won."

"All by myself?"

He smiled. "What, then? We've won?"

"Sure. Want to go take a shower together?"

At the end of the Pattern's first year of existence, we all knew we had something that was working. Something new. We were learning to do everything as we went along. Soon after Karl and I got together, we found latents with latent children. That could have turned out really bad. We discovered we were "allergic" to children of our own kind. We were more dangerous to them than their latent parents were. That was when Ada discovered her specialty. She was the only one of us who could tolerate children and care for them. She began using mutes as foster parents, and she began to take over the small private school not far from us. And she and Seth moved back to Larkin House.

They had been the last to leave, and now they were the first to return. They had only left, they said, because the others were leaving. Not because they wanted to be out of Larkin House. They didn't. They were as comfortable with us as our new Patternists were with each other in their groups, their "families" of unrelated adults. We Patternists seemed to be more-social creatures than mutes were. Not one of our new Patternists chose to live alone. Even those who wanted to go out on their own waited until they could find at least one other person to join them. Then, slowly, the pair collected others. Their house grew.

Rachel and Jesse came back to us a few days after Seth and Ada. They were a little shamefaced, ready to admit that they wanted back into the comfort they had not realized they had found until they walked away from it.

Jan just reappeared. I read her. She had been lonely as hell in the house she had chosen, but she didn't say anything to us. She wanted to live with us, and she wanted to use her ability. She thought she would be content if she could do those two things. She was learning to paint, and even the worst of her paintings lived. You touched them and they catapulted you into another world. A world of her imagination. Some of the new Patternists who were related to her began coming to her to learn to use whatever psychometric ability they had. She taught them, took lovers from among them, and worked to improve her art. And she was happier than she had ever been before.

The seven of us became the First Family. It was a joke at first. Karl made some comparison between our position in the section and the position of the President's family in the nation. The name stuck. I think we all thought it was a little silly at first, but we got used to it. Karl did his bit to help me get used to it.

"We could do something about making it more of a family," he said. "We'd be the first ones to try it, too. That would give some validity to our title."

The Pattern was just over a year old then. I looked at him uncertainly, not quite sure he was saying what I thought he was saying.

"Try that again?"

"We could have a baby."

"Could *we?*"

"Seriously, Mary. I'd like us to have a child."

"Why?"

He gave me a look of disgust.

"I mean . . . we wouldn't be able to keep it with us."

"I know that."

I thought about it, surprised that I hadn't really thought about it before. But, then, I had never wanted children. With Doro around, though, I had assumed that sooner or later I would be ordered to produce some. Ordered. Somehow, being asked was better.

"We can have a child if you want," I said.

He thought for a moment. "I don't imagine you could arrange for it to be a boy?"

I arranged for it to be a boy. I was a healer by then. I could not only choose the child's sex but insure his good health and my own good health while I was pregnant. So being pregnant was no excuse for me to slow our expansion.

I was pulling in latents from all over the country. I could pick them out of the surrounding mute population without trouble. It didn't matter any more that I had never met them or that they were three thousand miles away when I focused in on them. My range, like the distance the Patternists could travel from me, had increased as the Pattern had grown. Now I located latents by their bursts of telepathic activity and gave a general picture of their location to one of my Patternists. The Patternist could pinpoint them more closely when he was within a few miles of them.

So the Pattern grew. Karl and I had a son: Karl August Larkin. The name of the man whose body Doro had used to father me was Gerold August. I had never made any gesture in his memory before, and I probably never would again. But having the baby had made me sentimental.

Doro wasn't around to watch us much as we grew. He checked on us every few months, probably to remind us—remind me—where the final authority still rested. He showed up twice while I was pregnant. Then we didn't see him again until August was two months old. He showed up at a time when we weren't having any big problems. I was kind of glad to see him. Kind of proud that I was running things so smoothly. I didn't realize he'd come to put an end to that.

He came in and looked at my flat stomach and said, "Boy or girl?" I hadn't bothered to tell him I'd deliberately conceived a boy.

So Karl and I sat around and probably bored him with talk about the baby. I was surprised when he said he wanted to see it.

"Why?" I asked. "Babies his age all look pretty much alike. What is there to see?"

Both men frowned at me.

"Okay, okay," I said. "Let's go see the baby. Come on."

Doro got up, but Karl stayed where he was. "You two go ahead," he said. "I was out to see him this morning. My head won't take it again for a while."

No wonder he could afford to be indignant at my attitude! He was setting me up. I wished Ada was around to take Doro in. August wasn't at the school itself, but he was at one of the buffer houses surrounding the school. That was almost as bad. The static from the school and from children in general didn't hit me as hard as it did most of the others, but it still wasn't very pleasant.

We went in. Doro stared at August, and August stared back from the arms of Evelyn Winthrop, the mute woman who took care of him. Then we left.

"Drive somewhere far enough from the school for you to be comfortable, and park," said Doro when we got back to the car. "I want to talk to you."

"About the baby?"

"No. Something else. Although I suppose I should compliment you on your son."

I shrugged.

"You don't give a damn about him, do you?"

I turned onto a quiet, tree-lined street and parked. "He's got all his parts," I said. "Healthy mentally and physically. I saw to that. Watched him very carefully before he was born. Now I keep an eye on Evelyn and her husband to be sure they're giving him the care he needs. Beyond that, you're right."

"Jan all over again."

"Thanks."

"I'm not criticizing you. Telepaths are always the worst possible parents. I thought the Pattern might change that, but it hasn't. Most actives have to be bulldozed into even having children. You and Karl surprised me."

"Karl wanted a child."

"And you wanted Karl."

"I already had him by then. But the idea of having a child wasn't that repulsive. It still isn't. I'd do it again. Now, what did you want to talk to me about?"

"Your doing it again."

"What?"

"Or at least having your people do it. Because that's the only way I'm going to allow the Pattern to grow for a while."

I turned to look at him. "What are you talking about?"

"I'm suspending your latent-gathering as of today. You're to call your people in from their searches, and recruit no more new Patternists."

"But— But why? What have we done, Doro?"

"Nothing. Nothing but grow. And that's the problem. I'm not punishing you; I'm slowing you down a little. I'm being cautious."

"For what? Why should you be cautious about our growth? The mutes don't know anything about us, and they'd have a hard time hurting us if they did. We aren't hurting each other. I'm in control. There's been no unusual trouble."

"Mary . . . fifteen hundred adults and five hundred children in only two years! It's time you stopped devoting all your energy to growth and started figuring out just what it is you're growing. You're one woman holding everything together. Your only possible successor at this point is about two months old. There'd be a blood bath if anything happened to you. If you were hit by a car tomorrow, your people would disintegrate—all over each other."

"If I were hit by a car and there were anything at all of me left alive, I'd survive. If I couldn't put myself together again, Rachel would do it."

"Mary, what I'm saying is that you're irreplaceable. You're all your people have got. Now, you can go on playing the part of their savior if you do as I've told you. Or you can destroy them by plunging on headlong as you are now."

"Are you saying I have to stop recruiting until August is old enough to replace me if anything happens to me?"

"Yes. And for safety's sake, I suggest that you not make August an only child."

"Wait twenty years?"

"It only sounds like a long time, Mary, believe me." He smiled a little. "Besides, not only are you a potential immortal as a descendant of Emma, but you have your own and Rachel's healing ability to keep you young if your potential for longevity doesn't work out."

"Twenty Goddamn years . . . !"

"You would have something firm and well established to bring your people into by then, too. You wouldn't be just spreading haphazardly over the city."

"We aren't doing that now! You know we aren't. We're growing deliberately into Santa Elena, because that's where the living room we need is. Jesse is working right now to prepare a new section of Santa Elena for us. We've got the school in the most protected part of our Palo Alto district. We didn't manage that by accident! The people don't just move wherever they want to. They go to Jesse and he shows them what's available."

"And all that's available is what you take from mutes. You don't build anything of your own."

"We build ourselves!"

"You will build yourselves more slowly now."

I knew that tone of voice. I used it myself from time to time. I knew he was letting me argue so that I'd have time to get used to the idea, not because there was any chance of changing his mind. But twenty years!

"Doro, do you know what kind of work I've had Rachel doing for most of the past two years?"

"I know."

"Have you seen the people she brings in—walking corpses most of them? That is if they can even walk."

"Yes."

"My people, so far gone they look like they've been through Dachau!"

"Mary—"

"They turn out to be my best telepaths when they're like that, you know? That's why they're in such bad shape as latents. They're so sensitive, they pick up everything."

"Mary, listen."

"How many of those people do you imagine will die, probably in agony, in twenty years?"

"It doesn't matter, Mary. It doesn't matter at all."

End of conversation. At least as far as he was concerned. But I just couldn't let go.

"You've been watching them die for thousands of years," I said. "You've learned not to care. I've just been saving them for two years, but I've already learned the opposite lesson. I care."

"I was afraid you would."

"Is it such a bad thing?"

"It's going to hurt you. It's already started to hurt you."

"You could let me go after just the worst ones. Just the ones who would die without me."

"No."

"Goddamnit, Doro, they'd die anyway. What could you lose?"

He looked at me silently for a long moment. "Do you remember what I told you on the day, two years ago, when you discovered Clay Dana's potential?"

The crap about obeying. I remembered, all right. "I wondered when you'd get to that."

"You know I meant it."

I slumped back in the seat, wondering what I was going to do. I took his hand almost absently. "What a pity we had to become competitors!"

"We haven't. There's enough for both of us."

I looked down at his hand, calloused, with fingers that were too long. It hit me how much like my own, big, ugly hands it was, and I took another look at the body he was wearing—green-eyed, black-haired. . . . "Who is this you're wearing?" I asked.

He raised an eyebrow. "A relative of your father—as you've probably already guessed."

"What relation?"

His expression hardened. "A son. Your older half brother." He wasn't just giving me information. He was challenging me with it.

"Right," I said. "Just the kind of person I would be looking for. A close relative, a potentially good Patternist, and a likely victim to ease your hunger. You know damn well we're competitors, Doro."

I had never spoken that bluntly to him before. He stared at me as though I'd surprised him—which was what I had set out to do.

"Hey," I said softly. "You know what I am. You made me what I am. Don't cut me off from the thing I was born to do. Just let me have the worst of the latents. Rachel's kind. Okay that, and I won't touch any of the others."

He shook his head slowly. "I'm sorry, Mary."

"But why?" I yelled. "Why?"

"Let's get back to the house. You can start calling your people in."

I got out of the car, slammed the door, and walked around to the sidewalk. I couldn't stay sitting there beside him for a minute longer. I would have done something stupid and useless—and probably suicidal. He called to me a couple of times, but, thank God, he had the sense not to come after me.

I walked home. Palo Alto wasn't far. I needed to burn off some of my anger before I got home, anyway.

· Eleven ·

MARY

Karl was settling some kind of dispute when I got home. He was standing between two Patternist men who were trying to glare each other to death. Their communication was all mental and easy for me to ignore as I walked through the living room. I went to the library and began to call in my searchers. As usual, they were scattered around the country—around the continent. Doro had begun planting the best of his families from Africa, Europe, and Asia in various parts of North America hundreds of years before. He had decided then that the North American continent was big enough to give them room to avoid each other and that it would be racially diverse enough to absorb them all. Now I had people in three countries demanding to know why they should stop their searches before they had found all the latents they sensed—why they should abandon potential Patternists. I didn't blame them for being mad, but I wasn't about to tell them, one by one, what the problem was. I pulled a "Do it because I said so!" on them and broke contact before they could argue more.

Karl came into the library as I was finishing and said, "What are you doing sitting in here in the dark?"

I was in contact with a Patternist in Chicago who was crying in anger and frustration at my "stupid, arbitrary, dictatorial orders. . . . " On and on.

Just get your ass on the next plane to L.A., I told her. I broke contact with her and blinked as Karl turned on the light. I hadn't realized it was so late.

"Uh-oh," he said, looking at me. "I'll listen if you want to talk about it."

I just opened and gave it all to him.

"Twenty years," he said, frowning. "But why? It doesn't make sense."

"Doro doesn't have to make sense," I said. "Although in this case I think he has his reasons. I think it's interesting that he first denied that he and I were competitors."

Karl looked hard at me. "I don't think that's a point you should emphasize to him."

"I wasn't emphasizing it. I was letting him know I understood it, and that because I understood it I was willing to accept a reasonable limitation—willing to settle for just the worst of the latents."

"But it didn't do any good."

"No."

"I wonder why. It sounds fairly harmless, and he would be able to check on you just by questioning you now and then."

"Maybe it was something I said—although he knew it already."

"What?"

"That the really bad latents turn out to be my best Patternists. They're probably the victims that give him the most pleasure too, when he can catch them before they kill themselves or get themselves locked up. I'll bet that half brother of mine was a mess before Doro took him."

"Competition again," said Karl. "Possible." He looked at me curiously. "Does it bother you that the body he's wearing was your brother?"

"No. I never knew the man. Doro's appetite in general bothers me. He warned me that it would. But I can keep quiet about it as long as he isn't taking my Patternists."

"For all we know, that could be next."

"God! No, he wouldn't do that while I'm still alive. The only Patternist he's likely to take right now is me." Something occurred to me suddenly. "Wait a minute! He may have left me more clues to whatever the hell he's doing than I thought."

"What?"

"I'll get back to you in a minute." I reached out to the old neighborhood, to Emma. I could reach her fast now, because she belonged to me. I had a kind of link with her that would let me know the minute some other Patternist touched her, and at the same time let the Patternist know she was mine. I had that kind of connection with Rina too, since she was too old for me to risk her life by trying to push her into transition.

I read Emma, saw that Doro had been to see her just a few hours before. And he'd talked a lot. Now since he knew Emma was mine, knew that anything he said to her I would eventually pick up, I assumed that he had been talking at least partly to me. Perhaps more to me than about me. I looked at Karl. "This morning, Doro told Emma he was afraid I'd disobey him in this and make him kill me."

"Obviously he was wrong," said Karl.

"But he seemed so sure about it—and Emma seemed so sure. I can discount Emma, I guess. She's frightened enough of me—and jealous enough of me—to want me dead. But Doro. . . ."

"Do you have any intention of defying him?"

"None . . . now." I stared down at the table. "I wouldn't risk the people, the Pattern, even if I were willing to risk myself. I'm wondering, though. . . ."

"Wondering what?"

"Well, remember when we started this—when I pulled in Christine and Jamie Hanson?"

"Yes."

"And you and Doro and I tried to figure out why I was so eager to bring in more people. Doro finally decided that I needed them for the same reasons he needed them. For sustenance."

Karl smiled faintly, which had to be a mark of how much he had relaxed and accepted his place in the Pattern. "Don't you think fifteen hundred people might be enough to sustain you?"

I looked at him. "You don't know how much I'd like to say yes to that."

His smile vanished. "For the sake of the fifteen hundred, you'd better say yes to it."

"Yeah. I just wish I could be sure that *saying* yes was enough."

"Why wouldn't it be?"

"I might be too much like Doro." I sighed. "I'm supposed to be like him. He finally admitted that to Emma this morning. Have you ever seen him when he needs a change really badly?"

"No. But I know that's not a safe time to be near him."

"Right. If he's really in trouble, he's liable to lose control—just take whoever's closest to him. Usually, though, he prevents himself from getting into that situation by changing often and keeping to healthy, young bodies. I seem to prefer young minds—not necessarily healthy."

"But with so many young minds already here, there's no reason for you to defy Doro and go after more."

"There are more of them out there, Karl. I'm afraid that might be reason enough. Now that I'm thinking about it. . . . " I glanced at him. "You've felt how eager I am when I go after new people—the first ones two years ago, and the last ones this morning. I don't like thinking about what my life will be like now that I can't go after any more of them."

He put one elbow on the table and rested his chin on his hand. "You know, in his way, I think Doro does love you."

I stared at him in surprise. "What's that got to do with anything?"

"Am I right?"

"He loves me. What passes for love with him."

"Don't belittle it. I think it's the only lever you have that might move him—make him change his mind."

"I've never in my life been able to change his mind once he's made it up. His love . . . it lasts as long as I do what he tells me."

"All right, then; you may not have any influence. But you'll find out for sure, won't you. You'll try."

I took a deep breath, nodded. "I'll try anything within reason. But I don't think anything less than my complete obedience will satisfy him. I've made him wary and uncomfortable. I've been moving too fast, and letting him see me too clearly."

"It sounds as though you're saying he's afraid of you. And if you believe that, you're deluding yourself. Dangerously."

"No, not afraid. Cautious. He's alive because he's cautious. And I'm too powerful. Fifteen hundred people aren't giving me any trouble at all. Whatever the Pattern is, I'm not likely to overload it soon. Doro isn't worried that I can't handle the thing I'm building. He's worried that I can."

Karl thought about that for a long moment. "If you're right, if he is worried, it might not only be because you're competing with him and taking his people."

I looked at him questioningly.

"It might be because you could use those people against him. You can't hurt him alone, but if you took strength from some of us—or all of us. . . . "

"He made a point of telling Emma that wouldn't work."

"Did he convince you?"

"He didn't have to. I already knew better than to try anything like that with him."

"You had no reason to risk trying it before now. Now . . . you might have to try something. Or let us try. There should be enough Patternists now for us to overwhelm him without your help."

"No way."

"It's never been tried. You don't know—"

"I know. You couldn't do it. Not even all fifteen hundred of you together, because, as far as he's concerned, you wouldn't really be together. He'd take you one at a time, but so fast you'd fall like dominoes. I know. Because that's something I could do myself."

He frowned. "That's out, then. But I don't understand why he's so convinced that you couldn't defeat him using our strength."

"He said, 'Strength alone isn't enough to defeat me.' And part of the reason he gave is that I can't change bodies. But that doesn't hold up. I can kill his body with a thought, and that same thought will force him to attack me on a mental level. My territory."

"That sounds promising."

"Yes, but he knows it as well as I do. That means he has some other reason for his confidence. The only thing I can think of is my own ignorance. I just don't know how to take him. He's not a Patternist, he's not a mute—he's bound to have some surprises for me. If I go after him, the chances are I'll be dead before I can figure out how to kill him. He knows so much more than I do."

"But he's never faced anyone like you before. You'd be as new to him as he is to you."

"But killing is a way of life to him, Karl. He's damned good at it. And he has killed people who he thought were dangerous to him before. He claims I don't even have the potential to be dangerous to him personally."

"Do you imagine he's never made a mistake?"

"He's still alive."

"No wonder. Look how good he is at scaring hell out of his opponents before he faces them. If you accept him as all-knowing and invulnerable, you'd better be able to live without recruiting for as long as he says. Because you'll be in no shape to face him. You'll have already beaten yourself!"

We stared at each other for a long moment, and I could see that he was as worried as he sounded. "You know I'm not going to give him my life," I said quietly. "Or the lives of my Patternists. If I have to fight him, it will be a battle, not a rout."

"You'll take strength from us."

I winced, looked away. "Some of you at least."

"The strongest of us. Beginning with me."

I nodded. To protect them, I had to risk them. They could be killed even if I wasn't. If I was desperate and rushed, as I probably would be, I might take too much of their strength. And I would be killing them. Not Doro. They were my people, and I would be killing them.

Doro stayed at Larkin House that night. We still kept his room ready for him though he didn't use it much any more. He didn't intend to use it that night. Instead he came across the hall to my room. I was sitting in the middle of my bed in the dark, thinking. He walked in without knocking.

He and I hadn't made love for over a year, but he walked in as though there had been no break at all. Knowing him, I wasn't surprised. He sat on the side of my bed, took off his shoes, and lay down beside me fully clothed. I was stark naked myself.

"I checked on a few of your searchers," he said. "I see they're starting for home."

I didn't say anything. I had mixed emotions about his just being there. I had promised Karl that I'd use my "lever," try to change Doro's mind. Now looked like a good time for that. But, since he was Doro, I wouldn't get anything past him that I didn't mean. If I was going to be able to reach him at all, it had to be with truth.

"I'm glad you're co-operating," he said. "I was afraid you might not."

"I got the message you left with Emma," I said. "Although I think you laid it on kind of thick."

"I wasn't acting. I wasn't trying to scare you, either. I was honestly worried about you."

"Why make impossible demands of me and then worry about me?"

"Impossible?"

"Hard, then. Too hard."

He just looked at me—at what he could see of me in the light from the window.

"Hard on the others, too."

He shrugged.

"You've stayed away from us too long," I said. "It's easy for you to hurt us, because you don't really know us any more."

"Oh, I know you, girl."

That didn't sound too good. "I mean you used to be one of us. You could be again, you know."

"Your people don't need me. Neither do you."

"You're our founder," I said. "Our father. We teach the new

Patternists about you, but that isn't enough. They should get to know you."

"And me them."

"Yes."

"It won't work, Mary."

I frowned down at him. He was lying flat on his back now, looking up at the ceiling. "If you get to know us as we are now, Doro, you might find that we really are the people, the race, that you've been working for so long to build. We already belong to you, and you can be one of us. We haven't shut you out."

"It's surprising how eloquent you can become when you want something."

I hung on to my temper. "You know I'm not just talking. I mean what I'm saying."

"It doesn't matter. Because it's not going to change anything. The order I gave you is final. I'm not going to be talked out of it. Not by getting to know your people better. Not by renewing my relationship with you."

"What are you doing here, then?"

"Oh, I intend to renew our relationship. I just don't intend to let you charge me for it."

I kicked him out of the bed. We were positioned perfectly for it. I just let him have it in the side with both feet. He fell, cursing, and got up holding his side.

"What the hell was that supposed to prove?" he demanded. "I thought you had outgrown that kind of behavior."

"I have. I only give it to you because it's what you want."

He ignored that, sat down on the bed. "That was a stupid, dangerous thing to do."

"No it wasn't. You have some control. You can control your mouth too when you want to."

He sighed. "Well, at least you're back to normal."

"Shit!" I muttered and turned away from him. "Pleading for my people isn't normal. Acting like a latent is normal. Stay with us, Doro. Get to know us again, whether you think you'll change your mind or not."

"What is it you want me to see that you think I've missed?"

"The fact that your kids really have grown up, man. I know

actives and latents didn't use to be able to do that. They had too many problems just surviving. Surviving alone. We weren't meant for solitude. But the Pattern has let us grow up."

"What makes you think I haven't noticed that?"

I looked at him sharply. Something really ugly had come into his voice just then. Something I would have expected to hear in Emma's voice but not his. "Yeah," I said softly. "Of course you know. You even said it yourself a couple of minutes ago. It must have come as kind of a shock to you that after four thousand years, your work, your children, were suddenly as finished as you could make them. That they . . . didn't need you any more."

He gave me a look of pure hatred. I think he was as close to taking me at that moment as he had ever been. I touched his hand.

"Join us, Doro. If you destroy us, you'll be destroying part of yourself. All the time you spent creating us will be wasted. Your long life, wasted. Join us."

The hatred that had flared in his eyes was concealed again. I suspected it was more envy than hatred. If he had hated me, I would already have been dead. Envy was bad enough. He envied me for doing what he had bred me to do—because he was incomplete, and he would never be able to do it himself. He got up and walked out of my room.

KARL

In only ten days Karl knew without doubt that Mary's suspicions had been justified. She wasn't going to be able to obey Doro. She had begun sensing latents again without intending to, without searching for them. Sooner or later she was going to have to begin pulling them in again. And the day she did that would very likely be the day she died.

She and how many others?

Karl watched her with growing concern. She was like a latent now, trying to hold herself together, and no one knew it but she and Karl. She kept shielded, and she was actress enough to conceal it from the others—except possibly Doro. And Doro didn't care.

Mary had already talked to him and been refused. That tenth night, Karl went in to talk to him. He pleaded. Mary was in trouble. If she could even be given a small quota of the latents that Doro valued least—

"I'm sorry," said Doro. "I can't afford her unless she can obey me."

It was a dismissal. The subject was closed. Karl got up wearily and went to Mary's room.

She was lying on her back, staring up at the ceiling. Just staring. She did not move as he came to sit beside her, except to take his hand and hold it.

"What did he say?" she asked.

"You've been reading me," he said mildly.

"If I had, I'd know what he said. I was coming upstairs a few minutes ago. I saw you go into his room." She sat up and looked at him intently. "What did he say, Karl?"

"He said no."

"Oh." She lay down again. "I knew damned well he would. I just keep hoping."

"You're going to have to fight."

"I know."

"And you're going to win. You're going to kill him. You're going to do whatever you have to do to kill him!"

Like a latent, she turned onto her side, clutched her head between her hands, and curled her body into a tight knot.

The next day, Karl called the family together. Mary had gone to see August, and Karl wanted to talk to the others before she returned. She would find out what had been said. He planned to tell her himself, in fact. But he wanted to talk to them first without her.

They already knew why Mary had called in her searchers. They didn't like it. Mary's enthusiasm over the Pattern's growth had infected them long ago. Now Karl told them that Mary's submission could not last. That Mary's own needs would force her to disobey, and that when she disobeyed, Doro would kill her. Or try to.

"It's possible that with our numbers we can help her defeat him," Karl said. "I don't know how she'll handle things when the time comes, but I have a feeling she'll want to get as many of the people away from the section as she can. Doro has told us that actives couldn't handle themselves in groups before the Pattern. I know Mary's afraid of the chaos that might happen here if she's killed while we're all together. So I think she'll try to give the people some warning to get out of Forsyth, scatter. If any of you want to scatter with them, she'll almost certainly let you go. The idea of other Patternists dying either because she dies or because she takes too much strength from them is bothering her more than the thought of her own death."

"Sounds like you're telling us to cut and run," said Jesse.

"I'm offering you a choice," said Karl.

"Only because you know we won't take it," said Jesse.

Karl looked from him to the others, let his gaze pass over them slowly.

"He speaks for all of us," said Seth. "I didn't know Mary was in trouble. She hides things too well sometimes. But now that I do know, I'm not going to walk out on her."

"And how could I leave the school?" said Ada. "All the children. . . . "

"I think Doro has made a mistake," said Rachel. "I think he's waited too long to do this. I don't see how any one person could resist so many of us. I don't even see why we have to risk Mary, since she's the only one of us who's irreplaceable. If the rest of us got together and—"

"Mary says that wouldn't work," said Karl. "She says it wouldn't even work against her."

"Then, we'll all have to give her our strength."

"To be honest, she's not sure that will work either. Doro says strength alone isn't enough to beat him. I suspect he's lying. But the only way to find out for sure is for her to tackle him. So she will gather strength from some or all of us when the time comes. We're the only weapons she has."

"If she's not careful," said Jesse, "she won't have time to try it—or time to warn the people to scatter. Doro knows she's in trouble, doesn't he?"

"Yes."

"He might decide there's no point in waiting for her to break."

"I've thought about that," said Karl. "I don't think she'll let him surprise her. But, to be sure, I'm going to start work on her tonight—talk her into going after him. Preparing herself, and going after him."

"Are you sure you can talk her into it?" asked Jan.

"Yes." Karl looked at her. "You haven't said anything. Are you with us?"

Jan looked offended. "I'm a member of this family, aren't I?"

Karl smiled. Jan had changed. Her art had given her the strength that she had always lacked. And it had given her a contentment with her life. She might even be a live woman now, instead of a corpse, in bed. Karl wondered briefly but not seriously. Mary was woman enough for him if he could find some way of keeping her alive.

"I think Doro has made more than one mistake," said Jan. "I think he's wrong to believe that Mary still belongs to him. With the responsibility she's taken on for all that she's built here, she belongs to us, the people. To all of us."

"I suspect she thinks it's the other way around," said Rachel. "But it wouldn't hurt if we went to some of the heads of houses and said it Jan's way. They're our best, our strongest. Mary will need them."

"I don't know whether I'll be able to get her to take them," said Karl. "I intend to try, though."

"When Doro starts chewing at her, she'll take anybody she can get," said Jesse.

"If she has time, as you said," said Karl. "I don't want it to come to that. That's why I'm going to work on her. And, look, don't say anything to the heads of houses. Word will spread too quickly. It might spread to Doro. God knows what he'd do if he realized his cattle had finally gotten the nerve to plot against him."

· Twelve ·

MARY

When I woke up on the morning after Karl had talked to Doro, I found that my hands wouldn't stop shaking. I felt the way I had a few days before my transition. With Karl, I didn't even bother to hide it.

He said, "Open to me. Maybe I can help."

"You can't help," I muttered. "Not this time."

"Let me try."

I looked at him, saw the concern in his eyes, and felt almost guilty about doing as he asked. I opened to him not because I thought he could help me but because I wanted him to realize that he couldn't.

He stayed with me for several seconds, sharing my need, my hunger, my starvation. Sharing it but not diminishing it in any way. Finally he withdrew and stood staring at me bleakly. I went to him for the kind of comfort he could give, and he held me.

"You could take strength from me," he said. "It might ease your—"

"No!" I rested my head against his chest. "No, no, no. You think I haven't thought of that?"

"But you wouldn't have to take much. You could—"

"I said no, Karl. It's like you said last night. I'm going to have to fight him. I'll take from you then, and from the others. But not until then. I'm not the vampire he is. I give in return for my taking." I pulled away from him, looked at him. "God, I've got ethics all of a sudden."

"You've had them for some time, now, whether you were willing to admit to them or not."

I smiled. "I remember Doro wondering before my transition whether I would ever develop a conscience."

Karl made a sound of disgust. "I just wish Doro had developed one. Are you going out?"

"Yes. To see August."

He didn't say anything to that, and I wondered whether he realized this might be my last visit to our son. I finished dressing and left.

I saw August and spent some time strengthening Evelyn's programming, seeing to it that she would go on being a good mother to him even if Karl and I weren't around. And I planted some instructions that she wouldn't need or remember until August showed signs of approaching transition. I didn't want her panicking then, and taking him to a doctor or a hospital. Maybe I needn't have worried. Maybe Doro would see that he was taken care of. And maybe not.

I went home and managed to get through a fairly ordinary day. I passed a man and a woman to become heads of houses. They had been Patternists for over a year, and I read just about everything they had done during that year. Karl and I checked all prospective heads of houses. Back when we hadn't checked them, we'd gotten some bad ones. Some who had been too warped by their latent years to turn human again. We still got that kind, but they didn't become heads of houses any more. If we couldn't straighten them out, or heal them—if healing was what they needed—we killed them. We had no prison, needed none. A rogue Patternist was too dangerous to be left alive.

That was probably the way Doro felt about me. It went with

what he had told Karl. "I can't afford her unless she can obey me." We were too much alike, Doro and I. What ever gave him the idea that someone bred to be so similar to him would consent—could consent—to being controlled by him all her life?

I passed my two new heads of houses, but I told them not to do anything toward beginning their houses for a week. They didn't like that much, but they were so happy to be passed that they didn't argue. They were bright and capable. If, by some miracle, the Pattern still existed in a week, they would be a credit to it in their new positions.

I went with Jesse to see the houses he was opening up in Santa Elena. He asked me to go. I didn't have to see them. I only checked on the family now and then. And when I did, I could never find much to complain about. They cared about what we were building. They always did a good job.

In the car Jesse said, "Listen, you know we're all with you, don't you?"

I looked at him, not really surprised. Karl had told him. No one else could have.

"I just wish we could take him on for you," said Jesse.

"Thanks, Jess."

He glanced at me, then shook his head. "You don't look any more nervous over facing him than you did over facing me a couple of years ago."

I shrugged. "I don't think I can afford to broadcast my feelings."

"With all of us behind you, I think you can beat him."

"I intend to."

Big talk. I wondered why I bothered.

There were a few other routine duties. I welcomed them, because they kept my mind off how bad I felt. That night, I didn't feel like eating. I went to my room while everyone else was at dinner. Let them eat. It might be their last meal.

Karl came up about two hours later and found me looking out my window at nothing, waiting for him.

"I've got to talk to you," he said—just before I could say it to him.

"Okay." I sat down in the chair by the window. He sprawled on my bed.

"We had a meeting today—just the family. I told them what kind of trouble you were in, told them that you were going to fight. And I told them they could run if they wanted to."

"They won't run."

"I know that. I just wanted them to put it into words. I wanted them to hear themselves say it and know that they were committed."

"Everybody's committed. Every Patternist in the section. And all those who don't know it are about to find out."

He sat up straight. "What are you going to do?"

"First I'm going to clear the section."

"Clear it? Send everybody away?"

"Yes. Including the family, if they'll go. They won't be deserting me. I can use them just as effectively if they're a couple of states away."

"They won't go."

I shrugged. "I hope they don't wind up regretting that."

"I assume you're going after Doro in the morning."

"After everybody has had time to get out, yes. I want them to spread out, scatter as widely as possible, just in case."

"I know. I just hope Doro gives them time to go. If he notices that people are leaving—if he thinks of someone and that tracking sense of his tells him that that person is headed for Oregon, he's going to start checking around. He'll think you're sending out searchers again. Then, when he realizes everybody's going, he'll get the idea pretty quickly."

"We could see that he's distracted for the night."

He looked at me. I didn't say anything. Obviously this was no night to distract Doro with a Patternist. Karl gazed down at his hands for a moment, then looked up. "All right; it's done. Vivian will distract him. And she'll think it's her own idea."

We waited, our perception focused on Doro's room. Vivian knocked at his door, then went in. Her mind gave us Doro's words, and we knew we were safe. He was glad to see her. They hadn't been together for a long time.

"Now," said Karl.

"Now," I agreed. I went to the bed and lay down. It was best for me to be completely relaxed when I used the Pattern this way. I closed my eyes and brought it into focus. Now I was aware of the contented hum of my people. They were ending their day, resting or preparing to rest, and unconsciously giving each other calm.

I jerked the Pattern sharply, shattering their calm. It didn't hurt them, or me, but it startled them to attention. I felt Karl jump beside me, and he had been expecting it.

I could feel their attention on me as though I had walked onto the stage of a crowded auditorium. It was as easy to reach all 1,538 of them as it had been to reach just the family two years before. And there was no need for me to identify myself. Nobody else could have reached them through the Pattern as I did.

The Pattern is in danger, I sent bluntly. *It may be destroyed.*

I could feel their alarm at that. In the two short years of its existence the Pattern had given these people a new way of life. A way of life that they valued.

The Pattern may be destroyed, I repeated. *If it is, and if you're together when it happens, you will be in danger.* I gave them a short history lesson. A lesson they had already been exposed to once in orientation classes or through learning blocks. That, before the Pattern, active telepaths had not been able to survive together in groups. That they could not tolerate each other, could not accept the mental blending that occurred automatically without the control of the Pattern.

It might not be true any longer, I told them. *But it has been true for thousands of years. For safety's sake, we have to assume that it's still true. So you are all to get up tonight, now, and leave the section. Separate. Scatter.*

Their dismay was almost a physical force—that many people frightened, agreeing with each other and disagreeing with me. I put force of my own into my next thought, amplified it to a mental shout.

Be still!

A lot of them winced as though I had hit them.

I'm sending you away to save your lives, and you will go.

Some of them were upset enough to try to shut me out. But of course they couldn't. Not as long as I spoke through the Pattern.

You are all powerful people, I sent. *You will have no trouble making your ways alone. And if the Pattern survives, you know that I'll call you all back. I want you here as much as you want to be here. We're one people. But now, for your own sake, you must go. Leave tonight so that I can be sure you're safe.*

I let them feel the emotion I felt. Now was the time. I wanted them to see how important their safety was to me. I wanted them to know that I meant every word I gave them. But the words that I didn't give them were the ones they were concerned with. Most of the questions they threw at me were drowned in the confusion of their mental voices. I could have sorted them out and made sense of them, but I didn't bother. The one that I didn't have to sort out, though, was the one that was on everyone's mind. *What is the danger?* I couldn't miss reading it, but I could ignore it. My people knew Doro from classes and blocks. Most of them had had no personal contact with him at all. They were capable of shrugging off what they had learned—all their theoretical knowledge—and going after him for me. And getting themselves slaughtered. What they didn't know, in this case, could save them from committing suicide. I addressed them again.

You who are heads of houses—you know your responsibilities to your families. See that all the members of your families get out, and get out tonight. Help them get out. Take care of them.

There. I broke contact. Now the strongest people in the section, the most responsible people, had been charged with seeing that my commands were obeyed. I had faith in my heads of houses.

I opened my eyes—and knew at once that something was wrong. I turned my head and saw Karl standing beside the bed, his back to me, his body tense. Beyond him, at the door, stood Doro. It was Doro's expression that made me instantly re-establish contact with my Patternists. I jerked the Pattern again to get their attention. I felt their confusion, their fear. Then their surprise as they felt me with them again. I gave them my thoughts very clearly, but quickly.

Everybody, stop what you're doing. Be still.

They could see what I saw. My eyes were open now, and my mind was open to them. They could see Doro watching me past Karl. They could know that Doro was the danger. It was too late for them to make suicidal mistakes.

You won't have time to leave. You'll have to help me fight. Obey me, and we can kill him.

That thought cut through their confusion, as I had hoped it would. Here was a way to destroy what threatened them. Here was Doro, whom they had been warned against, but whom most of them did not really fear.

Sit down, or lie down. Wait. Do nothing. I'm going to need you.

Doro started toward Karl. I sat up, scrambled over close to Karl, and laid a hand on his shoulder. He glanced at me.

"It's okay," I said. "It's as okay as it's ever going to be. Get out of here."

He relaxed a little, but, instead of going, he sat down on the end of the bed. I didn't have time to argue with him. I began absorbing strength from my people. Not Karl. He would have collapsed and given me away. But the others. I had to collect from as many of them as I could before Doro attacked. Because I had no doubt that he was going to attack.

DORO

Doro stood still, gazing at the girl, wondering why he waited. "You have time to try again to get rid of Karl if you like," he said.

"Karl's made his decision." There was no fear in her voice. That pleased Doro somehow.

"Apparently you've made yours, too."

"There was no decision for me to make. I have to do what I was born to do."

Doro shrugged.

"What did you do with Vivian?"

"Nothing at all after I thought about it," he said. "Faithful little pet that she is now, Vivian hasn't looked at me for well over a year. Karl's women get like that when he stops trying to preserve their individuality—when he takes them over completely." He smiled. "Karl's mute women, I mean. So, when Vivian, who no longer had initiative enough to go looking for lovers other than Karl, suddenly came to me, I realized that she had almost certainly been sent. Why was she sent?"

"Does it matter?"

Doro gave her a sad smile. "No. Not really." In his shadowy way, Doro was aware of a great deal of psionic activity going on around her. He felt himself drawn to her as he had been two years before, when she took Jesse and Rachel. Now, he guessed, she would be taking a great many of her people. As many as he gave her time to take. She remained still as Doro sat down beside her. She looked at Karl, who sat on her other side.

"Move away from us," she said quietly.

Without a word, Karl got up and went to sit in the chair by the window. The instant he reached the chair he collapsed, seemed to pass out. Mary had finally taken him. An instant later, Doro took her.

At once, Doro was housed with her in her body. But she was no quick, easy kill. She would take a few moments.

She was power, strength concentrated as Doro had never felt it before—the strength of dozens, perhaps hundreds of Patternists. For a moment Doro was intoxicated with it. It filled him, blotted out all thought. The fiery threads of her Pattern surrounded him. And before him . . . before him was a slightly smaller replica of himself as he had perceived himself through the fading senses of his thousands of victims over the years. Before him, where all the threads of fire met in a wild tangle of brilliance, was a small sun.

Mary.

She was like a living creature of fire. Not human. No more human than he was. He had lied to her about that once—lied to calm her—when she was a child. And her major weakness, her vulnerable, irreplaceable human body, had made the lie seem true. But that body, like his own series of bodies, was only a mask, a shell. He saw her now as she really was, and she might have been his twin.

But, no, she was not his twin. She was a smaller, much younger being. A complete version of him. A mistake that he would not make again. But, ironically, her very completeness would help to destroy her. She was a symbiont, a being living in partnership with her people. She gave them unity, they fed her, and both thrived. She was not a parasite, though he had encouraged her to think of herself as one. And though she had great power, she was not naturally, instinctively, a killer. He was.

When he had had his look at her, he embraced her, enveloped her. On the physical level, the gesture would have seemed affectionate—until it was exposed as a strangle hold.

When Mary struggled to free herself, he drank in the strength she spent, consumed it ecstatically. Never had one person given him so much.

Alarmed, Mary struck at him, struggled harder, fed him more of herself. She fed him until her own strength and her borrowed strength were gone. Finally he tasted the familiar terror in her mind.

She knew she was about to die. She had nothing left, no time to draw strength from more of her people. She felt herself dying. Doro felt her dying.

Then he heard her voice.

No, he sensed it, disembodied, cursing. She was so much a part of him already that her thoughts were reaching him. He moved to finish her, consume the final fragments of her. But the final fragments were the Pattern.

She was still alive because she was still connected to all those people. The strength that Doro took now, the tiny amounts of strength that she had left, were replaced instantly. She could not die. New life flowed into her continually.

Furiously, Doro swept her into himself, where she should have died. For the fifth time, she did not die. She seemed to slither away from him, regaining substance apart from him as no victim of his should have been able to.

She was doing nothing on her own now. She was weak and exhausted. Her Pattern was doing its work automatically. Apparently it would go on doing that work as long as there were Patternists alive to support it.

Then Mary began to realize that Doro was having trouble.

She began to wonder why she was still alive. Her thoughts came to him clearly. And apparently his thoughts reached her.

You can't kill me, she sent. *After all that, you can't kill me. You may as well let me go!*

He was surprised at first that she was still aware enough to communicate with him. Then he was angry. She was helpless. She should have been his long ago, yet she would not die.

If he could manage to leave her body—a thing he had never done before without finishing his kill—he would only have to try again. He couldn't possibly let her live to collect more of his latents, to search until she found a way to kill him.

He would jump to Karl, and perhaps from Karl to someone else. Karl would already be more dead than alive now that she had taken strength from him. Doro would move on, find himself an able body and come back to her in it. Then he would simply cut her throat—decapitate her if necessary. Not even a healer could survive that. She might be mentally strong, but physically she was still only a small woman. She would be easy prey.

Mary seemed to clutch at him. She was trying to hold him as he had held her, but she had neither the technique nor the strength. She had learned a little, but it was too late. She was barely an annoyance. Doro focused on Karl.

Abruptly Mary became more than an annoyance.

She tore strength from the rest of her people. Not one at a time now. This time she took them all at once, the way Rachel had used to take from her congregations. But Mary stripped her Patternists as Rachel had never stripped her mutes. Then, desperately, Mary tried again to grasp Doro.

For a moment, she seemed not to realize that she was strong again—that her act of desperation had gained her a second chance. Then her new strength brought her to life. It became impossible for Doro to focus on anyone but her. Her power drew him.

Abruptly, she stopped clutching at him and threw herself on him. She embraced him.

Startled, Doro tried to shake her off. For a moment, his struggles fed her as hers had fed him earlier. She was a leech, riding, feeding orgiastically.

Doro caught himself, ceased his struggles. He smiled to himself grimly. Mary was learning, but there was still much that she didn't know. Now he taught her how difficult it was to get strength from an opponent who not only refused to give it away by struggling but who actively resisted her efforts to take it. And there was only one way to resist. As she sought to consume him, he countered by trying to consume her.

For long moments they strained against each other, neither of them gaining or losing power. They neutralized each other.

Disgusted, Doro tried again to focus on Karl. Best to get away from Mary mentally and get back to her physically.

Mary let him go.

Startled, Doro brought his attention back to her. For a moment, he could not focus on her. There was a roar of something like radio static in his mind—"noise" so intense that he tried to twist away from it. It cleared slowly.

Then he noticed that he had not drawn away from Mary completely. He was still joined to her. Joined by a single strand of fire. She had used her mental closeness with him to draw him into her web. Her Pattern.

He panicked.

He was a member of the Pattern. A Patternist. Property. Mary's property.

He strained against the seemingly fragile thread. It stretched easily. Then he realized that he was straining against himself. The thread was part of him. A mental limb. A limb that he could find no way to sever.

The Patternists had told him how it felt at first—that feeling of being trapped, of being on a leash. They had lived to get over their feelings. They had lived because Mary had wanted them to live. Doro himself had helped Mary understand how thoroughly their lives were in her hands.

Doro fought desperately, uselessly. He could feel Mary's amusement now. He had nearly killed her, had been about to kill the man she had attached herself to so firmly. Now she took her revenge. She consumed him slowly, drinking in his terror and his life, drawing out her own pleasure, and laughing through his soundless screams.

· Epilogue ·

MARY

They cremated Doro's last body before I was able to get out of bed. I was in bed for two days. A lot of others were there even longer. The few who were on their feet ran things with the help of the mute servants. One hundred and fifty-four Patternists never got up again at all. They were my weakest, those least able to take the strain I put on them. They died because it took me so long to learn how to kill Doro. By the time Doro was dead and I began to try to give back the strength I had taken from my people, the 154 were already dead. I had never tried to give back strength before, but I had never taken so much before, either. I managed it, and probably saved the lives of others who would have died. So that I only had to get used to the idea that I had killed the 154. . . .

Emma died. The day Rachel told her about Doro, she decided to die. It was just as well.

Karl lived. The family lived. If I had killed them, Emma's way out could have started to look good to me. Not that I would have taken it. I wouldn't have the freedom to consider a thing like that for about twenty years, no matter what happened. But that was all right. It wasn't a freedom I wanted. I had already won the only freedom I cared about. Doro was dead. Finally, thoroughly dead. Now we were free to grow again—we, his children.

About Octavia E. Butler

OCTAVIA E. BUTLER writes: "I am a 53-year-old writer who can remember being a 10-year-old writer and who expects someday to be an 80-year-old writer. I'm also comfortably asocial—a hermit in the middle of Seattle—a pessimist if I'm not careful, a feminist, a black, a former Baptist, an oil-and-water combination of ambition, laziness, insecurity, certainty, and drive.

I've had 11 novels published so far: *Patternmaster, Mind of My Mind, Survivor, Kindred, Wild Seed, Clay's Ark, Dawn, Adulthood Rites, Imago, Parable of the Sower,* and *Parable of the Talents,* as well as a collection of my shorter work, entitled *Bloodchild.* I've also had short stories published in anthologies and magazines. One, "Speech Sounds," won a Hugo Award as best short story of 1984. Another, "Bloodchild," won both the 1985 Hugo and the 1984 Nebula awards as best novelette. My most recent novel, *Parable of the Talents,* won the 1999 Nebula for Best Novel." **—Octavia E. Butler**

Of special Note: In 1995, Octavia E. Butler was awarded a MacArthur Fellowship. The program, funded by the John D. and Catherine T. MacArthur Foundation, rewards creative people who push the boundaries of their fields. In 2000, she received the PEN Center West Lifetime Achievement Award.